For my mother

In the Warrens of East London

by

Joyce Myerson

In the Warrens of East London

by

Joyce Myerson

AOS Publishing, 2024
Copyright © 2024

Joyce Myerson

All rights reserved under International
and Pan-American copyright conventions

ISBN: 978-1-990496-92-9

Cover Design: Jessica James

Visit AOS Publishing's website:
www.aospublishing.com

PART ONE

Chapter I

As he followed this perfect stranger, a young woman of the streets who sold her body to whoever was willing to pay, he reflected that perhaps this was the first time in his entire adult life—and he was already twenty-nine, a titled aristocrat with money to spare, a man with a profession, carrying his doctor's bag to prove it, although he rarely if ever practiced this profession—that he was acting honestly; even, he might say, honourably, if being honest was synonymous with being honourable. He was being honest because he was doing exactly what he wanted to do. And this woman had come up to him in the snow drifts of this ignominious street in East London, after he had decided to proceed on foot during the fiercest winter snowstorm he could remember. She had been clutching at her insignificant wrap, her face scarcely visible, snow descending furiously around her, all alone at this barely lit crossroads. He had wanted a choice of companions (he used that word because she had, asking him softly and rather tersely: "Would you like some companionship, my good sir?"), but she was the only one available. At any rate, she had intrigued him. The few syllables that she had uttered were crisp and clean, not the sounds one would expect in the slums of the city. What he could see of her face was also crisp and clean, no paint or rouge to speak of. She did not look hardened or exhausted by the poverty of her life. In fact, he would almost say that she was simply one of the most appealing creatures he had ever seen. She was clothed in simplicity, not destitution. He had felt a pull to her like metal to a magnet. Perhaps she was a hallucination, a mirage in the wasteland of his withered heart. And so, he moved along the street just behind her slim figure—not emaciated, no—feeling less cold than before, even anticipating the sensation of her lips on his own.

Finally, the woman (he so wanted to ask her name but did not know if that was the protocol in these situations of buyer and soon-to-be-bought) turned to him, and with a nod of her head, indicated the doorway to their right. She was about to push in the ugly wooden door, but Lucas stepped up beside her and pushed it in himself. It creaked on its hinges, and suddenly he was afraid of the certain squalor within. She was a little startled at his brusque but gentlemanly gesture and thanked him.

"It's just up the first flight of stairs, sir," she whispered to him. Why did she speak in such hushed tones? Again, he realized that he was drawn to the sound of her voice and the refined cadence of her speech. He felt as if he had been drugged and was imagining what he heard. Surely, she was a member of the lower classes. Look where she lived! Was he not hearing correctly? He had chosen this neighbourhood specifically because it would make him feel degraded. He did not deserve better.

After climbing to her floor, they walked down a darkened hallway to the last door. She fumbled with the keys. Was she nervous? Why would she be nervous? Had she not done this a hundred times before? As she turned the handle, she twisted her head sideways to him and looked deep into his eyes. His heart began to beat. What was she doing?

"My room is quite cold, sir. I have not been able to purchase wood or coal lately, but I have a warm quilt on the bed. Please do not let the absence of heat deter you from taking your...your...pleasure." She stumbled at the end of her sentence, unsure perhaps. Irresolute? Were they both losing their nerve despite her urging him to the contrary?

"I'll be fine, I'm sure," Lucas responded for the first time. His voice wavered. Everything seemed wrong, yet right. He entered the room one step behind her. He would do this.

Without looking around him at the stark interior, he searched in his vest pocket for the coins he thought would be her due. He was willing to pay her five times as much if she asked. He placed the money on the long wooden dining-room table along with his medicine case, the black leather one that his father had carried with him, with the initials L.L. in gold, the same initials as his own. The woman removed her wrap and shook the snow off it, glancing momentarily at the sum he had placed on the table. Her eyes opened wide. Had he miscalculated?

"If...if that's not enough...here, let me give you more. It makes no difference to me," and he pulled more shiny coins from another pocket and added them to the heap on the table. Before she could respond, he, too, removed his greatcoat, scarf, hat, and gloves. He handed them to her. She took them and hung them on a large nail on the wall. She stamped her shoes on the rug beneath their feet and he followed suit, aiming to get rid of as much snow as possible. When all that was done, he felt lost, like a small boy in an unfamiliar part of town, where a different language from his own was being spoken. But that wasn't the case at all. She spoke exactly the same language as he did, not a vowel or consonant alien to his ear.

She lit a lamp that stood on the table, and now he took in his surroundings as the glow hammered darkness away. He gasped. The place was definitely cold but there was life here. It was bare and spotless and orderly and poor, but its very cleanliness showed love and warmth. Besides the table, he spied a neatly-made bed to the left of the entrance. On the back wall was a big black stove, then a closed door, a basin on a pedestal, and cupboards up above. On the other side of the table was the empty fireplace, and after a space of about a foot, there stood a chest of drawers with another basin of water on top of it. The bottom drawer was open and nestled inside of it was...a sleeping baby! He looked at the woman in shock. She stood firmly facing him, her long dark hair cascading around her and shining in the lamplight. She was just steps from him, and he knew it was the moment to go to her and embrace her, but his feet were glued to the ground beneath. What is more, the makeshift bed of the child felt like an obstacle to their prescribed amorous encounter. When he hesitated to make a move, she dropped her head slightly and whispered, "I'm sorry."

At that instant, perhaps the sound of his mother's voice, perhaps the sensing of a stranger in his midst, caused the baby to open his eyes. He screwed them up, balled his little hands into fists, and let out a wail—an unhappy, suffering, feeble noise that immediately sent a shiver of recognition through Lucas. The baby needed something—warmth, nurturing, food? Lucas knelt down towards the child and gazed at him closely. He then looked up at the mother, who was also in the process of bending towards her little one. "Is he sick?" Lucas asked, because he thought that he was. He reached his hand over and gently touched the baby's head. It was hot and slightly wet.

Finally, the mother picked up her precious bundle and began rocking him as she stood up with him in her arms. Lucas also rose from his kneeling position. He wanted to hear the child's breathing, listen for congestion. "I think he may have a fever," he said, newly confident, hesitation gone. "May I listen to his chest? Please, I am a doctor." He reached over to take the little boy from her but waited for her to make the decision to trust him. The baby continued to cry, but it was not a healthy, vigorous sound. Instead of handing the baby to him, she explained the situation.

"Yes, he is feverish and congested. The house is too cold, and he hasn't eaten since early this morning. I have not been able to settle him until I left the house not two minutes before I saw you. He cried himself to sleep."

"Does he want to eat or is he refusing?"

"Oh no, he wants and needs to eat, but I have recently weaned him from my breast and have not had the money to buy him milk. That is why I...why I...left him alone...I would never have...have left him alone without someone if I wasn't desperate to solve the problem...of..." and then she began to cry. It was as if all her hardship could no longer keep a stranglehold on her sorrow. The floodgates had opened. And so, like him, she had been desperate. She had been willing to abandon all pretence at rectitude. She had been ready to throw her life away...to save that of her child. But how much more noble her reason! He had no such extenuating circumstances. He was just a self-centred pampered aristocrat with nothing to motivate him, nothing to give him a reason to live.

"So, you're not a...a..." She shook her head.

He wanted to put his arms around her, around them, and tell her that all would be well. Instead, he let her cry for a while with her baby hugged to her bosom, as he opened his father's well-stocked case. He pulled out an infant tonic and a small teaspoon. He tapped her arm to show that he was ready to administer the fluid to her sniffling son. He tried to make soothing clucking noises to the baby as he placed the spoon in his mouth. The baby swallowed but wasn't too fond of the taste, and again began to cry.

"Look, I have to go out and bring back some milk and food for yourself and the child. There is also the question of wood and coal. We need to boil some water for a bath for him, although I can see that you keep him clean." She nodded fiercely at this, proud of her knowledge of hygiene and its importance. "While I am gone, sponge him down with the water sitting in that basin over there, even if it's very cold. He is sweating and uncomfortable." She nodded at him, seemingly grateful for his taking charge, but he also could see that she was embarrassed by her penury. It did not matter. If she had pride, and she seemed to, she had better swallow it for the sake of her son. And anyway, at least for tonight, she had given *him*, Lucas the lost, a reason to live.

"Tell me where to go. I know little to nothing of these streets...." And for the first time he blushed, ashamed of himself and of his needs, needs that had brought him to the warrens of Whitechapel and to her. She gave him precise directions. He put his coat back on and wound his scarf around his neck. Before he opened the door to leave, he asked her one last question: "Where should I tell your supplier of coal and wood to send his wares? I cannot carry everything by myself."

"He has a boy with a wheelbarrow who will cart everything over to me. Just tell him to Nurse Gwynne's place. They know me."

He looked up in surprise. She was a nurse. What did that mean? Did she empty the slop pails at the hospital? Or was she educated—a Florence Nightingale of East London? He wanted to ask her, but later there would be time. And by her speech he knew she was educated. Where was the father of that child? Had he died? Had he abandoned her? Had they been married? No time for answers now. Now he had a purpose. He opened the door of her flat and set out to fulfil that purpose with a greater will than he had shown in a long time, perhaps ever.

The wind seemed to have died down and more people were about. There were even some ragged children packing snow into balls and throwing them at each other. Their existence was miserable, but at least they took pleasure where they could find it. All of a sudden, a ball meant for an urchin a few yards ahead of him hit his shoulder. The child who had thrown it looked stunned and a little uneasy. Lucas laughed, picked up some snow near his feet, patted it into a ball, and threw it back at his assailant. The boy ran from it, but it caught him on the back of his leg. He, too, laughed along with the other three or four children. As Lucas passed him on his way to the corner, he touched the boy's bare head with his gloved hand. He wanted to say something to him but the whole gang of them ran off together in the other direction. Lucas stared at them as they fell into a heap in the snow, shouting and laughing some more, then rolling around and finally making angel shapes with their arms and legs.

He smiled to himself. He had an indistinct memory of doing something similar with his mother one winter's day long ago, not in London, of course, but in Kent where their country estate lay, in his mother's beautiful garden alongside their home. He had been happy at that moment. Then she had disappeared from his life, and although his father's sister had been a more than adequate substitute for a mother, she was not *his* mother. He looked over again at the boys and girls cavorting in the snow, and wondered if they were happy, if they loved their mothers, and despite all the cold of their poor lives, if they felt warm and comfortable in her presence. He shook his head as if to empty it of these useless thoughts. He wanted to feel warm and comfortable tonight, nurtured, loved even, but instead *he* would provide warmth and comfort, and that was as it should be.

The street he walked along was narrow and intermittently lit, but without the snow it probably looked a lot more miserable and smelled a lot more dank. Instead, there was a freshness in the cold, crisp air and the various street-sellers somehow seemed more wholesome. The white was back in Whitechapel and he was glad of it. Up ahead he saw the coal and firewood merchant that Nurse Gwynne had spoken of. He entered the establishment to the jangle of a bell over the door. A boy of about eleven or twelve—a very black and dirty boy, his face and hair and clothes covered in coal dust, was lying in his barrow just inside the door and to the right. He sat up swiftly as Lucas entered, lifted his legs over the sides of the barrow, plunked his boots on the floor, and stood at attention.

"Can I help ye, sir? Ye be needin' any coal or firewood tonight?"

"As a matter of fact, yes," Lucas responded. At that moment a rather large and burly man, none too clean himself, entered the shop proper from somewhere in the back. Instantly he started yelling at the boy, but Lucas could make out very little of his speech, only that the child was called Phillip. Phillip immediately ran with a limp to the counter at the back where pails, shovels, balances, and weights were kept. He seemed to wince with every step. His elder also made his way behind the counter.

"Is there summat I kin do for ye today, sir?" He cocked his head sideways, perhaps finding it perplexing to see such a well-dressed gentleman enter his establishment. How would he go about explaining his purchasing interest for a woman such as Nurse Gwynne? What would they think?

Lucas cleared his throat. "I am here on an urgent quest for uh...my colleague, Nurse Gwynne. I am a doctor." The child and the man nodded in unison. So, they did know her. "Would it be possible to have your young man here cart uh...several...uh..." and here he looked back at the wagon where the boy had been napping, "perhaps three or four...loads of coal, firewood, and kindling to her flat? Uh... I will pay immediately and, uh..." He was making a fool of himself. He had never made such a purchase in his entire life. He had no idea what anything cost. He did not know how the coal or wood was ordered, in what quantities, how it was measured. But he forged on, nonetheless. He moved closer to the pair in front of him. "Could the boy stay a while after bringing the first load and light the stove, as well as start a fire in the fireplace, before he leaves to bring another...?" The boy nodded vigorously, making up for his stumbling gait. Shovel in hand, he began to fill a pail from the huge bags of coal around the outside walls of the shop. He then walked, hobbled really, towards the scale. Lucas now came right up to the man who stood next to the cash register and pulled out a bag of coins from the inside of his overcoat. The proprietor coughed.

"All right, so two loads o' firewood and kindlin', an' two loads o' coal? That be right?"

That was easy, thought Lucas. He smiled and nodded. The man wrote everything down on a piece of paper in a kind of abbreviated set of hieroglyphics. Phillip moved between the coal and the barrow, dumping the black rocks expertly within the large basin that he would eventually haul through the snow. Lucas turned to him and before Phillip hobbled back to the coal with his empty pail, he put his hand on the boy's shoulder, and looked into his face, "What, may I ask, is wrong with your foot or leg? You are limping badly, and it seems to hurt a great deal."

"Oh, don't ye worry none bout ol' Phillip, sir," jumped in the master of the place (his father?). "'E's always tryin' to get sympathy out o' anyone who'll pay attention." The man waved a hand at Phillip in a gesture of unconcern. "He's a bad'un, that'un." Lucas paid no attention to this outburst and continued to gaze at the boy.

"Nurse Gwynne is always tellin' me to stop by an' let 'er see me foot, but I, well…"

"There be no time for no nursin' in this business. You're 'ere to work an' that's …"

"But how can he work if he's in pain?" This Lucas directed at the owner. To the boy he said, "You must let us see to it tonight."

"Now wait a minute, sir, I'm not paying good money for no boy who shirks 'is duties and acts like 'e's sufferin' for no good reason. I give 'im room an' board in exchange for 'is work and 'e should be grateful." Lucas left Phillip to finish his job and came back to the man waiting to be paid. He paid the sum of money (how ridiculously little it was…to *him*, anyway), and since he supposed that the only way that he could persuade this irate man to let him see to the boy's injury was through his pocket, he made it very clear that he would not accept payment.

"I will not charge you a farthing for my services, but if you wish to keep Nurse Gwynne as a loyal patron of this establishment, you *will* allow us to examine the child's foot tonight after he has completed his duties for the evening. Do I make myself clear? And if we administer any kind of surgery, or poultice, there will be no charge at all. But Phillip *shall* be seen to, and tonight at the very latest. You should have listened to her before. The treatment might have been easier and less complicated had she taken care of it at an earlier stage." Lucas let out a long sigh. Why did this stone-cold man make him so angry? Why did he treat the boy so cruelly? And why did he, Lucas, feel so involved at that moment with the life of the woman he was just helping in a bad situation? He barely knew her, but something told him she would be a kind and compassionate nurse, and anyway, he had been persuaded that nursing was often more important than doctoring. Sometimes what the nurse could give was more valuable than what the doctor could give. It was not a popular opinion, but he held it.

As Lucas left the coal-monger's establishment, uncomfortable with his level of irritation, he recalled his sister reading from some of Florence Nightingale's writings on the subject of the importance of nursing in the life of a patient. Perhaps her view was not entirely scientific, given that it would be difficult to quantify exactly what the nurse offered up in the act of comforting and caring for her patient, but he understood that this immeasurable something was of great value. Just thinking about her wandering through the hospital wards in Scutari with her lamp in the middle of the night to check on her charges, soldiers either in the process of healing or dying, gave pause. Those soldiers who had returned after that terrible war in the Crimea, just two short years before, in 1856, had testified to the unbelievable curative powers of her presence lighting their sorry lives. Since her return, Miss Nightingale had not ventured out much, but her letters and tracts and political urgings to renew, for example, the state and the architecture of hospitals, had been circulating amongst the medical community's practitioners, and Isabel was forever commenting on her intriguing ideas, trying, no doubt, to arouse his interest. He had listened well to his sister, and had even agreed with many of her convictions, but it had never translated into his actually acting upon those ideas. He certainly agreed with Miss Nightingale's belief that the cleaning of drains was closer to God's will than the missionary's zeal to convert the heathen. She had got that right, and he had even seen the effects of good sanitation methods as opposed to prayer in the healing of many illnesses. But in all honesty, he was just too far gone into his daily despair to extricate himself from it and become an activist in favour of her pragmatic ideals.

For some reason, today or tonight, something had changed in him. Had it been his decision to seek the comfort of female flesh?

It had been a decision, taken over several days, as he had been contemplating an end to his pain. Perhaps decisiveness of any kind, even the most immoral, was capable of removing the inertia and ineptitude he generally wallowed in. He now wanted, really wanted, to help this Nurse Gwynne, healer of the unfortunate poor of East London. Was that how she earned her bread? It could not have been very lucrative seeing that her would-be patients had nothing or extremely little with which to pay for her services. As he moved along towards the store which she had indicated would provide him with the necessities she required—bread, milk, butter, tea—a female costermonger selling meat pies eyed him hopefully, and he thought, well, why not? Perhaps a few of these pies would make some sort of difference to the physical well-being of the woman he was engaged in helping. He motioned to the pie-seller that he was interested in her wares. She moved towards him along her snow-covered path, and he pulled out some coins from his waistcoat pocket. "How much for two, no, three...?", for suddenly he thought of Phillip, probably half-starved by his nasty employer. The woman told him the price, and again Lucas was surprised by how little things seemed to cost in this part of town. He thought of meals he had consumed in various inns and what they had cost him. Perhaps there were many more potatoes and much less meat in these particular pies. As he gave her the coins, and she placed one on top of another into the cloth bag with which Nurse Gwynne had provided him for his purchases, he decided to discover what he could about her role in the lives of her fellow citizens of these impoverished streets. "Uhm, do you know a certain Nurse Gwynne, miss?"

"Why, o' course, I do. Every 'un knows o' Nurse Gwynne in this town, sir. Do ye need 'er services?" She looked him up and down now, finding it a little difficult to believe that such a prosperous-looking gentleman could not find a doctor to pay for whatever it was he needed.

"Uh, well, uh, I am a doctor, and I, too, know of the healing that she provides you. It was just that I was not sure if...as you say...everyone was aware of her skills."

The woman smiled. "It's nice of a doctor to give Nurse Gwynne 'er due. Not many o' Miss Nightingale's nurses 'ave made it to Whitechapel to...ye know...do what it is they can fer us poor folk. She's a rare 'un, is she."

Lucas was intrigued. "You mean, Nurse Gwynne has been to the war, has nursed in the Crimean war?"

The pie-seller now showed surprise. "Ye mean ye didna know that she nursed where'er that last war took place?!"

"No, I did not, but I will make sure that she tells me of her experiences. And, just one more thing, if I may. If you say, uh, that she treats all you poor folk, how is it that she can survive? Surely it would be very difficult for you to pay her for her services?"

"Well, I, fer one, work meself to the bone to provide fer me blessed wee 'uns, but a meat pie now and then in payment when they's feelin' poorly be well worth the trouble," the woman proudly responded.

Lucas nodded. He smiled at her, thanked her for her information, and proceeded towards the establishment two doors up from where they had been chatting. He was getting more and more captivated by the talented and accomplished Nurse Gwynne. To think that she had known, no, had *worked with* his sister's very own heroine! Isa would be fascinated. But how would he manage to invent a plausible story as to his meeting with this nurse? Would he have to keep it a secret from Isabel?

Chapter II

On his way back to Nurse Gwynne's rooms, or more precisely room, Lucas was feeling a kind of excitement. He was bearing gifts, and it made him feel beneficent, although his gifts had hardly cost him much. He couldn't exactly say that they represented the fruits of his labours. But, no matter, it did not do to dwell on such a matter. He was doing something. And in a few hours, he would be tending hopefully to Phillip's ailment. He would be useful. At least he could be useful on this strangest of days in a series of miserable ones.

The children previously playing in front of her dwelling were no longer there, but their escapades in the snow could be traced every which way. It made him smile to himself, a rare occurrence lately. What could all this mean? Why was he so interested in this young woman's life? Did it mean that he could somehow have a future in this world, he who had been thinking most definitely that he no longer had a future, if he had ever had one, after that terrible day when he had caused the accident? Why must that definitive moment in his history keep such vigilance over his days on earth, squashing them somehow, squeezing the very life out of them? He shook his head. He wanted to scatter those thoughts, join them with those jumbled footsteps of the children who had spent their freedom mauling each other playfully in the snow. And perhaps, he and Nurse Gwynne might join their bodies into one underneath that quilt of which she had spoken. He shivered suddenly, and not from cold. And yet, what about the father of that little boy? Would he be a deterrent? This afternoon, he had not been, when she had deemed it absolutely necessary to feed her child and heat her home.

Lucas pushed the cumbersome door open with his shoulder, his hands filled with more than one bag. He noticed Phillip's barrow just inside the entrance. He must be upstairs lighting the fires and heating up the stove. Lucas very nearly ran up the flight of stairs leading to Nurse Gwynne's flat. At the end of the hall, he put one of his parcels down and knocked at the door. But it was not Gwynne herself who opened the door. Nor was it Phillip, but a strange woman, a toddler in her arms. He bent over to pick up the bag he had left on the floor, saying nothing.

"Quickly, quickly, Doctor, or ye'll be lettin' out all o' this lovely warmth that our Phillip is makin'," the stranger urged him. He obliged her and moved quickly into the house, searching for a sign from Gwynne regarding how he was supposed to react to the appearance of this woman in her home. Gwynne was at the stove. A pot of water had obviously just begun to boil, and she was grasping the handle of the pot with her apron and then going over to the basin on the floor to fill it with the water. After she completed her task, she turned to him and gave him the sincerest smile he had ever seen. She was happy to see him! After all, he was supposedly bringing sustenance for her beloved baby. But maybe she had worried just a little bit that he would not reappear, except that he had left his doctor bag on her dining-table. Phillip was picking up his empty pails and heading towards him and the door.

"I still 'ave another trip to make, sir. I'd best be goin'."

"But Phillip, when you return, do not forget to remind your master that you will not be going home immediately. There is the matter of your injury. I am determined to see what I can do to make you more comfortable."

"Yes, sir, I will." He was out the door in a flash, obviously worried about displeasing that master. Lucas placed all the bags on the dining-table and removed his outerwear, before addressing the mother and child on his right.

"Pleased to make your acquaintance. I am Doctor Lucas Lacey. Is there something amiss with your child?" He looked down at the little girl, mucous from her nose copiously running down over her lips, onto her chin, and further down onto her mother's hand beneath her chin. And then the child started to cough. She buried her face into her mother's chest, no doubt covering her mother's shawl with all her various excretions. "Well, I guess, she and Master uh..." he interrupted himself and raised his eyes to Gwynne. What was her son's name?

"Charles," Gwynne immediately replied and pointed to him seated on his makeshift bed, watching all the comings and goings, with his head listlessly leaning against the upper drawer, too weak to hold it up by himself.

"—uh, she and Master Charles have much in common." While his mother prepared to heat the milk with which she would feed him, Lucas listened to the girl's chest with his rather new bi-aural stethoscope, a gift last year from his aunt. After that, he administered to the child a teaspoon of the same tonic that he had to Charles. She, too—Selina was her name, and Jane, her mother's— made a face at the taste, but complained less than the boy had done. At this point, Gwynne came over and took the two-year-old from her mother, saying that she was about to give both babies a bath since it was nice and warm beside the roaring fire in the once-cold grate.   While she undressed Selina with the help of Jane, Lucas went over to the stove and poured the heated milk into a metal cup Gwynne had prepared for her child. He left it on the dining-table, and to the sounds of the little girl kicking her legs in the water, he went over to Charles and carefully lifted him up into his arms. Charles made no fuss. In fact, he intently watched everything Lucas was doing. Finally, Lucas brought the warm milk to Charles's lips and the boy slurped away, completely comfortable in the crook of Lucas's arm. Lucas sat down on one of the chairs and chatted nonsense to the little boy. He could feel Gwynne's eyes on him and Charles as she stood up, allowing Jane to take care of washing her little girl.

"Oh, by the way," Lucas interrupted the peace spreading around them, speaking to Gwynne, "when I passed by the shop where they sell used clothing, I went in and bought some clean cloth nappies—I suppose you can never have enough of them—and a sweater, leggings, and thick socks for Charles. I hope you can make use of them."

"Oh, my," she uttered, covering her lips with the palm of her hand. She blushed. "You are too generous, Dr. Lacey."

"Lucas, call me Lucas. And you have no idea how little my generosity was used in making those purchases. My generosity cannot compare with your own in helping the people of your neighbourhood." He stared into her eyes, trying to make her see the truth in his words, how much he admired her, and her selflessness in making available all she had learned from her nursing experience in the last war. He had done little himself with all the knowledge he had garnered from his own studies. She looked confused. Of course! She could not have known that he had questioned the pie-seller in the street. Not wanting to embarrass either her or himself with a disclosure of his investigations into how she earned her meagre living, he suggested that she boil water for tea and place the meat-pies that he had bought into the oven for heating up. He mentioned that besides tea and milk and butter and bread, he had bought some Wensleydale cheese, which he hoped she loved as much as he did.

Gwynne may have been thoroughly confused by all his purchases, but she did go over to them and begin unpacking the bags he had filled. There was also a pot of jam. He had wanted to buy chocolate powder as a hot beverage for all of them, since he considered it to be most healthful, but there had not been any in this part of London. He would have to bring some tomorrow. Tomorrow? Did he plan on coming back tomorrow? Well, he did have to see his patients, perhaps Phillip included. He looked up at Gwynne. She was staring at him. Had she read his thoughts? He felt as if she had, digging deeply into his psyche with her unfathomable nursing skills. Gwynne walked back to the stove to heat up some milk for their little patient, who was now being towelled down by her mother. She then went over to the package of nappies on the table. He had bought twenty, so she could afford to offer one to the other needy mother in the room. When the kettle began to whistle, she filled the tea pot and brought it to the table. The pies were warming nicely in the oven. She brought some cups to the table and asked if they all wanted milk in their tea. Lucas nodded. Charles had finished drinking. He looked a great deal better. It was time for his bath. His mother lifted the basin and went through the door beside the stove, presumably to drain the water out of it. When she returned, her friend was pouring tea, and he was busy undressing Charles. He handed Charles over to her and he filled the now-empty basin with a mixture of hot and cool water. She then bent down with Charles and carefully placed him into the tub. He obviously enjoyed the sensation of the warm water, and with more life than he had previously demonstrated, began slapping the water beside him with his little hands. Gwynne laughed. How lovely that laugh! She could be made happy by such small things—a baby, *her* baby enjoying the comfort of the warmth around him. Lucas sat down again and took the cup proffered by the other mother. Selina was now dressed in clothes none too clean. At least the nappy was clean. The baby was sitting on her mother's lap. Lucas decided to cut some pieces of cheese. There was no knife on the table, but he had a pen knife in his jacket pocket. He took it out and cut some slivers. He offered one to the little girl and told her mother to try one as well. He then got up and took an empty cup from the table and filled it with some warm milk for Selina, who was happily munching on the cheese. If only he could be made so easily happy. Why was it so much easier for everyone else to find just a little bit of happiness? Why was it so difficult for him?

Chapter III

Lucas and Gwynne were sitting and drinking some well-deserved tea. Gwynne felt happily tired from her exertions. Lucas had performed the small surgery on poor Phillip's swollen foot admirably. She herself had sewed the sutures and Lucas had watched, totally absorbed by her skill in this area. She had sewn countless injured limbs during her stay in that dreadful hospital in Scutari and later in the General Hospital in the Crimea. Eighteen months in hell it had been. But she had learned her lessons well. No one could take that from her.

Their three charges, Charles, Selina, and Phillip, were sleeping peacefully in her own bed. There would be no moving them tonight, and no place for either Lucas or herself to fulfil the obligation which she owed him. Lucas had just mentioned that he would have to visit the coal merchant and give him the news that Phillip would not be available to him for a few days. He would also have to bring some sort of crutch for the boy if he was to get around.

"I had better go now before the horrible fellow closes up shop. I will buy Phillip some clothes and undergarments at the used-clothing shop. He's wearing my shirt and I think I'd like it back." They both laughed at this pleasantry. After Phillip had had a bath and had his hair washed, probably for the first time in years, it was unthinkable for him to put his old clothes back on. They were best burned in the fire. Lucas seemed to have endless amounts of money. As far as she was concerned, he was spending it rather wisely, although perhaps you could say that his initial purchase, that of herself, could be considered less wise. She was concerned now about how she would repay him. She could not repay him for his generosity, but something about the man told her that he would not exact anything from her without her consent. What was he doing in this part of the city anyway? If he wanted a woman, surely he could have found a brothel of harlots more suited to his means. There probably existed dozens of them for the very rich in London. And yet, he did not seem to be a man who went in for that sort of thing. Although she had rarely encountered a true gentleman in her life, Lucas certainly lived up to the "gentle" part of that word. Never had she seen a more gentle man around children. He had fed her own child! He had been so delicate with Phillip. He had talked to and soothed the boy continuously through his ordeal. The surgeons she had known were not always competent, never mind gentle. But perhaps they had been inured to all the blood and broken bones around them. She did not really know how much doctoring this young man had done in his life. Truth be told, however, she liked him. There were few men that she did, for they rarely considered the consequences of their actions, especially towards women. Even her own father had often hurt her mother's feelings without a thought. He liked the fact that she earned money as a governess to his patron, and that his daughter was able to learn beside the two boys of the household. Lord and Lady Ridgley, who employed them, were kind enough to allow his daughter to be educated and to have access to their well-stocked library, but that did not mean that he felt obliged to demonstrate his gratitude in some way to his wife. As far as he was concerned, her mother was fortunate to be married to a man of such skill, a wheelwright by trade, in the services of one of the wealthiest men in all Derbyshire. She had a good life, and he didn't seem to think that he owed her any respect. She was his wife, and most definitely his servant.

When her mother had told her father that Gwynne would be going back to London after the war to be a nurse instead of remaining in Derbyshire to be a governess, he was furious with them. How dare they make such a stupid decision. "Life," he had proclaimed, "would be so much better here in Derbyshire. I can't believe that you have consented to our daughter going. We need her here." He was so angry that he headed for the door. As he slammed it shut behind him, he shouted, "Women have no brains! I would rather spend my time conversing with carriages and carts!"

Gwynne did not like to think about her father or her life in Derby. She might be poor now, but she was no man's servant. This doctor, however, seated across from her, and now rising to go out into the elements once again on another lofty purpose, was different, strange even. He never treated her in a superior fashion. He was quite self-deprecating, in fact. And he was just himself. He showed his emotions—his surprise at her real circumstances, his anger at Phillip's master, his wonder at her competence, his concern for the welfare of the people who had suddenly appeared in his life. And he had put her needs and that of her son before his own. Who was he? Why was he so willing to be her benefactor today? What had she done to deserve this? Would he take advantage of her, ultimately? She suddenly looked up at him with fear in her eyes as he pulled on his greatcoat. He saw what she was feeling, she was sure of it.

"I...I promise I will be back with those garments for Phillip. You will not need to wash those rags for him. He deserves better. What a horrible life he has had, first in the Workhouse and then as a slave to that dreadful master. You will not have to take care of him alone. It was *my* idea to treat him, and he will be *my* responsibility. You do know that don't you? I certainly feel the need to do more for him. I am not sure why exactly, or what I can do, but being privy to the abuse of that horrible coal merchant has made me almost wish to extract him from his present situation. Perhaps you think that I am being foolish." He came closer to her now, wanting obviously to convince her of the seriousness of his intentions towards Phillip. But what about his intentions towards her? Could she trust this man? He heaved a great sigh and then made a most startling revelation. "You do not know this, and how could you? But you have done more for me than anyone I can think of right now. I am indebted to you. I was on the brink of something today, something enormous, and...and...you...you somehow caught me by the tails of my coat before I fell into the abyss." He wiped a hand over his eyes as if wiping away a bad dream. He then placed his hands on the back of the chair in front of him. "And what is even more extraordinary is the fact that I can say this to you, without subterfuge, without any of the artifice of my class." He stared into her eyes, and she nodded her understanding, for in a way, she, too, had not felt any shame with him. She had made clear her needs and her willingness to sink to the level of a harlot with him. She had accepted his money and his food and his nappies! She had not lost her self-esteem, her pride, indeed herself with him, and well she could have, if it had been any other man who had followed her into her home and her life. She realized that she wanted to know his story, his history, why he had felt such despair. Perhaps she did not deserve to know it, for he had given her so much already, but she would ask him just the same.

"When you come back...tonight...you...if you want...could tell me what has happened to you...why you were on the brink of whatever it was." Here she stopped for a moment, suddenly ashamed of her candour. She dropped her eyes from him and looked at her hands in her lap. How could she have said that? It was like asking for his soul. But he replied:

"Yes, I think I would like that. I don't know how you know that I would want to talk about it. I don't think that I even knew before you said it." She heard him sigh deeply, and so she raised her eyes again. They both gazed at each other for what seemed, to Gwynne, a considerable length of time. Something was happening. Something was happening to him. Something was happening to her. She had known all along that going out this afternoon to find a man to pay her for her services would change her life forever, might make her never want to know a man in that way ever again. The experience with Charles's father had left her changed, yes, but she had recovered something that she had lost to him through her son. She could never say "their son", for that man, that gentleman, still did not know that he was a father and never would. She hoped never to see him again, and why would she? He would probably never set foot in East London, even though Lucas, this particular gentleman had. He was probably married now, anyway, and still seducing servant girls or raping governesses or anyone that worked for him because he thought that it was his right. It was what she hated most about him—his certainty of entitlement. The first time he had forced his wishes on her, she had told her mother, who promptly sent her off to London to work in Florence Nightingale's Institution for Sick Gentlewomen in Distressed Circumstances, basically a home for ailing impecunious governesses. Fortunately, her mother, a governess herself, and known to Miss Nightingale in their youth in Derbyshire, had written a well-received letter of introduction to the exemplary woman. Prickly though she was, she allowed Gwynne to work in this institution. Later, after much pleading on the part of Gwynne, who was only twenty at the outset of the War, consented to take her along to work in the Barrack Hospital in Scutari, across from Constantinople on the other side of the Bosporus. It was there that they treated the soldiers fighting the Russians in the Crimea. The problem was that when she came back to England, she went home to her family in Derbyshire, a place she should have avoided at all costs, because the young master, the very man who had introduced her to her inferior position in the world, taking advantage of his superior position, was at home at that moment from university. He managed to find her alone one day in the kitchen when all the servants had gone to church. He was angry that she had disappeared years before, and that anger translated itself into unspeakable violence. First he beat her, and finally violated her once again. This time he had impregnated her. Her mother sent her with all the money she could spare back to London and to a dear cousin, a woman who had been living in the very flat she and her son now shared. The arrangement was fine at first. Gwynne was able to work in a hospital as a nurse—after all, she had trained in the War—but it was merely drudgery. Nevertheless, her wage helped sustain their little household of two. When the fact that she was with child began to show prominently, Gwynne began to work as a healer in the neighbourhood, the poor coming to her humble abode to trade whatever they could afford for her invaluable skills. Six months earlier, Gwynne had been left alone with Charles to fend for herself, largely depending on the generosity of her extremely poor patients, who gave her very little or nothing at all. This day had marked her utter destitution, hence her decision earlier that afternoon. At this moment, however, staring into the face of the magnanimous Doctor Lacey, she no longer felt so destitute. She was warm. She had eaten. And her son, too, was on the mend, having not only supped at the gentle hands of her benevolent saviour, but having also been medicated with some sort of liquid remedy and clothed in some cosy woollies. The future was uncertain, but at least for a short time, she could feel as if she had been restored to a minimum of wellbeing. It would give her strength.

Lucas hesitated momentarily, but then proceeded to button his overcoat in preparation for his journey into the wintry wilds of Whitechapel. She stood as he wound his scarf around his neck. She felt a desire to be close to him, so she went to the other side of the table and picked up the gloves and hat that he had left there upon coming in the last time. At the door she handed them to him.

"I hope it is not colder than before. And you have one less layer, since you are not wearing a shirt."

He smiled at her as he took his winter paraphernalia from her. "I will be fine, although I am not looking forward to my talk with Phillip's master. Who knows how that man will react?"

Gwynne shrugged her shoulders. She felt as if she were keeping him from leaving, because, frankly, she wanted to be in his company, so she stepped back from him. He gave her a nod, turned away from her, and opened the door.

Chapter IV

The man in the used clothing store had a practically complete outfit for a twelve-year-old boy, the height and approximate weight of Phillip. Lucas realized that he would have to ransack the clothing that his uncle and aunt had saved from his own childhood if he wanted to decently clothe Phillip in the near future. Had he made the right choice about Phillip? What would Gwynne think? When he arrived at her flat and had removed his overcoat, and she had asked him about what had taken place at the coal merchant, he answered her by showing her the piece of paper with which that nasty fellow had provided him.

"This is the document that shows that the Whitechapel Workhouse relinquished Phillip as an apprentice to Mr. Housman and that Phillip became his responsibility at the time. Why do *you* have it?"

"Because I basically bought Phillip from him—for all of five pounds."

"Five pounds?!"

"Is that too much or too little? I have no idea, and frankly I don't really care what he charged me. The thing is—" here Lucas swallowed hard, as if fully absorbing the momentousness of his decision only as he began recounting what had transpired to Gwynne. "He's all mine now and...hopefully...if possible, I can give him a better life." Somehow, *he* felt like a little boy now. Who buys a child but someone who has not really lived in the world at large? He was a novice at life, at work, at responsibility. He was untried and miserably unprepared. The only thing he was good at was suffering. He took a deep breath. "Do you think I have done the wrong thing? Mr. Housman was ill-prepared to give Phillip an hour off, let alone a few days. I did not exactly have a choice." Lucas looked hopefully at Gwynne, seated to his left, her back to the fire. He was at the head of the table. Before she could give him an answer, he turned to gaze at the boy sleeping at the edge of the bed, the boy he had just taken under his wing. Did it mean he would have to be like a father? Could he just be a teacher to him? He could teach him how to read and write, but where would he live? Would he live with the servants of the family household in Chelsea? Would he have him live with him in his rooms, which he still continued to rent even after he had graduated from medical school and had stopped working in the hospital nearby? Would Phillip become some kind of servant to him? He turned back to Gwynne to get some answers from a woman who, though younger, had a great deal more experience with life. She was busy putting more wood on the fire. He watched her graceful movements. He loved the fact that she did not wear the whalebone corsets and hoops so fashionable these days among the women of the noble classes. It wasn't just the creaking when they sat—it was also the voluminous skirts that hid the body beneath. Poorer women could not afford whalebone. For him it seemed a part of Gwynne's total honesty.

She finally sat down and smiled at him. Did she think he was a fool? And if he told her of his other plans, just recently hatched, as he trudged through the cold and the snow, how would she react? But he had to tell her, because without her, there would be no plans, no future, no possibility of extricating himself from his debilitating spiritual—no other word for it—predicament.

"There is something else that I wish to tell you, that I need to tell you, something that could involve you, if you're interested." Her expression became serious. She moved her chair closer to the table and placed her joined hands on the surface. Did she look worried? "I need to do something useful with my life, the way that you do, and the only thing I know how to do is be a doctor. But, in truth, I really only enjoy the company of children. It's true. Perhaps it is something you have surmised."

Gwynne nodded. "Your skill with treating children, no, just in being with children is very noticeable. I have never known a gentleman, and I have been acquainted with a few, to take much interest in children, let alone their daily physical needs. Gentlemen do not think about nappies. Do they ever actually feed a child?" Lucas shrugged. "Well, if they do, I presume, only with some kind of encouragement from a mother. You do not seem to need any such encouragement. In fact—" here she smiled broadly at him, demonstrating again, it seemed, that she actually liked him. "I would say that it gives you pleasure to please a child. It is as if the cloud that has descended on your life is lifted when you engage in any way with one. Am I right?" She leaned her head slightly towards her shoulder as she made this query. It was such a charming gesture that Lucas felt his heart begin to thump. Every gesture of this woman affected him. He so wanted to touch her. He wanted to be sure that they were in this reality together. He did not want her to be a figment of his imagination. He moved his hand ever so slowly across the table and allowed his fingertips to seek out hers. He felt an electric current fly up his arm to his neck and throat. He could barely speak. She did not remove her fingers from his touch.

Lucas nodded. In a gruff voice, he spoke: "Yes, I guess you are right, although before tonight, I could probably have never expressed it. As a student doctor, I sometimes treated children, and I definitely enjoyed talking to them, trying to make them feel comfortable with me, if they were not too sick to notice me." Although he was totally focussed on what he was saying, his gaze was fixed on the touching of their hands, and on this special communion between them. "Would you like to work with me, be my helpmeet, on...on a totally equal footing, that is, you and me, and these children...?" He gestured to the ones in the bed, and then to all the imaginary others outside the glow of this tiny universe they inhabited together. "We...we could start a surgery, no, a real hospital for children, the ill-fed, ill-clothed paupers of this community that have come to know you as Nurse Gwynne.

Side-by-side we could treat them, nurture them...and in turn, they could renew my faith in life."

"You do know that there is not a farthing to be made in treating the destitute impoverished children of East London. Their parents, if they are not orphans, can barely afford to feed them, let alone pay the expense of a doctor, or even a humble nurse such as myself. You do remember what I was forced to do this afternoon, don't you?" Lucas took a sharp intake of breath. How could he forget?

Still mesmerized by the sight of their converging fingertips, Lucas answered her. "Oh, I have no intention of exacting any payment. It would be a charity hospital, at first funded by myself, and later by the philanthropy of the upper classes. I feel sure that I could get my aunt and my sister to broadcast the necessity of their support. I can seek counsel from my solicitor about the registration of such a charity. And you and whoever else we would need to work with us would be paid a decent wage and never want for anything. You will never have to throw yourself to the wolves again, Gwynne." And then he became bolder and took her hands fully in his. The desire to convince her was so strong that he barely heard the knock at the door, but when it became insistent, they both looked up at each other. "Another patient at this late hour?"

"Perhaps," replied Gwynne.

"I will answer the door. You stay here." Lucas rose and headed for the door. He turned the handle and when he opened it, he saw a short, stocky, middle-aged man, looking almost like a mummy, so wrapped up was he against the frigid air. The man looked startled to see him there.

"Uh, Miss Gwynne, please. Is she in?"

"Yes, she is. Are you seeking medical attention?"

"No, I am not. I am her landlord. I saw light under the door, and I decided to see if I could manage to squeeze the rent out of her at this late hour. It is almost Christmas and I have received nothing for weeks and weeks." He looked Lucas up and down.

"You seem to be a man of the world. Surely you understand the necessity of meeting one's obligations. I can no longer afford to be patient, my good sir, whoever you may be."

As Lucas moved over to let the importunate man in, he could see the man's gaze fall on the numerous shillings that he, Lucas, had left on this end of the table hours ago—and it seemed like days since that had happened. "Well," the man uttered with excitement, "perhaps Nurse Gwynne was prepared to see me tonight." He rubbed his hands together and finally looked up at Lucas, so difficult was it to tear his eyes away from the sight of all that money, and then turned his head to take in Gwynne at the other end of the room. Gwynne looked bereft and uncomfortable, but Lucas took the situation in his stride. After all, he was a gentleman, and in matters of money—he had just spent five pounds of his on a lifelong purpose—he had learned how to behave.

"Oh, by all means, sir, my colleague Nurse Gwynne and I were just discussing the need to pay you what is owed." Lucas made a slight bow and then offered his hand. The landlord shook it eagerly. "My name is Dr. Lacey. Your tenant and I have worked together on many an occasion in various hospitals."

"Gaunt is my name. Pleased to make your acquaintance." Mr. Gaunt looked sceptical of Lucas's expressed motive for being in a young woman's home at this hour of the night but kept any comment to himself. He moved towards the money, picking each coin up after he removed his gloves. "One...two...three weeks...and may I take this and next week's, as well?" He eyed Lucas and not Gwynne as he made this request.

Lucas nodded his approval. "Of course, and...actually...the reason I am here...and since you are here...I was wondering if you would be so good as to inform me if you have any other premises to let in this area...to serve as our surgery, since I do not think that Nurse Gwynne can continue to operate out of her home any longer."

The man opened his eyes wide. "Here? You want to open a surgery here?!"

"Actually, something more in the vein of a small charity hospital...for, uh...sick children, that is."

"A charity hospital for the children of Whitechapel?!"

"Why so surprised? Can you think of a borough more in need of such an establishment?"

"Well, no, I suppose you're right." Mr. Gaunt had finished gathering up the coins and was dropping them into the pocket of his overcoat. "Far be it from me to discourage you...If you have the money, I have the space. Nurse Gwynne knows that right next door in this very building there is a rather large and empty flat I have not rented out in a long while. It was just waiting for you, my good sir. The inhabitants of this neighbourhood do not seem to be able to afford such a commodious and healthful suite of rooms. Would you care to have a look now? I always have my keys." Gaunt jingled them in his pocket. "We could take my lamp and see if it takes your fancy."

Lucas turned towards Gwynne. "Shall we go now, or shall we wait until tomorrow to see it in the daylight?"

"I cannot leave the children unattended, but you may go—"

"—and tomorrow we can look again together. I would not make any kind of decision without you."

Looking slightly aghast at the quick turn of events, Gwynne nodded to Lucas, and armed with her permission and approval, Lucas followed the landlord out of her flat. What a day and night this had been! And it was not yet over.

Chapter V

When Lucas and Mr. Gaunt left, Gwynne immediately got up to fill the kettle from the pail on the floor near the stove. Lucas had gone several times down the back stairs to the pump in the courtyard to fill her pail, especially when they had had to bathe the children. She had never known a man, except a paid servant, to haul water for someone like her. No one had had to ask him, either. Surely, he did not help his own servants to fetch water. Perhaps he even had indoor plumbing, something she had recently heard about. This particular representative of the upper class was so unusual. And the offer he had made her! To work alongside him, equal to equal! Even Miss Nightingale— a woman who always insisted that she should be in charge of everything concerning the running of a hospital—would have been astonished. Miss Nightingale had always had to fight for every change she wanted. And now this doctor just declared that it would be so. She would not have to fight for anything. Of course, perhaps it would not turn out like that. Perhaps he was just saying it. But taking orders from a man like Dr. Lacey would be a great deal easier than it had been from the likes of the doctors at the Barracks Hospital. They had been uncouth and rude from the first day. It was true that conditions had been horrible, and no one had actually had enough to eat. In the winter it had been hard to keep warm. Perhaps in some nobleman's drawing room, these surgeons would have behaved otherwise. But she had known the real and not the fake, well-mannered doctor, the one easily capable of touching her and making advances that never seemed to stop, no matter how insistent she had been in her rejections. Even the older doctors, with wives and children at home, groped her when they could, bribing her with any treat they could think of to be able to lie with her. Some of the nurses did give in, just to have that extra morsel of food, to have the gin offered to them. It had been a hopeless situation, and she never blamed the other women for their desires. But she knew that in her heart of hearts she blamed the men, those so-called gentlemen. The soldiers on the other hand showed their gratitude constantly, if you held their hand, for example, during a particularly painful or gruesome procedure. The youngest even fell in love with the nurses. Many were sad at the loss of one of their limbs, and a smile from a nurse meant a great deal. She hoped they did not go home to beat their wives. Gwynne shivered at the thought. Perhaps you could not trust any man, not just gentlemen, to control their hands when they felt deprived of something from a woman they felt was obliged to yield to their demands.

Lucas had done another extraordinary thing. He had pledged to take care of Phillip. He had paid a man like Housman for the privilege. Yes, it was easy for him to spend his money. He seemed to have so much of it. But most gentlemen his age, especially the idle ones, like Edmund, father to Charles, spent it on their personal pleasures. What would they do with Phillip? What was to be his fate now? Surely it would be better than the one on offer from his master, Housman. She could help with Phillip, although she had no right to presume that she would have any say in his future. She mustn't get her hopes up. She mustn't think that just because Lucas said something today, it would happen tomorrow. Gentlemen were supposed to keep their word. But what about the promise to protect those under your roof? How many times had Edmund's parents been forced to protect *him* from some monetary demand from a poor girl in their employ who had been taken advantage of by the superior braggart and lout of a son that he was? What about protecting the girl herself? Was that not a responsibility of the gentle classes? Gwynne shook her head as if she had been having the conversation with another self. It did no good dwelling on the injustices of this world, nor did it do her any good to think about Edmund, free and unfettered, sowing his seed or seeds indiscriminately around the country and beyond.

If Lucas wanted her to work for him, she would. She would fulfil her duties as a competent and reliable nurse for him. She would interpret the needs of the poor for him, too. He did not seem to have much experience in the realities of East London life. She smiled as she took the kettle off the hob and poured some water into the teapot. He would be the apprentice in many ways. She swished the water around, poured it out into a basin, then added the tea and filled the pot. She brought it to the table. The cups were still there, and she poured a bit of milk into each one. Even the tea he had bought was better than any tea she had drunk in years. Where had he found it? Did the shop where she usually went carry this sort of better-quality product? It must...but the proprietor had obviously never offered it to her.

Gwynne sat down again, wondering why it was taking so long for Lucas to return. In the silence she listened to the steady breathing of the three children. Sometimes either Charles or Selina coughed. There was still congestion in their lungs, but a good night's sleep, something that Charles had not had for quite a while, would be very beneficial. She thanked Lucas silently for coming to her aid this afternoon. She realized that she wanted him to continue to be in her life at least for a bit longer. The world had suddenly become so much more interesting, much less repetitive. He surprised her every time he opened his mouth. She believed, too, that he would share something important with her before the night was over. He had said that he wanted to. Perhaps their intimacy would end after they became employer and employee. The thought saddened her. She desired to know him better. He had suffered, too, in a very different way than her, but he had known real sorrow in his life. And why did he speak of an aunt and a sister and not a mother? Had he experienced unspeakable loss? What had befallen him in his past that he was still trying to grapple with? Why had he come here, practically to her door today, when he had a whole city of experienced prostitutes to choose from? She shivered from the sense of mystery surrounding this man, so unlike any man she had ever known.

Chapter VI

After bidding farewell to Gaunt, Lucas knocked again at a door at which he had knocked countless times today. He felt buoyant and heartened by the dialogue he had had with the man. Possibility was gladdening his previously heavy heart. He was so anxious to speak with Gwynne that he did not wait for her to open the door to him. He pushed it inwards and there she was, her hand extended, just about to turn the handle. He smiled broadly at her but excused himself for not having been able to delay his eagerness to be with her. He said all that, too. Would there be no end to the surprising honesty that had sprung up between them from the beginning? He knew that he held his true self back from just about everyone, even from his sister, fearing always that he would disillusion her. But with this woman he felt no such fear, perhaps because she had already seen the worst of him. He had nothing to lose. It was possible that neither did she.

She, too, smiled openly. "You were confabulating with my landlord ever so long. Were you successful?" Before he answered her, she took his hand and guided him to the fireplace where two chairs sat in front of it. "Let us sit here. I have noticed that the bottoms of your trousers have become wet after so many times in the snow today. There must be a whole foot of it out there by now."

"Indeed," he replied, happily following in her wake. When he sat down, she offered him a mug of tea and encouraged him to remove his shoes as well. Perhaps, she said, his socks were also wet. He did as she bade him. Then she took a mug for herself and sat down beside him. He sighed deeply and took a gulp of tea. It warmed him as it went down. The rooms next door had been frigid, and he still did not have a shirt on, only his waistcoat above his under-vest, and then a wool frock coat that was not meant for such inhumanly cold temperatures. He felt at ease and stared into the fire. If all went well, this woman and her feminine comfort might become a quotidian dream come true. He then could become a truthful person, a man of some validity, and no longer a man of ineptitude. He had big hopes. Were they too big? Would she discover his weaknesses? Would he disappoint her, too? This was not a woman easily taken in, and buying the trifles he had bought today would not be enough to convince her of his worth.

"Tell me of the rooms next door. They must be of a certain size, since until three months ago, they were inhabited by three separate families who could not afford to live on their own."

"According to Gaunt, they could hardly afford to live there at all, even with sharing the rent. It was getting increasingly difficult to collect it from them. They were in the habit of paying whatever they could on a weekly basis, but in the end they all up and left."

Gwynne grew still. "I myself might have been thrown onto the street had you not come to my rescue today," she softly whispered, head down, eyes on the mug of tea in her lap.

Lucas nodded and then blurted out, unthinkingly: "The landlord just assumed that I was the wayward husband and father finally come home. He kept saying that you were a good woman and did not deserve bad treatment from anyone. I assumed he was lecturing me for my failure to keep you safe and secure."

"What!? He thought *what*!?"

"It was merely my conjecture, but it seems logical enough. I'm sorry if it hurts you." He twisted his body around towards her. "Truly, I am sorry. Perhaps I should not have spoken. I do not seem to be able to control my tongue with you. Things just come out." He hesitated a moment before adding: "It is a blessing, actually, not to have to censor myself. It gets so tiring to pretend all the time. Do you know what I mean?"

But she did not answer him. "Did you disabuse him of such a notion?"

"Well, he never said it overtly, so I...I...did I do the wrong thing? I...I...guess I was being selfish. It was easier. I *am* truly sorry. We can tell him the truth tomorrow when he comes again in the afternoon, before it gets dark, to let you look at the premises yourself." Lucas began to tremble. Please don't let this stupid mistake ruin everything, he prayed.

Gwynne scratched her head and looked away from him for a moment. To Lucas, she looked confused, surprised, startled, but not angry. Please let that be true.

"Whyever would you let him think such a thing? I know that this is only the East London slums, and your friends and family are hardly likely to set foot in our vicinity, but surely you have some sort of reputation to uphold? Gaunt could talk to acquaintances, mention your name...."

Lucas nodded his head. Before he replied, he took a sip of tea, needing the time to manufacture a logical response. Why had he been so comfortable with linking himself to this woman in a more than professional way? It was quite simple, really. "I...I...guess it felt good, even with the veiled reprimand from him for having abandoned you for so long." Now they both turned towards each other, she looking sceptical and guarded. Lucas, feeling contrite, brushed his free hand over his eyes and face. He looked down. "What you must think of someone like me. In reality, I am more destitute than you are." Before he went on, he sighed deeply, worrying about how she would perceive him. "It did feel good, though. It felt as if I had my boots bolted to the earth. I had weight. Oh, it is so much better being this errant husband to you and father to Charles, than being Lucas Lacey, a man with no purpose, a man of little consequence." And now he felt as if he wanted to cry. But that would not be fair to her. His lack of clarity with Gaunt had been unfair to her as well, and maybe to a man she had once loved. Was that man dead? Had he been a soldier at war in the Crimea? And what had he, Lucas, done to her, to their budding relationship by admitting such an astounding truth about himself? "I am so sorry for having disrespected you and your...your...real husband." She said nothing for a long time. She did not forgive him or chastise him. They sat in silence, continuing to sip their drinks. Finally, he stood up and placed his cup down on the table. She leaned over and put hers on the floor beside her chair. "Say something, Gwynne. Where is Charles's father? Why has he left you to fend for yourself? Is he dead? Did he die in the war? Please tell me." He sat down again and leaned over to her, wishing to touch her. Hadn't she taken his hand earlier to bring him to the fireplace? She had been so spontaneous. He allowed his fingers to gently brush her shoulder, feeling again the rush of an electrical charge up his arm, as if he had been struck by lightning. Slowly he allowed his entire palm to rest onto her shoulder. And then he stopped moving. He waited.

Chapter VII

When she felt the gentle pressure of Lucas's hand on her shoulder, she knew it was a gesture of compassion, not of possession. She may not trust men, but she knew that this time, in this place, kindness was what was being offered her. It brought tears to her eyes, and she made a desperate attempt to keep them from spilling over. No one knew her story here, except for her cousin, who was no longer here. Perhaps her cousin had informed some friend, but she, Gwynne, had never been asked outright. The inhabitants of this slum assumed what they wished in her case. They respected her and did not need to know another sad story in a world full of sad stories. Everyone had suffered here, from the vegetable sellers, no more than eight years old, to the women who took in washing to earn their living, to the coster-mongers who sold household gadgets or used clothing. True, she was educated, and they were not, but they were well-aware that misfortune could befall anyone.

At this juncture in time, Lucas turned his chair to face her, and their knees brushed. He had told her that he wished to recount his misadventures tonight, but now he looked just ready to listen. He did not speak or urge her once again to answer his questions.

Gwynne leaned her head back until it met the top of the high-backed chair. He would see her tear-stained face, but she didn't care. She had nothing to hide and nothing to lose. And if she laid blame at the foot of a gentleman of the moneyed classes, so be it. It was the truth. Edmund was to blame. It was his nature. He was a bully and a thug. He enjoyed hurting others. Sometimes she wondered if he enjoyed that more than his carnal pleasures. She was inclined to think that it was so. She remembered the gleam in his eyes when, as a young boy, he cut up small animals, dissecting their organs to view their inner workings. She, too, was fascinated by these scientific exploits, and along with his slightly younger brother, the sickly Thomas, looked on as Edmund carried out his needless surgeries. She felt ashamed of her interest but could not help herself. Eventually she sought out illustrated books on animal and human biology from the manor library because she was so interested. But Edmund's excuse was never scientific. He was maiming, mutilating, injuring. That was all that interested him. And on that fateful day, after her return from the War, when he backhanded her over her face, yelling gross expletives at her, as if she had abandoned him, and they had had some kind of agreement that she was his, the leer on his face was unmistakable. He was expressing an obscene joy in causing her pain. And when he thrust himself into her, her distress only ignited him more.

And thus, she began to recount the story, the long, sad story of Gwynne and Edmund to Lucas, from the time of their childhoods. "Once I was twelve and he sixteen, I sensed a change in him. Chasing his brother and me around the garden was no longer thrilling, and neither was scaring us when we played in the woods. It was as if only hounding us, harassing us could give him any type of satisfaction. He waged a campaign against me, taunting me, doing all within his power to seduce me. His brother could not defend me. My mother was already out of the picture. We had a male tutor who also gave lessons in science, mathematics, philosophy, and Latin, besides French and literature as my mother had. She was governess now to the children of the boys' much older sister. By the time I was thirteen, I could no longer stand the attention I was subjected to by the young master." Gwynne was very careful never to say the name of Charles's father. Perhaps Lucas knew him. Perhaps they had been at Oxford together. "I informed my mother that I wished to help her in her duties towards the four children now under her wing. My father was definitely pleased. Sometimes I spent whole days with the children, two boys and two girls all under the age of seven, and let my mother have time to herself. When I wished to study, I took myself off to the library and either read there or took the books home if my tormentor was around and not at his lessons." Here Gwynne let out a deep sigh. Now she was nearing the dreadful part. If she hadn't yet painted a picture of that young man's propensity to cruelty, it was about to be revealed in all its ugly glory. When she finally reached the moment of the most momentous example of the intercourse between herself and Edmund, her voice began to falter. She was fifteen when it had happened, when Edmund's reign of terror had reached its zenith. In truth, she was tremendously adept at avoiding him, but this fuelled his rage even more, and on that fateful day, when he accosted her in the woods as she was on her way home to the cottage less than a mile from the manor, he railed at her first for not showing the gratitude he deserved. After all, his parents had allowed her the benefit of *his* education, *his* tutor. She was a mere dependent and yet she got so much more than any other! His voice grew louder, and his hands grasped her shoulders. He shook her with all the vehemence of someone wronged. But how had she wronged him? She was not his betrothed. She was not on this earth for his enjoyment. She said nothing, letting him grow more and more violent. Ultimately, he threw her to the ground, and before she could scramble onto her feet again, he was on top of her. Her writhing beneath him in an effort to escape increasingly inflamed him and the young lad of nineteen could not curtail his desires. As she spoke to Lucas of her ordeal, her chest began to heave. Telling her mother was a most natural thing to do. It had come out in a wail of agony. Telling this man was very different. She was no longer a child. She was not pouring her heart out to a beloved cousin. She was a full-fledged woman in the grips of an old story that never seemed to die, and he, her interlocutor, was a superior man of means, an equal of Edmund's, and although he had been so unbelievingly caring of her and Charles up until now, he might feel attacked in some way, as if what she had been telling him was somehow a slur on his class and his gender. Because it was—it *was* an attack on his class and his gender. He could not fail to take it any other way. She had not been watching his reactions, and after she had reached this point in her monologue, she dropped her head into her hands. She was overwhelmed with emotion. After all this time, the memory could still sweep her up and transport her back in time to that day of horror.

Lucas never removed his hand, but nor did he utter anything. When she finally raised her head and turned her face to glance at him, he looked totally stricken and aggrieved, stunned into silence. The hand that had been on her shoulder now softly grazed the side of her face. He was as close as he could be to her.

"My story is not over because it was not on this occasion that Charles was conceived." Lucas nodded. He had worked that out. He sat very still. She could feel him willing her to continue although his voice could not articulate any words of encouragement. So Gwynne narrated as best she could the rest of the story—the fortuitous meeting with Florence Nightingale, the experience of the medical horrors of war and cholera, the second violent onslaught from Edmund, and her life in Whitechapel up until the moment she had waylaid him in the small square near her home.

"I have no idea what characteristics of his father Charles will possess. He is only eleven months old. So far, I see nothing in him that resembles that...that—"

"—inhuman blight on society," Lucas finished her sentence.

Gwynne was a little startled at his intensity. Again, she turned to him and saw that he, too, showed the anger that welled up in her when she thought of Edmund.

"You did not deserve such treatment, such maltreatment. No woman deserves that."

"I know," was all she said. She could not absolve Edmund. She could not excuse his actions. He was what he was. And he was by no means a gentleman. It was clear that Lucas comprehended this, and she was grateful for that. She was exhausted now. So much emotion, not just of anguish, but also of resentment. She did have Charles, though, and that was a blessing. So, she had to admit it. "I do have the blessing of Charles. I am grateful for him every day of my life."

"Despite the fact that he represents an enormous financial burden."

"He is no burden to me. He is precious, and I am determined to give him a good life, no matter how difficult it may seem."

Lucas nodded his head slowly. "You are an astonishing woman. That man did not succeed in demeaning you. He did not succeed in defiling you. You are above reproach and…and…I am proud to perhaps be able to stand with you and work with you in the near future, although I myself have no such qualities of unsulliedness. I cannot claim to have been untainted by life, for unlike you, I have succumbed to all my weaknesses of character. Today, tonight, more than ever, you have made me ashamed of my very nature, for I, like your abuser, am a man, and a man of the noble class."

"But you have never used your superior strength, I assume, to make a woman feel inferior, powerless, and a victim of debasement."

* * *

Before he could answer her, Lucas groaned. She had given him so much to think about! "Well, no, but I have never done anything to prevent such monstrous acts, nor have I spoken out against them, knowing full well of their existence. I am not guiltless." Should he tell her of his uncle's offer to let him sit in the House of Lords instead of him, and his very own sister's urging him to do this so that he might work for change in their country? His sister! She had a formidable mind. She was inquisitive, well-read, knowledgeable, a seeker of intellectual truth, constantly trying to engage him in all about which she thought. Their aunt and uncle had brought them up after the untimely and tragic death of their parents when he was six and Isabel not quite two. The pair encouraged both of them to learn and read and study, but, of course, for Isa it was more difficult to find a channel for all her investigative prowess. *She* should have been the doctor. *She* should have gone to university and pursued a career. She would have been the brightest student in the class. She seemed to care about everything and everyone. She cared a great deal about him, and all he could do was disappoint her as he supposed he had so far disappointed their loving guardians. He could not find fault with either of those truly noble human beings.

Lucas was torn as to whether he should admit all his debilitating flaws, but before his mind could come to a conclusion, his mouth was uttering the words, and his voice was intoning all the grievances he had against himself. It was as if he could not stop himself. Somehow, he was going to bare his soul to this woman. He had let down his sister by refusing his uncle's offer. It was not as if Isabel herself could fight for the things she believed in. She could visit the poor of their village in Kent. She could in some insubstantial way help those abandoned girls who had borne children out of wedlock. She could bring food to them or medicine when they fell ill, but her dreams were so much larger. Only Lucas could live them out on the political stage, but his heart had been asleep. He felt deeply guilty for all these failures.

There was also the matter of his shame over his imagining this woman naked in his arms, in his or her bed, and there for his enjoyment. Of course, he would never push her to do something against her will, but his desires were definitely carnal. Never before had he felt so drawn to a woman. Sometimes he wondered at himself, at his lack of interest in all the women that had been paraded before him at balls, at grand dinners, in the drawing rooms of the wealthy. His aunt was despairing of him ever taking a wife. But this woman! She was like the answer to all his dreams and wishes. He yearned for her. He did not wish to be out of her sight. But she had just recounted the most gruesome of experiences at the hands of a monster. How could he confess to her the sinfulness of his desires in relation to her? But before he had to make up his mind about whether to be honest about his feelings, carnal or otherwise, towards her, Gwynne intervened in his monologue on all the infamies he had perpetrated through inertia.

"It does not surprise me that you feel that way. It is apparent that you are a man consumed with remorse and grief for something you have committed in the past. Perhaps you may be entitled to forgiveness since you feel such regret. But I have no idea what a man like you could have done to merit such self-loathing. You are nothing like the man that has clouded my entire existence. And even if your sister, Isabel, may be somewhat disenchanted with you for not rallying to her causes, they are still *her* causes. If you cannot find the energy for political involvement, then perhaps the only other thing you may be able to do for her is to help her find some way for her to express herself more fully, despite the limited opportunities for women." She stopped momentarily, but Lucas knew she had more to say about him and he wanted to hear it. He wanted to hear what a woman with whom he had been so forthcoming and sincere would have to offer him in terms of absolution.

"Please go on."

Gwynne took a deep breath. "It is not really a totally formulated thought, but I was wondering if it was your sense of guilt that brought you...here...today...yesterday, actually, for we are deep into the night, and in a few hours, it will be dawn." She leaned her head to the side in that enchanting spontaneous act of inquisitiveness that had so charmed him earlier.

"If you must know, I came here in thrall to a simple call of nature. Wasn't that obvious? I wanted something from the universe that I had not had before, and which I thought I deserved before I took my departure from the universe. Was it a desperate act or was it a selfish act of a man who no longer had the will to go on?"

"Departure from the universe?" was Gwynne's response. "But what do you mean? Do you mean what I think you mean?" She looked shocked.

Lucas only nodded. He leaned forward and put his elbows on his knees, with the palms of his hands supporting his head. He stared ahead of him but saw nothing. Perhaps most recently that was how he had been meeting the world, with eyes open but blind to anything outside himself. He had been heading toward crisis. But why now? He had his whole life ahead of him, a life full of promise. He had everything a man or woman could want—a loving family, a life of ease surrounded by beauty, a completed education leading to a career that could be filled with satisfactions, what with all the new discoveries of the mid-nineteenth century—but it seemed he wanted none of these things. He only wanted to stop suffering, and now...maybe she was right. Maybe all he wanted was this woman's forgiveness. And where would that lead? Gwynne's voice broke his inner musings on possible self-inflicted departure or possible attachment, and what she uttered startled him. It put him most definitely on the path to attachment.

"When people leave this world, when they die...you mustn't think that they are privy to what goes on here without them. Because they aren't. The world just goes on without them. You would not live out your days in limbo, free from pain, but still listening in on the conversations of those you love. Free of pain you may be, but free, as well, of any consciousness of life in this world. I do not believe that you are ready for that, Lucas, for that total detachment from yourself and others." Lucas lifted his head and acknowledged with a nod that she was right.

Chapter VIII

It was broad daylight and Mr. Gaunt, Gwynne, Lucas, with Charles seated on his shoulders, jabbering away in his personal language, Phillip hopping around on his new crutch, provided by his benefactor and new master, Jane, and her entire family—baby Selina, husband Jonathan, and fourteen-year-old son Robert—were all examining the rooms next door to hers as a possible home for Lucas's hospital for children, actually Lucas's *and* her hospital, for he kept insisting that it was a joint venture. She felt tired, for she had not slept a wink the night before, but also exhilarated. Lucas had left early in the morning after telling her the story from *his* past that had haunted him all his life. What a pair they were! Lucas, unfortunately, had been more consumed by the accident that had brought his parents' life to an end than she had been by her entanglement with Edmund. In fact, Charles had helped her in this. She had not had the time to wallow in self-pity. She couldn't torture herself over what had happened. She had to take care of her son. Yes, she felt anger and some sorrow, but too much had happened to her afterwards. In many ways the war that she had participated in had taught her enough of life to understand that there were greater sorrows than her own. Yes, she had felt bereft when her dear cousin Charlotte had left this little home of theirs. She had fallen in love with a valet to a nobleman, eventually marrying him and going into service herself in the same household somewhere in Kensington. But Lucas's universe had been much narrower. After he had finished his studies and practical experience in the hospital, leisure time had been his constant companion. For Lucas it had proved disastrous. But now he seemed so animated. He was embarking on his career. He would have responsibilities. He could prove he was a good man.

Jonathan, a carpenter and builder by trade, but recently at a low ebb in his professional life, with little work coming his way, was buoyed by the fact that he would be very much needed to create the right kind of ambiance for a hospital out of this flat. Walls would have to be moved or added to make a room where children might sleep, a special room containing all the equipment and cupboards available from Lucas's father's surgery, a room with several baths for the bathing of their little patients who would invariably need to be scrubbed, a bedroom for a night-nurse, a waiting-room for the parents of the children, and beds on wheels would need to be constructed at the right height for the children— a whole long list of things that Jonathan was being asked to do. Fortunately, his young son was his apprentice, and he, too, would have plenty of work. Since they would need help as well in the daily running of the hospital, Jane had offered herself as someone who could bathe the children, scrub the floors, cook the meals, in fact do anything necessary, for she, too, wished to be gainfully employed, and help lift her family out of the dry well of poverty. Both she and Gwynne had babies, but somehow they knew that all the adults, including Lucas, would care for them. And then there was Phillip, who was already declaring that he would fetch water, keep the fires and stove going, haul coal, take care of Charles and Selina, and help with the sick children. He seemed so happy about his wonderful new circumstances. To work with Nurse Gwynne and Doctor Lacey! What more could he ask for? She knew that Lucas had not imagined forcing Phillip to work. He was so young. But she had managed to make him understand that this was life in East London. Children worked, and the fact that Phillip would never be exploited or hurt in any way, that they both would make time for him to learn, to read, to write was a great fortune for the boy. Perhaps she and Lucas could find out about Phillip's mother. Was she still in the Workhouse? Could they remove her and give her employment? They would have to see what Phillip's feelings were about her, discover what he wanted. Now he was telling everyone that he wanted to be the night watchman. Someone would have to sleep here from now on and guard the place. A bed by the fireplace was all he needed. It was a thought. They did need to decide where Phillip would sleep. Would he be going home every night with Lucas?

Lucas sought her eyes as Phillip was prattling on about his future tasks. She smiled at him, and he returned the smile. Every one of their three patients, including the previously sick Charles and Selina, was on the mend. She felt a closeness with this man, a closeness hard to explain, seeing as they had only met the day before. But what a meeting it had been, full as it was of confessions and heretofore deeply hidden secrets! He had said that he had never before been so utterly honest with anyone. He had never been himself in this way, not even with his beloved sister. They both had felt a tremendous degree of relief at being able to unburden themselves. As she had pointed out to him, no one could ever be as harshly judgmental as he had been in regard to himself. This comment had led to his full disclosure of the terrifying incident that had marred his life and enveloped his emotional being in a shroud of misery.

He had begun with telling her this heartbreaking fact: "I never spoke of what had happened on that day of horrors. Perhaps, at age six, I couldn't really be lucid or comprehensible. I just went to bed for weeks, living and re-living the event in my head. Doctors came and went, but I refused to speak. Finally, I left my room and went to the stable where the only other survivor, one of the horses, was also recovering from the shock. I took a stepladder and climbed up until my face was parallel with his ear, and with my arms wrapped around his neck, I whispered to him of our common experience. I recalled everything for him, for us. I painted the whole gruesome picture...and I thanked him for being alive and allowing me to cling to him in the aftermath. I told him I would never abandon him, that he would be *my* horse forever, that we were inextricably linked by fate, that he was my best friend in the world, and that I needed him desperately." What a strange admission! And somehow, she knew that this friendship with the horse, which he called Davey, was something that kept him alive and sane and whole for years and years. The horse grew old, and still Lucas clung to him for survival. When he went away to university, he returned at every available moment to ascertain whether his horse was still alive. As a child, when his aunt and uncle saw how important the horse was to him, they encouraged him to start riding a pony, a much smaller animal, which he could eventually ride with ease. They were happy that Lucas had found something—riding—into which he could channel his sorrow, and, as far as they were concerned, it seemed to work well. He grew happier and livelier with each passing day that he spent on his pony or talking to Davey. The stable-boy, a young man of twenty-five, rode Davey to keep the horse active while he waited for Lucas to be big enough to ride him. Finally, that day came when Lucas, a strapping lad of fourteen, mounted Davey for the first time, and man and beast rode off as one into the lands surrounding the Lacey estate. Lucas described for her his joy at being able to sit atop the proud animal and fly through the countryside. They were unified in motion just as they had been in tragedy. Riding Davey was like communing with his dead parents, showing the universe that he could keep them alive in the fusion between himself and his horse. As long as he could feel Davey beneath him powerfully devouring the miles and miles of forest and meadow, he was able to feel hope. Eventually he learned to ride him without a saddle so he could be even closer to the animal just as he, a frightened six-year-old, had been when he lay atop him, with their hearts pounding together and their bodies half-submerged in the lake, where all the others, his mother and father, and the other horse harnessed to the carriage lay drowned. Such was the extraordinary relationship between the two that she could not fail to ask Lucas when the horse had died. When he revealed to her that Davey had died the Christmas before, the room seemed to grow stiller. The crackle of the fire and the breathing of the children were hushed by the power of this statement. Lucas had lost his living connection to his parents one year ago. Was that when he began to slide into despair? Could the demise of this animal have pulled the earth from under his feet? Neither of them spoke for minutes following Lucas's declaration of this simple fact. Then Lucas, who had been recounting the story with his head fallen forward, as if speaking not to her directly, but more to the ground or to the spot where the floor met the fireplace, lifted his head, and she turned hers towards him. Their eyes met and neither of them had to answer the silent question. The truth of his condition was in the air between them, and the air vibrated with their mutual understanding.

Chapter IX

At dawn, Lucas returned to the family home in Chelsea. He bathed and changed his clothes and substituted his fashionable shoes for a pair of hunting-boots for the rigours of the wintry weather. He then chatted with Mrs. Blunt, the ever-faithful cook whom he had loved all of his life. Afterwards he headed back to Gwynne's home with a mid-day feast prepared by the endearing Mrs. Blunt. He wished all the people involved in his forthcoming scheme to heal the dirty, hungry, sick, and sometimes abandoned children of East London to celebrate fully with him in the humble home of the nurse who had so recently nursed him in his hour of need. They were seated around her dining-table while Gwynne carved the roast and placed the many slices it entailed into her guests' plates together with gravy, roast potatoes and carrots, and Yorkshire pudding. When they had been busy perusing the premises adjacent to hers, this meal had been left cooking in her once-cold but now well-heated stove. Everyone was talking and laughing, and the adults, too, were partaking in the several bottles of claret that Lucas had also brought from the well-stocked cellar of the Chelsea mansion. Never had he found a better, more real joy in the consumption of a typical English repast than in this very meagre but wholesome environment in the heart of the London slums. And he had caused this happiness. These people, including himself, would be fully employed in the very near future, and that gave hope and pleasure to one and all. He had carted all these edibles in the family carriage, and it had been a strange sight to see it entering the modest and unassuming street of his imminent workplace. The coachman and his personal valet had helped to carry everything up the stairs, and even Gwynne, who had once inhabited the halls of a noble domain, was shocked at the sight of so much livery and the like, but she acted promptly, and quickly filled her stove with the proffered trays. Only when his servants had left did she actually exclaim, along with Phillip, her surprise at Lucas's munificence: "Is this all in honour of the enterprise to which you are so committed to carry out?"

Lucas nodded. "And if all goes well...that is...should you be enthusiastic about the proposed site for this enterprise next door, then, of course, celebrating is a must. Perhaps tomorrow, I will transport my father's complete surgery, and hopefully we can be set up, if not immediately as a hospital, at least as a place where we can diagnose and heal whatever or whoever comes our way."

Phillip, in all the flurry of activity, was trying to manoeuvre on his new crutch. He was dressed in the suit of clothes Lucas had purchased the day before and seemed very pleased with himself, although there was still a slight lingering pain in his ailing foot. But he had nothing to complain about. Gwynne had explained to him that he never had to go back to work for the uncaring likes of Mr. Housman, and although she had not exactly explained what Lucas wished of him, he was prepared for anything, being a survivor of the workhouse. He certainly had never eaten better.

Lucas, surveying the hearty appetites of his new friends around the table, thought back to the early hours of the morning when he felt there was so little or nothing to smile about, as he recounted to Gwynne the harrowing experience of witnessing the horrors of death at the tender age of six. He would never have thought that one day, twenty-three years after the fact, he would be confessing to a near but dear stranger the exact circumstances of his heavy heart in relation to all things connected to his continued existence upon this earth. How that had happened was confounding, but he knew in his heart of hearts that it had something to do with this woman's uniqueness, perhaps with her having jumped the boundary between the life of the fortunate and the life of the less fortunate, and her own capacity to defy the odds and survive in the treacherous waters of personal integrity and freedom—freedom from the constraints of the prevailing social order. She was who she was without artifice. She had the strength to live with discomfort and poverty. Her economic circumstances did not prevent her from engaging in activities to help others with little financial reward for her effort. She had been prevailed upon to surrender her body to a brute of a man, but she had not succumbed to an invasion of her soul. She was intact. Knowing this to be true had perhaps allowed him to unburden himself and reveal that his ill-fated childhood ordeal had in fact attacked him at his very core, and the result was that he was no more intact than the carriage that had cracked under the weight of itself, as it toppled dizzyingly into the rising waters of the pond near his home in Kent. That disastrous day had wormed its way into his soul, and it would take a revolution of sorts for him to become whole again. And that revolution was beginning. In truth, it was all that mattered now. He, too, would defy conventional wisdom. He would not become a doctor to those who could pay. He would devote his energies to those whose hold on health was tenuous in the best of circumstances. He was convinced that malnutrition and the grime of poverty was the leading cause of the ills of his soon-to-be little patients. He was no politician, as his sister wanted him to be, but he could in his small way, and with the help of Nurse Gwynne, right some of the wrongs that his sister railed against. And so, listening and talking to these humble creatures around Gwynne's table made him feel for the first time in a very long time that, in the end, he could make his own good fortune, that he could fight to breathe air, and not be tempted to let himself drown in the murky waters of his past.

It had been unbelievably hard at first, trying to utter the syllables that would free him from his haunting nightmare. They escaped his lips in dribs and drabs, and he had had no idea whether he would be able to fully disclose whence his shame and remorse originated, but eventually, through the gentle coaxing of his audience of one, he was able to divulge the whole horrible truth—and the fact that he felt culpable in terms of the fatal outcome. Because, in his mind, he *had* put everyone in danger.

The three of them, his father, his mother, and himself, had been returning home to Kent on that fatal spring day, from an excursion in London. His baby sister had for the first time been left with his Aunt Edith and Uncle Graham so that his parents could experience some little freedom from the incessant needs of a two-year-old. Of course there were servants, many servants in both family homes, but his mother worried over her little daughter, and Lucas's father had thought that, if they were away from Isabel, his wife would worry less. Also, she could pay more attention to her six-year-old, who, he could attest, was feeling a little left out since the birth of his sister. Today Lucas would probably admit that, in reality, his mother never stopped being her attentive self, but, at the time, he was a little morose about Isabel's entrance onto the family scene. Often his guilt extended to this misassigning of blame onto his probably blameless mother and certainly blameless sister. It all got confounded together until his self-loathing encompassed just about every misdeed he had ever committed from the age of four to six. How tiresome, he thought today, he had been, when pondering, when muddling over all his perceived wrongdoing. How could he have taken himself so seriously all these years? Why was he so prone to examining and re-examining all the permutations of his actions and non-actions? No one else in his family was like that. His father had a scientific mind and, yes, he pursued truth in his profession and was exacting, but that did not mean that his mind went over and over and over again the same old images and feelings from his past. He didn't dwell, as Lucas did, on something in an endless circle of futility. If one avenue of thought was futile, his father abandoned it. But that was not Lucas's way. And from what he remembered, his mother was all clarity and light. She knew her duty. She fulfilled it and had not had a guilty conscience for one single moment—as far as the boy he had been knew. Then there were his aunt and uncle, who had just stepped in so easily to discharge their fraternal responsibilities to his parents, without a word of rebellion against circumstances. Their whole lives had been transformed, uprooted, altered irrevocably in an instant. But they never complained. They gave their love to Isabel and himself unstintingly. No guilt there—unless you considered the possibility that they perceived his own unhappiness and were at a loss as to what to do to help him. But they acted! They never gave up with him. They pursued all the avenues open to them in the quest for that one thing that would render him happy. Immediately following the tragedy, when they discovered his love for horses, or, more exactly, a specific horse, they did everything in their power to indulge that interest, or passion, as they saw it. No, they did not falter where he was concerned. They gave and gave, and he, Lucas, continued to falter, and be his agonizingly self-consumed, blundering, hopeless self. And his sister! Well, she was one of the most engaged and committed human beings he had ever known. There was no comparison between the two of them. She was never idle. As for him, only his mind was never idle, giving in as it always did to his guilty conscience and never letting him escape the turmoil of repetitive self-evaluation.

Thus, Isabel was not with them in the carriage his father was driving himself, on this day, on the last leg of the journey home. They were a few miles from their destination, and since it had stopped raining, which it had done for most of that day, he, Lucas, had begged his father to allow him to ride up front instead of inside the closed carriage with his mother. He wanted to see their house as they wended their way over the last hillock and the unobstructed view of it would adorn his excited vision from the vantage point of the driver's seat. After all, his father had decided not to take the coachman. His father had decided that steering a pair of horses was a job for him on this trip. Probably, he, too, wished to be met by the wonderful sight of their country estate in all its green glory. Unfortunately, the road was especially muddy and churned up by the preceding traffic along it, probably farmer's carts and the like. And controlling the horses as they stumbled along in the quicksand-like earth beneath their feet was becoming more and more difficult for him—experienced driver though he was. They had just turned onto the embankment above the pond whose water, due to the excessive rainfall this particular spring, was higher than usual. This was a part of the road that generally, unless exceedingly dry, could be treacherous, because where the side of the road ended there was no gradual grassy falling-off towards the water. It was more like a straight cliff about two metres high. It was certainly not the bluffs of Dover, but a carriage toppling over could be damaged a great deal, perhaps irreparably, and the passengers, depending on the weight of the entire structure, could also be severely hurt in the process. Up until this time, however, no one had ever died or drowned, but some had been seriously injured. It was all up to the skill of the coachman, but this particular coachman, at the precise moment of reaching this test of his abilities, had more on his mind than merely the controlling of the pair of horses. At this juncture in the journey, Lucas had chosen to stand up rather than stay seated. Had he wanted to see better the desperate attempts of the horses to regain their footing in the slippery, sucking mud? Had he been afraid and jumped up, unable to contain his emotions? What had prompted his sudden movement? The exact motive for his untimely action escaped him to this day, but he knew that it was his own decision, and not the jerking of the horses that had forced him upwards. He was on his feet, not thrown into the air by the swaying of the vehicle. But his choice to do this had disastrous consequences, for his father's reaction was to protect his son from falling over. Instead of trying to steady the animals with both his hands on the reins, he reached out with one of them for his precarious, unstable son in an instinctive attempt to hold him down. But he never had time to grab an arm or a jacket sleeve or a hand. What actually happened—and in a way it saved Lucas's life—was that his outstretched hand pushed Lucas with all the force of the falling carriage way out into the deeper water, where Lucas became submerged momentarily, eventually coming up for air, but never was he at any moment hit by any part of the wooden vehicle as it crashed over the edge, breaking apart along the way, as it hit the rocky shore as well as the bottom of the pond. Lucas stood on the floor of the little lake, the water slapping his face, but not over his head. He sucked the air in great gulps after his hurtling dive, and he watched the carriage splinter all around his parents. He could not really see his mother within, but whatever luggage was inside must have landed on her head and body in the crash, knocking her unconscious and burying her in the water that eventually covered everything. His father was thrown onto the rocks and the carriage came crashing down on top of him. The horses screamed, and Davey, the more fortunate horse because he was installed on the outer side and not on the side closest the water, splashed down on top of his teammate, who struggled beneath him, trying to come up for air. Since they were harnessed together, there was no way that he could free himself from the water. Lucas was bewildered by all the gory mess he had created. He was unable to move. He did not know where to go first. At a certain point he realized that his parents were both completely below the top of the water and they were no longer moving. Only the horses were writhing, one piled on the other, one alive but terrified, and the other one fighting to breathe. Lucas understood that he had to free him from his restraints so that he could swim away from the weight of his shackled brother-in-arms. Eventually Lucas's limbs loosened, and his brain began to work again. He pushed himself towards shore, but when he reached the horses, there was no movement from beneath, and he had no idea where the harnesses were attached. His little hands were useless for this monumental task. So, he clambered onto the side of the living horse, his face buried in his mane, his arms around the body as far as they would go, feeling the ribs rise and fall beneath his own small chest, and stayed clinging to the animal until they both calmed down. He believed the horse whinnied his thoughts to him, communicated through the vibrations of his torso underneath him. Somehow, he learned his name—Davey—in the process. They lay there like that for he knew not how long—but certainly until darkness—channelling to each other their sorrow for the loss of human and animal. It did not matter to Lucas if it took hours or days to be rescued, for he was already rescued atop the breathing, grieving animal. They were locked in an embrace that nourished and saved. Time did not exist. There was only their inhalation and exhalation. When rescue finally arrived and men tried to extricate him from the warmth of Davey, Lucas screamed and screamed. They did finally dislodge him, but Lucas would not budge until the harness was loosened and Davey could also be saved from the cold water. The men wrapped him up in blankets and one carried him away, but Lucas's arm extended back to Davey, and he kept on screaming until Davey stood, was able to walk on firm ground, and was helped to climb back up to the road. The men assured him that Davey would be brought back to the stable, be kept warm and fed. Before he passed out from exhaustion and fright, Lucas saw again in his mind the destruction of the two people responsible for his life, the crashing of wood and flesh, the slow drowning of a noble animal. When he lost consciousness, he did so because he had to. He could not take in anymore of the wreckage that he had triggered.

When he finished describing for Gwynne the whole of the incident that had wrecked his life and stolen that of his parents, she seemed lost in thought, trying to make sense of his outpouring, but there was no hesitation on her part to touch him, to gently stroke his head, to let him know that she was there, listening to his pain. He had never felt so completely understood by any human. The only other being that had ever touched him so was a beloved horse.

Chapter X

Lucas, from his side of the table nearest to the door, was asking her about Florence Nightingale and her ideas regarding the ideal set-up of hospitals. She was at the head of the table, the stove belching heat and comfort on this day, so close to Christmas but seeming to herself and her guests just like Christmas, better than most Christmases spent in this dark corner of London. They were certainly a happy lot. The prospect of continuous though hard work was welcoming. Before Lucas had entered their lives—what was it? —a day ago? —they had been dragging themselves around, weighed down by their impecunious circumstances, or, as in the case of Phillip, by the cruelty of a harsh master. This celebratory meal was a testament to the belief that one should never give up. Gwynne found herself smiling as she expounded on the essence of her greatest teacher's ideas regarding how hospitals should be built.

"Since Miss Nightingale believes in the importance of wholesome air, she would have hospital rooms filled with light streaming in from high windows, with ceilings higher than usual, so the windows could rise to capture all of the day's radiance."

"Somehow," intervened Lucas, "I don't think that is going to be possible next door. Perhaps we could build bigger windows, but the views from the windows would still be bleak. And we couldn't change the height of the ceilings. I guess the filling of the place with light will have to come from the soul of the place, from something we would have to create with our attitudes to the children." He smiled broadly at her from across the length of the table. Gwynne returned the smile, giving him, she knew, exactly the approval he craved from her. In truth, it was not too difficult to please this man. She just had to be truthful. Jonathan was commenting on the possibility of raising the height of the windows and Lucas was listening intently to his suggestions regarding increasing the number of windows, especially at the back of the rooms, since the front faced the hallway and the staircase. Lucas nodded and made it clear that he would definitely consider implementing Jonathan's suggestions.

As Gwynne rose to clear some of the plates from the table, Lucas addressed her again. "But would you not say, Gwynne, that some of Miss Nightingale's ideas on bad air-good air were also mistaken? In your hospital at Scutari, we now think that it was the tainted water from the cesspool running underneath the structure that may have caused the rampant cholera among the patients. Miss Nightingale was not aware that the water was not wholesome, and all those, dare I say, ridiculous attempts to kill the 'bad' miasmatic air by having the wounded soldiers smoke their pipes continuously to rid the air of whatever substance might be causing their sickness were all for nought. I, for one, also believe that hospital cleanliness, the personal hygiene of the hospital's inhabitants, as well as healthy sunlight go a very long way to helping the healing process, but I think the bad air debate has been lost and the contaminated water theory is winning the day. Do you agree?" Lucas looked slightly unsure of himself at that moment. After all he was criticizing a national heroine, a woman revered, a woman who had contributed so much to her own education. Gwynne suddenly felt a desire to be alone with Lucas to show him perhaps through touch that he had not in the least offended her sensibilities.

She placed the dirty plates on the counter next to the basin closest to her stove and then returned to her seat. All eyes were on her. Did the others in the room understand the controversial issue that Lucas had brought up? Probably not, so she decided to enlighten them and have them participate, if not vocally in the conversation, at least mentally. "I do agree, Lucas, and I believe that Miss Nightingale has only ever disagreed with the theory that disease is transmitted through touch. If we would talk to her today, I am sure she will have read Dr. Snow's work on the transmission of cholera through foul water and not foul air and will have given it its due consideration. Unfortunately..." Here Gwynne turned her head from side to side to include everyone in the room. "Dr. Snow's proofs continue to be negated by public health officials because they are found to be distasteful and because he showed that bloodletting is useless, and we know how much bloodletting is a beloved practice of so many physicians in this country." Besides Lucas, who was nodding in agreement with her, the others in the room looked slightly dumbfounded. So, Gwynne went on. "You remember the cholera epidemic in Soho four years ago?"

"How could we e'er forget? Hundreds died includin' the child o' me oldest friend, a music-hall singer," Jane announced. "Mary was 'eart-broken. We all were."

"And scared." Jonathan, her husband, piped up. "It spread no matter who ye were and got ye no matter 'ow rich an' mighty. Beggin' your pardon, Dr. Lacey."

"No need to apologize, Jonathan. You are absolutely right. And so is Nurse Gwynne. It is most unfortunate that the conclusions to the exhaustive research of John Snow, who published a very intelligent book on the subject a few years ago, are not more frequently acted upon, and those who continue to believe that cholera and other diseases are somehow breathed in are still preaching their absurd theories."

"Well, then, what did 'e say, this doctor, about why some be stricken?" asked Jonathan. Lucas silently urged her, with a simple nod of his head, to tell the story. Perhaps she *could* make a story of it.

"Well, in that last deadly epidemic, most of the cases were clustered around the Broad Street water pump at the corner of Cambridge Street. Dr. Snow thought it an obvious place to start. Apparently, a mother had washed her baby's dirty nappies in the well there. This particular baby had contracted cholera. The waters of the cesspit, because of the faulty brickwork, seeped out and mixed with the supposedly clean drinking water, and the baby's disease was spread to all the people that drank that water, probably in much the same way that it had occurred in my hospital in Constantinople. However, it must be remembered that all of Miss Nightingale's hygiene policies eventually contributed to the waning of the spreading of diseases on the wards there."

"And more proof of Snow's research also came from another interesting source," added Lucas, at this point. "There was a brewery in the vicinity that used the same water. However, during one of the processes in brewing, the water is boiled at a very high temperature. None of the employees of the brewery came down with cholera, the reason being that they received beer daily, along with their wages, as a form of payment. These people never drank the water in its original state. If they drank water, they probably drank it from a well near where they lived. Eventually the authorities closed off the pump at Broad Street, and the epidemic was stopped, but to actually say out loud that what was in that baby's nappies caused the problem was a little too indelicate for the British public."

Jonathan, Jane, Robert, and even Phillip began to laugh at this, despite the gruesomeness of the subject. Finally, Jane spoke up. "Most folk need a wee bit o' the reality o' East London to wake 'em up. Rich folk 'ave no idea, do they? The maids that be emptyin' their chamber pots certainly do." Gwynne noticed Lucas blush a bit, but he smiled and acknowledged the truth in Jane's words. Pampered though he may be, thought Gwynne, he would always accept the truth. Now Lucas asked a rather strange question:

"Do you think, Gwynne, that despite perhaps a slight difference of opinion regarding the theory of bad air causing particular diseases, Miss Nightingale might grant us an audience so that we may discuss with her all manner of things regarding our children's hospital? I know that she has been feeling poorly since her return, probably suffering from Crimean fever, and does not venture outside her home here in London, but I hear that a select group of people have been able to visit her. Surely your previous intimate relationship with her and all of your shared experiences would be good cause for her to wish to see her former pupil and discover what has become of you. What we could learn from her might prove invaluable. Strictly speaking, we would be seeking her advice. Of course, just to meet her would be, for me, unbelievable good fortune. Just think what I may be able to glean from her distinguished and well-informed mind."

Gwynne was caught off-guard by this suggestion. It was not that she had *not* wanted to seek out her old employer after coming back from the Crimea. In fact, she *had* wanted to renew the acquaintance. Miss Nightingale had been such an important person in her life, and the strength of their relationship had never waned in all the years they had known each other. What had previously stopped her was first her pregnancy and then Charles himself. Miss Nightingale would probably have been appalled by her new circumstances, and how could she keep the fact of a baby in her life from the woman? She would never lie to her, and the thought of revealing the whole story terrified her. All that fear was likely showing on her face right now, because Lucas was looking at her with concern in his eyes. She could not, in front of all these others, disclose the secret of her trepidation. She would have to tell him later.

"Well, ye-e-s, that is something we could consider. I wouldn't want to disturb her if she is unwell, but I would imagine she would be interested in our little mission. She has always been interested in the Ragged Schools here in London where the poor have basically been allowed to send their children to receive a modicum of learning. Let's discuss this later, Lucas. I will think of a letter that I might write to her asking permission for an interview." With this Gwynne lowered her eyes to the table, unsure how to continue this discourse. But the others, realizing her discomfort, proceeded to change the subject. Glad of this, she rose from the table and put the kettle to boil on the hob for tea. Did they think that she and Miss Nightingale had had some sort of falling-out? Better that than explaining that she was ashamed of her present situation. Of course, she would divulge all to Lucas. She would not be afraid to tell *him* of her misgivings where Miss Nightingale was concerned.

Chapter XI

Finally, she and Lucas were alone. Charles was napping. Actually, it had been Lucas who had sung him to sleep while she washed the dishes and straightened up the flat after the meal. Phillip had gone out, crutch and all, to order coal for the premises next door and some firewood for the one big fireplace. He would also get the chimney sweep to clean out the chimneys before they would start to heat up the rooms. Hopefully the sweep would come before nightfall, because Phillip was determined to sleep on the premises and guard it with his life. The rooms came with two beds and mattresses, as well as a large central table, not too different from the one in her apartment. Phillip was therefore also tasked with buying some bedding for himself—linen, pillow, and blankets. Since he only had one hand at his disposal, the other firmly attached to his crutch, he would request delivery, and since all and sundry in the neighbourhood trusted her, Doctor Lacey being an unknown quantity, he was sure that payment upon delivery would be acceptable. Despite his lingering pain, he was cheerful and very much full of hope and eagerness for his prospects.

As soon as he had gone, and she and Lucas were seated on their respective chairs in front of the wood fire, he immediately asked her about what had transpired earlier when they were talking about Miss Nightingale. Why had she expressed discomfort on the subject of renewing contact?

She sighed before answering, then she looked at him meaningfully. "Would it surprise you if I said that I was embarrassed? I was about to become a mother and it was visible to everyone. The people in this part of the city didn't much seem to care, what with all the misfortune befalling the entire population of East London. But Miss Nightingale would care. And me without a husband! She is such a proper lady. Explaining the circumstances of my condition would have been agonizing. I suppose I could have visited her after Charles's birth and left him with my cousin for a few hours, but I would have had to tell her the truth. I could not leave out such an important detail of my present state of affairs, could I? The choice was either reveal all or not go. I chose not to go."

Lucas moved his chair inches closer to her. "And what about now?" he asked in a whisper, as if he did not want the room to hear her answer. She knew exactly what he meant. How well she understood the messages he sent her. It was uncanny, their ability to communicate. But she had to make things clear to him. "Lucas, Miss Nightingale is *not* like Mr. Gaunt, or...or...even Jane to me. I deeply admire her. I cannot just let her imagine that you are Charles's father and that we are married. None of that is true." Her voice faltered at this juncture. Why had that been so hard to say? It was as if she was afraid to hurt him. He had felt somehow rewarded that others had placed him alongside her in that family way. It had made him feel substantial that he was connected to two real live human beings. Why didn't the other real live human beings in his sphere of life provide the same measure of solidity for him? It was his turn to sigh now, and he pulled slightly back from her. "No, Lucas, don't do that. Don't pull away. We must only have truth between us if our association is going to work."

Lucas nodded. "I know. Isn't it strange that I am so dependent on our honest exchange with each other, one without pretence of any kind, and yet...and yet...I seem to need the fact of a connection to your child...I mean I have a connection to him, an inner one, but I seem to need a pretend outer one. Why is that?"

"Lucas," she responded immediately, slightly tugging at his arm so he might come back into their intimate huddle, "you are looking for a new identity, one completely different from your previous one. A father is a worthwhile identity, one that has a real place in this world. You just want a real place in this world, and you are finding it now. It may take time, but it will happen. I am sure of it. And hopefully you will be happy living inside of this identity." She wanted so to stroke his face now. She felt such an urge to hold him in her arms and be held by him. This was new for her. She kept away from men as a general rule. She avoided their touch. They might hurt her, if not now, then one day. But she felt drawn to this man's flesh as well as his spirit. She felt that his embrace would not hurt. It would heal. She shivered.

"Are you cold, Gwynne? Let me get your shawl." He got up from his chair, went over to the hooks by the door, and took her knitted shawl from its usual place. As he walked back to her, she wanted to stand up and take him in her arms. His thoughtfulness was so touching. She rose, but then fear gripped her. Could she be so bold? She wanted to be like that. She wanted to be a modern, self-assured creature, but she was, in fact, no such thing. She was a woman wronged, and it would be hard for her, perhaps harder than for Lucas, to clothe herself in a new identity.

When she took the shawl from him and wrapped it around her shoulders, craving his arms around her rather than this scrap of wool, she thought he just might come to her and enfold her in an embrace. He looked about to make such a move, but he hesitated, a sense of caution on his face, and they both resumed sitting again before the fire. She must somehow make him know that she was not breakable, at least not with him.

After a few moments of silence and mutual deep contemplation as the flame danced before their eyes, Lucas sighed and turned to face her.

"It will be Christmas in a few days. I have to go and spend it in the country with my family. Tomorrow morning, I will bring my father's entire surgery, shelves, desk, patient-bed, glass bottles of various solutions and unguents, and other essential paraphernalia from Chelsea and set it up in the smaller room next door. It is now being dismantled, prepared, and boxed for delivery in our carriage." He sighed again and leaned back in his chair. She thought that he wanted to ask her about Phillip.

"Do not worry, Lucas. You may leave Phillip in my care. It would not do to pounce upon your aunt and uncle and sister with a surprise ward. Besides, he is still healing, and this is his place now, his home. He is so proud of his new responsibilities, self-inflicted though they may be, you couldn't pull him away from the hospital if you tried. He so wants to be part of the initial installation. And I will take good care of him in your absence. I will be as devoted to him as you are, and as he is to us."

Lucas sat up straight now. He had been clearly moved by her little speech. But he began to shake his head. "Dear Gwynne, it is not just Phillip who has found a new home here with you. *I* don't want to leave the day after tomorrow. *I* want to stay here. *I* am being dragged away by duty and tradition, when I would much rather be working by your side, cleaning, scouring, and preparing for our new patients, because I am sure they will be coming. Phillip is out there probably announcing to the entire neighbourhood of our barely-begun enterprise, don't you think?" She chuckled at this vision of Phillip he conjured in her mind, waving his crutch like a banner, announcing to one and all of what was coming to pass. Lucas laughed, too. There was something he needed to know, though, and she had to tell him.

"Lucas, despite all that you say—and I understand every sentiment uttered—you must not reject those that love you. You must let them share in your newfound hope for your future. They should come here and see the place when it will actually be ready—your sister especially. They may want to help with the search for funding. You cannot pay indefinitely all the expenses—"

"—oh, but I can," Lucas interrupted somewhat guiltily. "I have a huge inheritance from my parents, and I have barely spent a farthing of it. The stewards, accountants, and solicitors of our estates continue to extract profits from our land, from investments, from the labours of those who work for us. Neither my uncle nor I have any truly extravagant needs, except for the smooth running of our households and occasional trips to the continent. And why should the children—" he turned to face her full on, wanting to bring home his important point. "Why should the children of this humble little borough want for medical care when I have never wanted for anything my entire life?" She wanted to add, 'except for a mother and father', but could not bring herself to hurt him with that truth. She just nodded at him and then brashly took one of his hands in both hers.

"I am fully cognizant, Lucas, of your generosity, of...your...*need* to be generous. But you also have to give back to your guardians. They must know that their kindness and devotion to you has been worthwhile. You must give them an inkling of their success. They deserve it. I am sure that they are truly wonderful people. Do not cheat them of a little joy. Go home to them for Christmas and give them the best gift that you can possibly give them."

Before he took his leave of her, however, there was a knock at her door. It was for the delivery of coal next door. Mr. Housman had obviously got a new boy. He told them that Phillip had brought the chimney sweep round the back where there was a ladder to get on the roof. A few minutes later another boy arrived with the bedding that Phillip had bought. Lucas paid for everything and then he left, promising to return in the morning with the equipment for their surgery. He seemed loath to leave, but Gwynne managed to get him out the door. She wondered if one day he wouldn't leave. It was a thought that did not frighten her. In fact, it gave her solace. She wanted to stop fighting with the world, with the male world, and perhaps Lucas was her means of doing that.

Chapter XII

When Lucas got out of the hansom cab in front of the door in Chelsea, he realized that he did not want to enter the house yet, not that anyone from his family would be there. They were all already in Kent, since the House of Lords had stopped sitting for the Christmas break a few weeks prior. He usually came home when the family was away and stayed in his rooms when they were in London. If his aunt and uncle felt slighted by this, they never said as much. His sister never asked him why he preferred it this way, but he could feel that she envied him his freedom—an unmarried man had his money and his life, whereas an unmarried woman had nothing, just the rules and regulations that society imposed upon her. Gwynne's life had had its limitations, still did, poverty and deprivation playing a big part in that, but she certainly had more freedom than Isabel. Isa could only wait to be married and fill her days with reading and good deeds to the best of her abilities, but Gwynne had experienced real life, hardship, and even death. He must introduce his sister to Gwynne, not that he really wanted to share his nurse-friend with anyone, but it was time to do something for Isa, now that he had begun to take care of himself. Gwynne had been right. The members of his family deserved a little pleasure or satisfaction of a kind that perhaps he could give them.

Today had been warmer, certainly above freezing, and although it was very dark already, Lucas decided to walk around the block before he went in. He stood for a moment looking at the imposing building that had been in his father's family for many decades—a well-built, solid mansion with the requisite wrought-iron fencing; rather beautiful he had to admit, the four white Grecian columns at the entrance that spoke of wealth and position, the triangular marble pediment that of course went with these columns, although it was free of sculptures that might have been there had the building been built in Ancient times and not in the previous century.

Despite its handsomeness, Lucas could not bring himself to enter via the front door tonight. When he was ready, he would come in through the back of the house, as servants and tradesmen were wont to do. It pained him to think that since there were two classes of people in the world, the plebeian and the patrician, someone like Gwynne and his other new friends might be forced to go in by the back. *He* had a choice, but they would not. He decided there and then that if Gwynne were to ever come here—and why wouldn't she?—under no circumstances would he give in to the differentiation that society proclaimed existed. Gwynne was beyond category, beyond societal rank, and to him, she was becoming much more than a confidante, friend, and colleague.

Trudging through the melting snow, Lucas was reminded of his university friend Rupert Keynes, whom he had not spoken to for ages. How long had it been, a year? Here was someone who was truly passionate about architecture, someone who could say whether some architectural detail harked back to Leon Battista Alberti or Filippo Brunelleschi or Andrea Palladio.   Sometimes Lucas had wondered why his friend had chosen medicine at all as a field of study. It was so obvious to him that the history of architecture and art was Rupert's first love. Of course, Rupert's parents could have had something to do with that choice.

When they had finished their studies, he and Rupert had taken a continental tour together. To go with Rupert through France and Italy had been more of an education than going to university. The cities and towns of these two countries became for Lucas a never-ending garden of delights. Rupert had dragged him around the most out-of-the way places to behold indescribable beauties of art and architecture. He must have written a hundred letters to his sister about all that he was seeing and experiencing, promising that the two of them would make this tour together in the near future. But that had never come to pass. Lucas had selfishly deprived Isa of a journey she would have loved, because in time, he had become so bogged down in his weighty sense of despair. What a cruel and thoughtless brother he had been! And furthermore, he had never introduced Rupert to his family. Rupert hated society, and his parents had lost hope in his ever finding a suitable wife, much like Lucas's own aunt and uncle where he was concerned. For the two of them, it had been something of a relief to abandon their families and tramp around Europe without a thought for what one's parents or guardians were planning for one's future. They had had a great deal in common and then they had lost touch. Lucas knew that Rupert had had no intention of joining his father's lucrative medical practice and instead had decided to devote himself to scientific research, and the development of new cures for specific illnesses.

As Lucas put his key into the back door of the family home, after his short contemplative perambulation around the neighbourhood, he decided that now was the time to renew this friendship, now that he felt that he could be made whole again by having a purpose in life. He realized how strange it was that he had never told Rupert, a friend and companion of many years, anything about what he was feeling, about why he could not get truly excited about anything in his life. He had merely followed Rupert, responding to the other's enthusiasms, enjoying being a part of someone else's loves and interests. Their mutual sense of rebellion was shared aloud, but not the guilt that ensued in Lucas's case, because his aunt and uncle were blameless. The emotions that truly mattered, these he had never expressed to anyone but Gwynne, someone he had known a mere few days and nights, and the bond he felt with her, he knew, must never be torn asunder. And he must never treat her as he had treated his sister. How could he ever make up to Isabel his unforgivable slight of her needs and wants? Perhaps in some way he could get her to be a part of this hospital for the sick and abandoned children of East London. He would have to ask her if she wanted to participate, at least meet Gwynne and talk to her of Florence Nightingale. And Rupert, too...he would get into contact with him again, tell him about his hospital when it was fully operational. He mused again that he had never once even whispered to Rupert that the only patients he ever wanted were the very small, the as yet not fully formed. He had never really admitted it to himself. How much he had recently learned about himself in the company of a humble but remarkable nurse, his very own lady with a lamp!

Inside Mrs. Blunt's warm kitchen, Lucas removed his greatcoat, hat, scarf, gloves, and boots. Before making his way into the interior of the house and up the stairs to his bedroom, he sat down by the fire. He built it up with new logs and waited for the cook to appear. He was feeling a little hungry, and perhaps there were some leftovers he could eat. When no one entered the kitchen, after about five minutes, he decided to go looking for some other inhabitants. Since the family was all in Kent for the holidays, few servants were left in the London household—Mrs. Blunt, who usually stayed here anyway, since there was a live-in cook in Kent, his personal valet, Peter, and Susan, the parlour maid, and maybe a few others, oh yes, the footman Gabriel, and the coachman, Reginald, and Martin, the stable boy, who would all be helping again tomorrow to move his father's equipment into East London. Of these, only his valet and himself would be heading down south on the train in two days' time. His uncle's coach would pick him and Peter up at the Ashford station.

In the servants' dining-hall, he found Peter and Susan at the table in a tête-à-tête. Because he was not wearing any shoes, they had not heard him. Peter all of a sudden moved in closer to Susan and kissed her on the mouth. Lucas could tell that she returned his ardour. When Peter moved away from her, he sighed and put both his hands on her face and looked into her eyes. So, Peter and Susan were in love! Lucas cleared his throat, and immediately Peter bounced to his feet and Susan looked down in embarrassment.

"I am sorry to have disturbed you," Lucas began. What was he supposed to say? Suddenly Mrs. Blunt appeared in the dining-hall as well and took in the meaning of the situation.

"All right, all right," she hastily interrupted. "This was bound to happen sometime." She turned to Peter and Susan. "I told you to tell him, didn't I?"

"Tell me what?" asked Lucas.

Both Peter and Susan were tongue-tied, so Mrs. Blunt again took over. "My dear sir, these two lovebirds wish to be married, but they are afraid your aunt will not allow it. Many houses do not like married servants—"

"—but that's ridiculous," interrupted Lucas. "And anyway, our housekeeper and butler are married."

"They came as a married couple without children before you were out of britches, my dear Lucas, and so...Peter and Susan here have been feeling uncertain. I told them to ask you. At any rate," Mrs. Blunt smiled broadly, "I would never let you refuse them."

Lucas laughed. "My dear Mrs. Blunt, you do not have to order me to accept their wishes to marry. I am perfectly capable of making a logical decision by myself." Lucas turned to the happy couple. "Don't you worry. I will let my aunt know that I have given you my blessing. And anyway, Susan, don't you have parents?" Susan nodded. "Well, I think that your young man should ask them rather than me for your hand in marriage."

"Oh, sir, they live down south not far from you in Kent, on the way to Dover. I 'aven't seen them in many a year."

"Well, why don't you and Peter go there for Christmas and get married down there? Take some time to yourselves. I will see to the railway tickets with Peter tomorrow after we come back from East London. Would you like that?"

Susan looked as if she were about to jump for joy and cry at the same time. Peter's grin was a mile wide. He took Susan's hand in his. It felt good to make two happy people even happier. He looked up at the cook. "Have you all had supper yet?" Mrs. Blunt shook her head. "Is there any food for us?"

"Of course there is, Lucas. Can't you smell it?"

"Well, then, let's all eat together here in celebration of Peter and Susan's upcoming marriage. In two days' time we will travel together down to Kent by train."

"Susan, come and help me bring in the dinner." Mrs. Blunt said to the maid, and they took their leave of the men.

"And I will find a good bottle of claret in the cellar. Come with me, Peter." Peter followed him down into the wine cellar where they decided on a suitable bottle for their meal. Upstairs, Peter opened the bottle and the two men sat down. Lucas realized that he had never really talked man-to-man with Peter. He was always his loyal servant, but never a sounding board as Isabel's lady's maid, Rebecca, seemed to be to her. Lucas wondered what Peter thought of his recent few days spent in East London. Did Peter judge him or even really think about him at all? And what did he know of Peter's background? Had he come to the Lacey household via Kent as well?

"Peter, do you also hail from Kent as most of our servants do?"

"No, sir. I'm from Spitalfields, meself. I grew up in poverty and escaped. I don't really like to remember me childhood. At ten, me mother died of the cholera."

"I am so sorry to hear that, Peter," Lucas said, and he was. What a terrible blow it must have been.

Peter nodded in acknowledgement of Lucas's heartfelt words, knowing full well that his master had also lost parents. "Me dad and I were left adrift for many a month after that. Finally, me father decided, since our lives in East London were going nowhere, to try to seek employment in Dover where a cousin of 'is lived and worked at the docks. 'Ad me mother been alive it might have been an impossible journey, seeing as we 'ad to walk most of the way there, not 'aving enough money to spend on transportation, food, and lodging. But farmers along the way gave us rides in their carts, sometimes fed us, and offered us accommodation either in their barns or their 'ouses." Here Peter took a deep breath, lost for a moment in contemplation of his difficult childhood. Lucas waited for him to continue. Finally, it hit him that the head of their stables in Kent, the man in charge of taking care of all their many horses and the upkeep of the stables, must be none other than Peter's father. He was always simply known as Mullins: his last name. Lucas had never made the connection before. In fact, he probably hadn't much cared about the relationship between all the servants that his family employed. How insensitive of him. Isabel would have known everything she could about these people and where they came from. She cared about them. This failing of his was perhaps what had made him so ready to give up on life. He gave nothing to others. He had been as hermetically sealed in his own little world as a fish in a fishbowl.

"So how did you and your dad end up in service in our household?"

"Well, at first, me dad worked at the docks in Dover with 'is cousin. That lasted about six months. 'Orses were always 'is first love. 'Ere in London, 'e worked as a groom for the 'orses that pull the 'ansom cabs and omnibuses—'ard work, with little remuneration. When in Dover, he 'eard about a job at a particular stable in Maidstone. We lived there for about three years, and I was even able to attend school. Somehow 'e learned that there was an opening as a groom at your uncle's estate, Ashford-way. And so, we ended up there. Eventually I went into service, too, just being a kitchen-boy in the beginning, then a footman, and finally your valet."

"So, me dragging you into East London of late, has that proved trying?"

"Not really. I think that what you are doing is admirable, m'Lord. Someone like you and Nurse Gwynne would've been a boon to all us poor folk in my days."

So, Peter had thought about what he was doing. His valet's positive acknowledgement of his project felt good. "Thank you, Peter. I value your opinion." Peter looked a little taken aback. Lucas continued, "I am sorry I have never told you that before. And your father, well, he has been an important person in my life. As a child, riding was a particular joy for me—"

"—Oh, m'Lord, I forgot to mention. I 'eard from Martin t'other day, when 'e returned 'ere from Kent, last week, that your Uncle 'as bought a new 'orse, and me dad 'as been training 'im for you to ride this Christmas. Martin says 'e is some beautiful animal." Peter smiled broadly, and Lucas was about to ask a few questions about the animal when the women returned from the kitchen, pushing a serving cart with four plates of ham, mashed potatoes, and French beans, as well as four wine glasses.

Eventually all four of them were seated and eating and toasting and drinking. Towards the end of the meal, Susan asked him how long he was planning to stay in Kent and if he would return to Chelsea or to his rented lodgings. "I want to be back here as soon as possible. I want to start working in Whitechapel in the New Year, but I am anxious to be here when we are getting the place ready for our future patients." They all seemed well-aware of his new endeavour. Peter must have filled them in on all that had been happening in the last few days. "I would love to come back here in a few short days, but I guess that would meet with hearty disapproval from the family. So, I was thinking four-five days at the most...and I don't know exactly where I will reside...probably..." Lucas scratched his head. He hadn't thought that much about it. All he had thought about really was getting back to Gwynne and the hospital as soon as he could.

"Only four-five days, m'Lord?" Mrs. Blunt and Susan echoed each other.

"Well, there is just so much to do."

"So, Susan and I could spend that much time in Dover, and return by the same train to London with you?" Peter asked.

Lucas nodded, but he then asked if Susan was meant to help the family in the country. "Doesn't my aunt need you in Kent, Susan, for the next few weeks before they return to London for the sitting of the House of Lords in the New Year?"

"Sir, the reason I am here is to care for your needs either in your central lodgings or here. Someone has to keep the place clean for you. Didn't you realize that?"

"I notice that you are sometimes in my rooms, and sometimes the other parlour maid Lucy is there."

"Sometimes your aunt sends Patricia, and sometimes Helen to care for you. We rotate."

Lucas pondered this arrangement, of which he had had no awareness previously. The women were just there, and Peter was just there. He had hardly noticed. How complicated the running of three households could be. His aunt ran things so smoothly. He was certainly well taken care of. He hadn't realized that his needs were so great. Peter interrupted his musings.

"M'Lord, are you sure I should leave you this Christmas? A young man needs 'is valet, especially when there may be guests and special dinners."

"You don't think that I can dress myself?"

"I think you can dress yourself, sir, but your clothes 'ave to be spotless, and pressed, and your boots do not get polished by themselves."

Lucas blushed. He felt like a spoiled child. He *was* a spoiled child. Embarrassed by this new knowledge of the importance of servants in his life, Lucas responded to Peter's query, however with the certainty that Peter's needs at the moment were of a much higher order. "Peter, I want you to be married. That is much more important than the shine on my boots. One of the footmen, Michael, perhaps, who takes care of visiting gentlemen sometimes, can serve as my manservant for those few days." Peter nodded, relieved that he did not have to give up his forthcoming marriage to pamper a helpless master. Lucas then turned to

Susan. "I was wondering, Susan, if it would be more to your liking if you could permanently be assigned to me in the future. This way, you and Peter would always be under the same roof. I will mostly stay at my lodgings and you and Peter can have the largest of the servants' rooms, or...whatever you wish. And if and when you have children, he, she, or they can have the other servants' rooms." Susan was smiling and nodding. "Besides, I may need both of you for other responsibilities when my hospital project really gets underway."

Mrs. Blunt intervened at this point. "Things may get complicated with the coming of children, sir. Taking care of children *and* taking care of you..." She did not need to finish her sentence for Lucas to get the gist of her meaning.

"Am I really such a difficult master to deal with? You are making me feel decidedly dependent." He thought of Gwynne and Jane, who managed to work and bring up children in much more dire circumstances.

Mrs. Blunt put an affectionate arm around Lucas's shoulders. "I love you, my dear boy, and, no, you are not a demanding master, just a little oblivious perhaps about all that goes into making your life smooth and easy."

Lucas sighed. And then he had a happy thought. "And when I have children one day, they can all grow up together somewhere, and enjoy Mrs. Blunt's cooking, and I will always make sure that they are all healthy and happy." Susan, Peter, and the cook began to laugh. It was really time for him to live on his own with his very own household. But first he must make a family. He had never thought about that before this moment. He had been too engrossed with the possibility of walking out on life, not with the prospect of bringing more life into the world.

Chapter XIII

"I would like to be back here by the twenty-ninth of the month, Gwynne, the thirtieth at the latest. The thought of you and Jane and Jonathan and Robert and Phillip doing all the work of setting up the place without me at your side is...is...appalling—unfair at the very least."

He was beseeching her to understand his haste at getting back to London before the New Year, and although she was beginning to feel that life seemed much fuller with this man in her presence, she decidedly did not wish him to experience guilt if his aunt entreated him to stay longer with his family. She was conscious of how fragile Lucas's hold on life could be, even if he had now discovered a way to use his knowledge and skill to the betterment of the children of the East end.

"Don't you want me here...especially now?"

"Of course I do...and the thought of you leaving is...is...upsetting...distressful, if you will," she was searching to find the exact word that would convey her meaning best, but feared that she was not succeeding. "But if you hurt your aunt or your sister in any way, I know that when you come back here, you will carry that burden with you. Just don't make any plan. Test the waters, so to speak, when you are there. Reveal to them, certainly, that you are anxious to get on with your life...but...buy a railway ticket back to London *after* you see how they react. If Peter and Susan have already left Dover to meet you, they can stay a few more days with you in Kent, if it is necessary to keep everyone there happy. It won't really matter to either of them."

Lucas sat down heavily on her bed. She could see that he was tired from the move of his father's, now his own surgery, into its new home next door. They were all pretty exhausted. Jane's family had gone home, and Phillip was already asleep in his own room. Charles had been a little unsettled by the end of the day, with all the excitement of so many people in his life. Lucas had brought a crib for him from the home in Chelsea. His aunt was probably saving it for his or Isabel's future children, but Lucas was convinced that no one would mind if Charles used it now. That, too, had excited her little boy, and it had taken him a while before he fell asleep, but now he was sleeping deeply. She was so grateful to Lucas for thinking of Charles. She wondered a bit at his growing attachment to her son. She had never noticed a man taking a profound interest in a child, even if it were his own. But Lucas seemed interested in everything that the children around him did—Phillip, Selina, as well as Charles. He was truly suited to this work he had chosen to do.

Gwynne took a chair and placed it in front of Lucas and sat down. She was noticing how much she longed to be near him when he was around. It was never really enough to be in the same room as him. He, too, seemed to move towards her when there was an opportunity to be closer. It had been like that all day, almost as if they were dancing together as partners. At some point, they were forced to acknowledge and address other people, but, in time, they wended their way back to each other. Was her suggestion to him to stay as long as he had to in Kent just a way to assert her independence? Was she afraid of losing that because this man had found a way into her heart? Was he going to be more than an employer? Did she want him to be something more or did she want to be her self-sufficient self again—a woman who yearned for no man?

He finally looked up at her after a momentary silence and spoke. "I suppose one can never really escape the tyranny of wanting to please others. Since I have never known before what it was that I actually wished for from life, I spent my time trying to be what others wanted me to be. I never actually succeeded, though. I suppose you are right. I will always feel the weight of disappointing them, my sister, my aunt, my uncle. I do so want to be free of guilt." Lucas passed a hand over his face and sighed into it. Gwynne took that hand into hers and held it on her lap.

"Listen, Lucas, there is no need to feel so much guilt." Gwynne tried to organize her thoughts as lucidly as possible. There was something she wanted to tell him, something she had been thinking about a great deal. She began her little speech slowly and softly. "I believe," she began almost in a whisper, "that all of your feelings of never being able to pay back the love and devotion bestowed upon you by your aunt, uncle, and Isabel are a result of never being able to forgive yourself for causing, as you see it, the accident that took the lives of your parents and that of a horse. You have never felt that you deserved their love because, at the age of six, you had done a deplorable thing. Am I right?"

Lucas swallowed hard, seemed on the verge of speaking, but then gave up and just nodded. To Gwynne, it was as if he could not trust himself with words at that moment. His face was so full of emotion and expectation. He was waiting for her to continue. He knew that what she was about to reveal would be of great importance to him. Gwynne took a deep breath.

"What I am about to tell you may surprise you, because my interpretation of the day in which your parents died is completely different from your own. But I have thought long and hard about it and have come to an alternative conclusion which, by virtue of my greater objectivity in the matter, I deem to be the more probable one." Lucas was so totally absorbed in what she was saying that he was listening almost breathlessly, certainly unmoving. "I believe that when you stood up at the front of the wagon in that fateful moment on that fateful day, you were responding naturally to the situation. You felt in your body the precariousness of the carriage's hold on the road. Your father did, too. Standing up was not a wanton act. It was justified by the real sensation that the world was about to collapse. You needed to be on your feet to meet the threat. When your father let go of the reins with the hand nearest to you, he wasn't about to clutch at your clothing to keep you in your seat, to keep you in the carriage as if it would readjust itself and find itself back on the road to safety. He touched you, didn't he? You felt his hand on your chest?" Again, all that Lucas did was nod. Gwynne extended her own hand towards his chest and pushed him away from her. "Did you feel it more or less like that?"

"Ye-e-s, but—"

"—but nothing. He wasn't trying to keep you with him. He was trying to save your life the only possible way. In order to survive, you had to fall as far away from the debris of the wreckage. You knew how to swim, did you not?"

"Of course. I had been swimming for two years by then."

"Right." Gwynne nodded at him. "Your father saved your life by pushing you into the water. The momentum of the fall propelled you even further, and thankfully you escaped the consequences of the crash against the rocks and the ground directly beneath the cliff, something which your father did not. He released the grip on the reins purposefully to deliver you from harm because he *knew* that he could not prevent the fall any longer. Unfortunately, he did not have the time to follow you, to dive into the water as far away as he could. Had he done that, had he saved his own life, then perhaps he could have also managed to rescue your mother. She was knocked unconscious by whatever hit her on the head—a piece of the broken carriage, a falling box containing something heavy. But she may not have drowned as a consequence, had your father had the opportunity to pull her out of the water. She may have been concussed, but she would have been breathing air. You could not have done any of that. You were only a small child. But he was a strong man. Perhaps he might even have had enough time to also release the other horse from bondage. We will never know. But the fact remains, you did not cause the accident. The accident happened. You reacted instinctively. Your father saved you, but failed to save anyone else, including himself. Perhaps, in that split second, his thought was only for you." Gwynne was nodding again to demonstrate her certainty. "Fortunately, he had the time and the wherewithal to take care of you as was his duty. You owe him your life. But all the death on that day was not in any way due to you. You were just as much a victim of the accident as those that did not survive." Gwynne paused for a moment then placed her hand gently on Lucas's face. She saw shock there. She saw that he was on the verge of breaking down. "And now you must take that life that your father bestowed on you for a second time and live it to the fullest. That is your duty to him, Lucas." She then removed herself from the chair and sat down directly beside him on the bed, gathering him in her arms as she did this. Lucas held nothing back. The side of his face lay on her shoulder, and he cried into her neck, his arms clinging to her as if she were his pillar of safety, the one thing that could deliver him from his lifelong torment. Gwynne held him, willing all of her strength to sustain him. She had spoken the truth. She was sure of it. He had only to believe her and sail into the open waters. In a way, she knew that he had already liberated her by allowing her to vent the emotions of fear, and hatred, and anguish caused by another man. She had never before been so aware of the power of truth, its power to redeem, and its power to restore. She hoped that she would never evade or falsify events or feelings when dealing with Lucas. Was that possible? Did all men and women lie, especially to each other? Their story, hers and Lucas's had begun in absolute honesty. In a way they had been utterly naked with each other—all the social contrivances and niceties of class and rules of behaviour totally absent from their exchange. She had not fulfilled their bargain, however. She had not lain on this bed with him and given up her body to him as promised. Something told her that she would; perhaps not today, but some day, when they were ready, they would both move in the open waters. They would defy convention again. Did Lucas know this? She did not think so. He would be too worried about her, about appearing like Edmund in her eyes, like a brute of a man taking his way with a woman without concern for her wishes. In time he would be ready. And in time so would she.

PART TWO

Chapter XIV

"My dear, dear Isabel, it is my most fervent wish that you should meet this...this...friend of mine, this Nightingale of a nurse, who has for a long time been conferring her well-honed skills on the poor of the East end without my aid, but who now will have me at her side to assist her in her tasks, specifically with children, of course, since I have recently come to learn that I want to practice my profession uniquely in the company of children." After this rather long sentence, Lucas sighed and pulled slightly back from his sister, as if giving her the space to take in all that he was saying. He knew he had conveyed a great deal of information in that one sentence—first, his utmost respect for Gwynne, second, his discovery of what he wanted to do in life, and third his distinct desire to share something of his newfound lease on life with her, someone he feared he had neglected for far too long. Perhaps he had shared something more than a mere sense of respect towards Gwynne, because his feelings, especially now, after their last encounter in her home, where he had broken down so utterly and completely, were so obviously of a higher and more all-encompassing order. As usual, it had been hard to tear himself away from her. He had felt such gratitude, as well as such naked need for her that he could barely control any kind of restraint in his profuse expression of indebtedness. Their long embrace only convinced him more of his longing to not only live out his professional life with her, but also his emotional and sentimental life. He was still trying to interpret all that had happened. On the train he scarcely spoke at all to Susan and Peter, reliving in his imagination all that had transpired in the arms of Gwynne. He knew that he had to leave her then. He could not, after all, spend the night in her bed, whether he touched her or not—although touch her and kiss her was exactly what he wished wholeheartedly to do. Did he really want to do exactly that—live with her the way that Peter wished to live with Susan? Could he actually marry her? Could he actually give up his aristocratic life of ease, that of an Earl, no less, and live out his days with her in the warrens of East London? She was certainly not a lady of the drawing-room, nor would he want her to be. That would be preposterous! She was so much more. And he could never expect her to devote herself totally to him, his needs, and his happiness. She was not that kind of woman. She had a mission in life, as did he, now that he was in her orbit. There was so much to think about. Unfortunately, the only person with whom he could discuss all this with total frankness was the woman in question herself. He could only recount a fraction of all of it with Isabel. Poor Isabel! She, as a female member of the upper classes, was forced to sacrifice too much. He had to convince her to not just work to make a success of the charity that would sustain his children's hospital, as both she and their aunt enthusiastically promised to do, but also to somehow *be* a part of it, lend her superior intelligence and refinement of mind and spirit to the venture. But in what form could this participation manifest itself?

He was sitting opposite her, in a comfortable armchair in the second-floor drawing-room, she in the settee to his right, the fire blazing before them. Dinner was over. The invited guests were in their own chambers, as were his aunt and uncle. Only he and Isabel were awake and alone in this magnificent room. It had all the trappings of wealth and the beauty that comes with the means to furnish a room elaborately but in good taste. He almost hated it, the whole dreary life of earls and lords and ladies. Looking at his sister, in her perfect gown of a pale lilac colour, absolutely in the latest fashion, with her painstakingly curled and coiffed hair, blonde like his own and their mother's, worked on probably for hours by Rebecca, her devoted lady's maid, he could only see the tightening of society's yoke around her—each pin, a bar of her prison, each piece of whale bone, a symbol of captivity and oppression. Tonight, in her splendour, she had seemed a blur in the domestic landscape, her face clouded over and indistinct. It had made him think of the absolute clarity of Gwynne's face, the exquisite starkness in the contrasts of her features, her dark, long hair in the evening after work, loose and flowing in the glow of the oil lamp, her smooth, fair skin, and her intensely green eyes—no heaps of time spent in dressing to advantage only making her less distinctive in the process. No, he did not have to search for the real Gwynne. She was always there. Of course he had had glimpses of his sister's true self, of her intellectual brilliance all through his life. And he wanted it to shine through always, not only when the company had gone to bed. She deserved the opportunity to freely express herself whenever and wherever she wanted, but stuck in this palace, it was not meant to be. All of a sudden, he had the desire to show her his admiration and respect and belief in her ability to climb over the walls of her prison. He wanted to embrace her, and so he rose from his seat and dropped down beside her, stretching his arms around her and squeezing her to his chest. "Oh, Isabel, you deserve so much more than this wretched life of yours behind the walls of this castle. You need to spread your wings and give the world the privilege of your mind and soul. I wish I could free you from the tyrannical grip of rules and obligations. I have not loved you well. I have not served you well. I will never forgive myself if I cannot right the wrongs with which society has burdened you."

Isabel reciprocated his brotherly ardour and circled her arms around his broad shoulders. "There is little that you or anyone can do. A woman is always relegated to the drawing-room, whether in the house of her father or the house of her husband." She sighed into his neck and then pulled away from him. "Do not fret so, Lucas." She smiled at him in her supremely generous way, giving him the beauty of her intelligent eyes. "You have always loved me well. I know of no other woman who has a brother like you, who listens so closely to all my childish utterings." She stroked his hair and then placed her lips on his cheek.

"But I want so much more for you. I mean I want others to hear what you have to say about all manner of things—philosophy, politics, literature, foreign literature...." Lucas protested ruefully.

His sister sat up straight and cocked her head to the side as she eyed him carefully. The gesture reminded him of Gwynne. Did all women do that? How had he failed to notice before? "You know, Lucas, there is something decidedly different about you, and I don't just mean your enthusiasm for this East end project of yours." She brought her hand to his head and caressed his hair, the colour of which made them noticeably siblings.

"Different? How?" he questioned her.

"Your demeanour, the way you behave towards...others...not just us, everyone around you." She tried to express her thought in words, but her hand gestures showed how difficult she was finding it to answer him.

"So, I am different with others, but how am I different with others?" He continued to press her for a fuller response.

"Well...I would have to say that you are just more open, more vocal, freer, less cautious. Don't worry, dear brother, I...rather like this new you, and...and I think you are happier. Am I right?"

Lucas leaned against the back of the settee, obviously pondering her assessment of his altered behaviour of late. So, his emotional nakedness with Gwynne had somehow translated to a freer nature in the drawing-rooms of society. He actually hadn't noticed. He realized, however, that he was censoring much fewer thoughts when communicating idly with his interlocutors. Before, it didn't really seem to matter to him how completely or incompletely he responded to his companions in conversation. Usually he chose to be quite aloof, since he didn't really care about that of which he was speaking. But it was true, he would have to say, that on this trip home for Christmas, he participated in conversations around the dinner table, for instance, in a more natural way. Perhaps he had stopped judging his acquaintances.

Perhaps he had stopped judging himself. Slowly, Lucas nodded. "Yes, I have changed, Isabel. And I am much happier." He smiled openly now. Isabel had every right to know the truth.

"I am wondering, Lucas, if this Nurse Gwynne has anything to do with your transformation." She stopped and touched his arm momentarily. "You do not have to answer me. I do not wish to pry confidence from you, if you do not wish to give it."

"Ask away, Isabel. I do not want to shrink from the truth about my state of mind." He turned to look at his sister. He hoped that she hadn't actually known how much he had been contemplating ending it all in the past. She would have suffered dreadfully. But he supposed he could divulge at least some part of that despair, now that a new lightness of heart had crept into his life, after Gwynne's quiet interpretation of the single most harrowing experience of his life. What she had said to him about not being at fault for the tragic end to his parents' lives had caused a kind of revolution inside of him, and nothing was the same anymore. When he woke in the mornings, for the first moment, he was surprised at how buoyant he felt. It took a minute to place himself in time, and then he would say to himself, *Ah-hah! It is two days, or three days, or four since Gwynne turned my world upside down.* It was...wondrous, really. How could he explain all that to Isabel, who had never really known the exact origin of his dejection? Or did she? She couldn't. She wasn't there. She was too young. And besides, he had never really expressed anything about it. He took one of his sister's hands in both his own, squeezed it, smiled again, and pronounced in distinct tones: "If you must know, Nurse Gwynne, in her very special way, has nursed me back to health...I think...I hope. Perhaps I will not be such a burden to you now, Isabel. Perhaps I, for the first time in a long time, can be of help to *you,* for I may no longer be so centred on myself and what I lack in *my* life."

Chapter XV

"I couldn't convince her, Gwynne. I so wanted her to come back with me and see for herself what we are up to here, so that she could find a place for herself in our midst, but you know what it's like for unmarried ladies. The thought of her staying in the London house, even if I would go home to her every night, without the protection of my aunt and uncle, is somehow...just not *de rigueur.* She can only come back here when Parliament resumes sitting in the New Year, the last week of January, I presume, when the entire household has to return to London." Lucas shook his head in frustration. "How can she live like that? She is a mature, thoughtful, sober twenty-five-year-old. What do they think she will get up to? It is the young gentlemen of her age that should be watched over, for they are so much more likely to get up to behaviour of the unwanted sort—carousing, gambling, spending money recklessly without a thought in the world." Lucas flung his arms about to emphasize the wantonness of his peers. "My sister, on the other hand, has never spent a farthing on her own personal enjoyment without my aunt and uncle carefully evaluating the expenditure." Lucas was standing now as he tried to convince her of the ridiculous ways of upper-class society. If indeed that was all he wanted to do—convince her—then his rant was not exactly necessary, but she allowed him the space and time to vent. She nodded in agreement, however, from her seated position at the dining-room table. Lucas had returned two days before the end of the year, bearing gifts, of course, for the children in his entourage—a wooden pull-toy of a little dog for Charles, as well as more necessary items, like clothes for her little son, a beautiful doll for two-year-old Selina, and clothes for her, too, a set of carpentry tools for Robert, who had never owned anything of his own in his young life, using his father's tools since he began his apprenticeship, and a warm winter coat and new boots and a man's pocket knife for Phillip. The children were ecstatic. They were all next door with Jonathan and Jane, either working or playing. Jane was preparing the evening meal for everyone. When Lucas had left to go to Kent for Christmas, he had also left her a great deal of money to pay for whatever the hospital needed in the way of supplies—lumber, nails, screws, plaster and the like, food, and cleaning materials, as well as wages for herself and Jane. As for Jonathan, he would pay him when billed at the end of each month for his and Robert's services. She had kept an exact tally of all her expenses, but when they had gone to her room in order to look over the details of all that she had disbursed, he did not seem at all interested in numbers, and much more interested in filling her in on the details of his reunion with his family. His aunt and his sister were completely on board with their running of a charity. All he had to do was see his solicitor to set it up, and they would do the rest—seeking the funding necessary for maintaining the project. But mostly he wanted to give her an account of Isabel's what he called captivity within the tentacles of their class. At this juncture in his tirade, she could not fail to smile at his vehemence.

"Why are you smiling, Gwynne? It's not funny. She's exactly like a worm on a hook and I cannot seem to help her."

"My dear Lucas, I am only smiling because it is so unusual to see a man take up the cause for women's equality. I believe in it, too. And, if there is anything I can do for Isabel, I promise that I will endeavour to help her with all the energy I can muster. What, for example, do you think her role could be here, besides the one of trying to wheedle her acquaintances out of their precious pounds? Do you have anything in mind?"

Lucas sat down abruptly across from her. She had taken the wind out of his sails, it seemed. He put his elbows on the table and his face in his hands. When he lifted his head, he just uttered a barely audible, "No."

Gwynne reached over from her side of the table and took both his hands in her own. "Well, I have an idea, Lucas."

"You do? Really? Tell me immediately."

"Well, since you have been gone this last week, I have been treating several young orphans from the streets in our hospital. Ordinarily they might not have come to me, since they have nothing with which to offer in return. But now that Phillip has been broadcasting the existence of the hospital and the fact that our services are totally free, they have been coming with their scrapes, bruises, and even broken bones. It pains me to have to send them back out there after I have bandaged them up and given them a hot meal. Eight-year-old Malcolm, however, is our first real resident. He has been sleeping with Phillip, but I think that Jonathan has now completed a bed for him, made to your specifications, and Phillip will be going out to purchase some linens and blankets for tonight." She stopped momentarily here, drew breath, and began the story of this unfortunate lad, who was so undernourished and skeletal when he arrived that she did not know how his thin legs could have transported him here. He ate porridge, soup, overcooked vegetables, and a little meat, but slept most of the day, and was just beginning to look as if he might remain in the land of the living. When he was awake, Phillip moved him around the central space of the hospital to and from his bed, to have his bath, and to the examining room on the push-chair that Robert and Jonathan had constructed. He was just that weak. "But afterwards, Lucas, I really don't have the heart to throw him out onto the streets again." She pointed to the rooms next door. "Now that we have a real space where children without a home may sleep, how can we push them out the door? For as long as I have been doing this work here in Whitechapel, I have had no choice. Their illnesses have mostly to do with malnutrition and I have had so little to offer them. It has been heartbreaking knowing that they cannot get a real start in life when they have nothing and no means to really earn enough to feed themselves." It was her turn to drop her head, in a gesture of defeat, into her hands, which she freed from their grasp of Lucas's.

Lucas instantly followed up on her train of thought. "You think that we could allow them to remain here, perhaps expand the premises, when more rooms become free in this dwelling, and what...what would we do with them?"

Gwynne lifted her head and responded immediately. "We could start some sort of school, not too different from the Ragged Schools: teach them the basics of reading, writing, sums, knowledge of geography and the world. And perhaps your sister could do that if she wanted. I was thinking that for those children who are not orphans, they, too, could benefit from learning. Even...even their parents could come in the evening and learn to read and write. Think of how that might change their lives. Lucas, we could do so much more than fill their bellies or stop their bleeding after a street fight, or...or...bathe them before they return to the filth and vermin to which they are so accustomed."

It was Lucas's turn to smile. "What an idea, Gwynne! Yes, a place for them to live, under the care and tutelage of my sister! What an idea! You are brilliant!"

"But would she be interested?"

"It will be my job to convince her. Actually, I think *you* could be instrumental in demonstrating the value of such work. You live here, know the terrain, and have seen with your own eyes the hopelessness of these children's prospects for a brighter future. I know she would listen to you and respect your knowledge. You are the perfect spokeswoman for our cause."

Gwynne put up her palm to stop the flow of his compliments. "Do not get carried away, Lucas. We haven't met yet. Give her a chance to assess my powers of persuasion by herself. I have no idea how she might react to our plea to get her involved. She did not exactly jump at the chance to step out of her role as princess in the tower to follow you to big bad London. She may not relish the idea of working here day in and day out. It is not exactly like Chelsea. In fact, it is nothing like Chelsea here. There is not a Lord or Lady in sight."

Lucas sat down again to talk to her at her level, but this time he came to her side of the table and pulled out a chair next to her. He placed his hands on her shoulders and looked directly into her face.

"My dear Gwynne, you must not prejudge my sister."

"I know that you believe in the power of her intellect," she protested, "but to work here needs courage and fortitude more than intelligence." She pointed with her index finger to her heart. "More than anything, *I* would wish her to accept our proposal. Of course I want that. But I fear that in talking about these poor and ragged children, perhaps her future charges, I might scare her more than enthuse her. The truth about their lot is so appalling. And the truth is all I can tell her. There is nothing attractive about grime and poverty. Nothing at all. I do not know if I have what it takes to convince her. She might just want to run home and take a bath and wash off all the reality of Whitechapel." Was this the truth that she was telling him? The truth about *her*? What was scaring her so much about meeting his sister? When she thought of it, it seemed like a really good idea—certainly the part about a live-in school for orphans. She believed in that, for sure. But the thought of having Isabel, his beloved Isa, around here all of the time...was that what she really wanted? Inside her heart, she felt a tug of fear. Would Lucas's exclusive interest in her be diverted by the powerful attraction of his sister's presence? Would she be losing something of this, which could only be described as momentous emotion between them? When he had been gone, she had yearned for his return, the magnetism of his being, the intensity of their intercourse.

"Listen, Gwynne," Lucas began in a whisper. "I can only vouch for the power that you have had over me. If you transmit a mere tenth of that power towards her, she cannot fail to respond in the affirmative *and* with enthusiasm. In your quiet stillness, you are capable of delivering a message of such potency that no one could resist it. I truly believe that." His face was drawing so close to hers now that she felt that their lips were bound to meet...

With a bang of the door against the wall, Phillip burst into the room. "Dr. Lacey, Malcolm is awake now, if ye want to examine 'im. 'E's ready for ye. I can wheel 'im into your examining room, if ye'd like."

Lucas stood up as soon as they heard the noisy intrusion. He nodded at Phillip and followed him out. Gwynne continued to sit for a moment before she trailed after them.

Chapter XVI

After examining Malcolm, Lucas felt a debilitating sadness. How could anyone allow a child to practically die of starvation? He was sure that Gwynne was not the only mother in Whitechapel ready to sell her body in order to feed her child. But obviously, whoever had charge of Malcolm had none of that instinct to protect one's young. The eight-year-old spoke little of his previous circumstances, but Gwynne had assured him that Malcolm was talking much more than he had at first. Time would tell if his spirit would recover as well as his body. There were bruises everywhere on that body. At least Phillip's "owner" had not beaten him into submission. But Phillip, despite his good cheer, had emotional scars. Lucas felt ready to tackle the question of Phillip's mother, still an inhabitant of the Workhouse.

As soon as Phillip started wheeling Malcolm back to his bedroom, Lucas caught Gwynne's eye. She was helping Jane with the last-minute preparations for the dinner in which all would participate, except for Malcolm, who was being fed at about twice as many intervals per day—a little at a time, mind you. This practice instituted by Gwynne was working well, and although his schedule was off everyone else's, at least he was making progress. It was as if he was re-learning everything like a baby, and sleeping during periods between feedings.

He wished to broach the subject of Phillip's mother with Gwynne immediately. Perhaps he could even go as early as tomorrow to the Workhouse to find her, if Phillip showed an interest in seeing her again. He never spoke of her. Did he still love her? Gwynne understood by a movement of his head in the direction of the consulting room that he wanted to speak tête-à-tête with her. She whispered something to Jane, wiped her hands on her apron, and came towards him. Lucas entered the room and when Gwynne was within its walls, too, he asked her to shut the door. There were two chairs in front of his desk and they both sat down in them.

"Are you worried about Malcolm? Do you think that he is still in grave danger?" Gwynne asked in a worried tone of voice.

Lucas sighed and shook his head. "You have been doing all that could be expected. I think that he is recovering, although he was not far off from permanent damage to his vital organs. The word about our hospital got out just in time for him. Otherwise, he would have died on the street from hunger." Lucas shook his head again to show his bewilderment at the callousness of the human race.

"It is hard to believe, isn't it, that such a thing could happen in England in the mid-nineteenth century? We can be a hard-hearted lot."

"At the moment I am more worried about his mental state. I know you say he is revealing more about himself, and I am sure you are right, since you were here at the beginning, and I was not, but he does seem pretty walled into himself. We need to get him to trust us, to know that we care. Otherwise...I don't know how he'll turn out. I know what it is like to feel that no one can possibly have any idea what you are going through at that age. I at least...at least..." and here Lucas floundered, his own emotions blocking the completion of his sentence. He hugged himself suddenly, as if a blast of cold air had entered the room. The coldness of the grown-ups in Malcolm's vicinity seemed to have had a chilling effect on his insides.

"I can see he has really affected you as he did me," Gwynne interjected. "You were about to say that at least you had a horse with whom to share your sorrow. And you are right. Malcolm has had no one, but Phillip is really caring well for him, and, in fact, I think it has been good for Malcolm to sleep with Phillip. The warmth of another body that does not seem to want to hurt you...like a brother...can be very reassuring...comforting."

Lucas smiled weakly, and then nodded, acknowledging that once again she had got it right. Then he took a deep breath and began, "What I really wanted to talk to you about was Phillip." Gwynne looked up at him in that inquiring way of hers, with her head cocked to one side. When she did that, it was as if his heart skipped a beat. Did she do that just for him? "Remember we talked about his mother?" Gwynne nodded. "I think it is time to ask him about her. I would like to know if he would like to see her again. If she didn't beat him and was kind to him, but just could no longer support him, then he deserves a mother. Everyone deserves a mother, right?"

Gwynne looked thoughtful. "Yes, I agree. Are you willing to take her out of the Workhouse and bring her here to work?"

"Well, not if she has a propensity to drink and knock her son about," Lucas answered quickly. "But if it will make him happy, then yes, we can give her a job. Do you think that *I* should ask about her or *you* or both of us?"

"Let us see if we can get him to talk about her naturally at first. But if there is no way to do that, I think we could both draw him aside or go to my place and bring up the topic."

Just then they heard Jane calling that supper was ready. Lucas was glad that everyone would be at this meal, including Jonathan. He had something very important to discuss with all of them, but especially his builder. "Yes, let's do that," he responded, standing up. Gwynne was on her feet, too, and Lucas realized that he had not broached the topic of his feelings about her yet. Sometimes it just felt as if she knew everything about what he was feeling, and it wasn't necessary to voice the innermost workings of his being. He almost felt as if he *had* begun the conversation. But what would he actually say to her? Would he just say how much it hurt to be parted from her? And if he revealed all this and she did not reciprocate, would that change their working relationship? Would it make it unbearable to work beside her without the possibility of knowing that one day he would never have to separate himself from her? Was it better to live with the hope minus the certainty? Or was it just better to know even if the outcome would be so utterly painful? He did not know if he could bear a rejection.

"What is the matter, Lucas? Are you all right?"

"Dear Gwynne, I do not wish to importune you any longer on this day. In time we will speak more of many things. I am sorry that you seem to be the only one with whom I am able to converse on every topic under the sun. I have grown dependent on your ever-receptive ear."

"Do not be troubled about that, Lucas. My ear is yours." And when she blushed, he knew he loved her. There was no other word for what was inside his breast. He took her hand in his left hand, and with his right, he opened the door to the others. Let the world see them as a unified couple.

But no one seemed at all surprised that they walked into the dining-room hand-in-hand. The other adults, Jane and Jonathan, looked, saw, and barely demonstrated any acknowledgement. Perhaps there was a slight smile on Jane's lips, but that could have been because Selina was jabbering away at her from her husband's arms. Phillip and Charles were on the floor playing with Charles's new toy. Charles was laughing and Phillip was making faces at him. Robert was slicing bread and then he helped his mother by putting the food on the table. What a family they all were! Lucas turned towards his partner and she to him. They both smiled. Had she been thinking the same thing?

When everyone was seated around the table, Charles and Selina in their own highchairs built by Robert and Jonathan, and the food was being passed around, Jane mentioned that Selina had started to say all of their names. "Selina, what's your name?" She pointed at her little girl. "Lina!!" was the happy squeal.

"And who am I?" Jane pointed at herself. "Mama!!"

"And who is that?" She pointed to her son, still standing. "Obby!"

"Right! And who is that?" Jane indicated her husband. "Da!"

Everyone was laughing by now. Jane called to them with her hands up, "Wait, wait, the best is yet to come." Jane pointed to Charles, sitting across from Selina and next to her mother. "Who is this?" Selina threw her hands in the air and exclaimed, "Lali!"

"Yes, Charlie! And who is sitting next to Charlie? What is Charlie's mama's name?"

Selina clapped her hands, thoroughly enjoying the game, "Winnie!"

"Two more to go, Selina. Who is this big boy next to Gwynne?"

"Lip-lip!" This got a huge roar from her captive audience.

"And who is sitting over there at the end of the table?" She pointed at Lucas, and to everyone's surprise, Selina gave a full-throated, "Uke!" And then she repeated it yet again, "U-u-uke!" lengthening the single vowel. Her spectators were enthralled with her performance, and everyone clapped their hands. Jane tousled her daughter's hair.

Gwynne was the first to comment, "I don't think I've ever seen her so happy, Jane."

"Well, maybe that's because ye always see 'er sick!" More laughter.

But Gwynne insisted. "She really is thriving. I think that she feels the general sentiment of happiness and industriousness that is floating around here, and we all owe that to Lucas's generosity. Don't we?" Gwynne looked around Phillip to make sure that Lucas was receiving the full benefit of her statement. Everyone murmured in agreement.

Lucas put up his hands to quell their enthusiasm. He shook his head. "The operative word, Gwynne, is industriousness. It is because all of you care so much about what we are trying to do here that we will succeed, succeed in healing sick children because the warmth will come from us and not from the sun outside the windows. I really believe that, although Jonathan and Robert have my approval to increase the height of the windows as far as they will go." Lucas put down his fork momentarily. "I have something else I would like to discuss with all of you, especially Phillip." He touched the boy's head with his left hand. Phillip's eyes went wide. "I think that Phillip spends half the day going up and down the back stairs to the pump in the courtyard to bring up water. Am I right, Phillip?"

Phillip shrugged. "I don't mind. It's me job."

"Yes, it is, but I think you have too many jobs. I was thinking of telling the landlord that I would be willing to pay to pipe in the water directly from that pump so that we could have water continuously at our disposal here in the kitchen, and maybe in the bathroom, and in Gwynne's flat as well, perhaps the whole floor if the place on the other side of the hospital becomes free and we can take it over."

"Piped-in water? 'Ere in Whitechapel?" This query came from Robert.

"Yes, if it is possible, and I think it would be, seeing as the entire building is serviced by its own pump, and the water does not have to come from the pump up the road near the stores. Am I right, Jonathan?"

"Well, aye, it'd be a great expense, and it'd mean diggin' up the courtyard so that a pipe could be laid deep enough not to freeze in winter and diggin' a 'ole through the stone wall of the buildin' for the pipe that'd 'ave to be turned up to this floor. It could be done. We may 'ave to 'ave a bigger drainage pipe than the one in the floors at the moment. We oughten to place new ones under all the basins that'd 'old the water. That way drainin' the water from the large basins where the young'uns bathe would be easy. Aye, it'd mean a lot less running up an' down them there stairs for Phillip. I think 'e should be 'appy 'bout that."

"Well, then," Lucas continued, "I think I will have a word with Mr. Gaunt as early as tomorrow." He put an arm gently around Phillip and pulled him towards his chest. "You will be free from all that running up and down, although it is apparent that your foot has healed immensely well."

"Free to do what, Dr. Lacey?" Phillip asked.

"Why, free to study, free to do some learning."

"To become a doctor like you?"

"We'll see, my boy, but I feel that if you get some schooling, you will be free to choose what you want to do eventually."

Robert joined in the conversation as he sat down. "I'd like to get me some schoolin' too. I 'ave lots o' work to do, I know, but I want...I want..."

"What more could ye possibly want?" His father interrupted. "Right now, ye've got all ye'll be needin' for a while." Robert looked discouraged. He turned his gaze towards Lucas.

Lucas saw his beseeching look. He realized that the boy understood that he would be on his side. And he was, but how to convey his approval without hurting Jonathan? Jonathan and Robert were sitting across from him. He gazed at both of them. It was obvious that Jonathan was a proud father, and Lucas had no desire to usurp that position in Robert's life, but perhaps he could have a better life than his father, and perhaps Lucas was the one that could make that happen. He was just about to speak, when he heard Gwynne ostensibly coming to his rescue, since she was in no way competing for a son's loyalty.

"Jonathan, your boy is so very capable, so ready to grow and go beyond the confines of the East end. He truly desires to follow in your footsteps," Gwynne began, and as she said these words, Lucas saw that the boy was nodding in concert with this statement of hers. "However, perhaps with a little education, he may be able to procure work in a more consistent way. You have everything to teach him about building and carpentry and the like, but he may be capable of being a voice for your business. Who knows where he might be able to take your skills if—"

"—if 'e could talk, read, an' write like the two of ye," Jonathan broke in, waving a hand at both of them. Lucas was not sure if this was a compliment or an insult. Did Jonathan dislike the educated classes, thinking that they had an easier time of it than the poor of this neighbourhood?

Now it was Jane's turn to interject and in favour of their son. "Yes, that's right, me dear," she said looking at her husband. "S'a good thing to 'ave the advantages of an edication. 'E can learn the trade from you an' the ways o' the worl' from them."

"Or from some other teacher whom we can bring here to teach any child who wants to learn, like Phillip, Malcolm, or Robert."

"Like them Ragged Schools?" Jonathan asked, clearly knowing something about the possibilities of learning for the poor in this day and age.

"Yes," responded Lucas, "Something like that, but right here in the hospital, wherever we can set up a table, perhaps just in front of the ward to our right. I can see three or four or five pupils and a teacher fitting quite nicely in there."

Jonathan was nodding. He made it clear that before he built a table to that purpose, he wanted to finish making several beds for future inmates. Lucas was in agreement. He did not mention his sister, to whom he and Gwynne had not yet spoken, and who had not even arrived in London. There was time yet, but he was glad for Gwynne's intervention. She had made the idea of going beyond one's father palatable. A part of him wished everyone else would disappear at this moment so he could tell her this. He wished, too, that they could consistently and daily have some time to be alone together. Perhaps he could institute a meeting between the two of them in his office to discuss all manner of things—even personal ones—once a day. They might be interrupted by the arrival of a new patient, but he could live with that.

During the rest of the meal, there was more discussion about indoor plumbing and how it would make the women's lives more comfortable, not just Phillip's. Before they were finished eating, however, someone knocked at the front door and before Phillip could get up to answer it, the door swung open with a blast of cold damp air to reveal a thoroughly wet girl of about thirteen or fourteen, looking wan and bedraggled. She stepped into the warm room, but before they could greet her or she them, she seemed to lose strength in her legs and her knees buckled. Lucas and Phillip were the first to jump up and go to her. She moaned something incomprehensible to them before losing consciousness. Phillip immediately went to get the push- chair waiting by the fire for its next patient and Robert and Lucas lifted the child onto it.

"She must be chilled to the bone, Lucas. It is pouring outside, and by the look of the muddiness of her skirts, I would say she has been out in the storm and on foot for a long time," Gwynne remarked.

"Phillip, would you stoke the fire in our consulting-room while we try to bring her around?" In answer to Lucas's suggestion, Phillip picked up some logs near the central hearth and carried them into the other room. Lucas pushed the girl towards the blazing fire just behind the dining-room table. In seconds the child opened her eyes to see Gwynne's face smiling down at her.

"Am I...am I in the new Children's 'ospital?" Gwynne nodded, still smiling reassuringly, and Lucas responded:

"Yes, you have arrived and we will take care of you. What is your name?"

"Ally be my name, and I am ever so gl—" but a fit of coughing prevented her from finishing her sentence. Jane brought over a cup of tea and when she finally stopped coughing, Gwynne managed to get her to drink some of the warm liquid. Ally drank it hungrily.

Another child weak from lack of nourishment, thought Lucas, looking up at Gwynne who seemed to communicate silently to him a similar judgement. Lucas just hoped that when they examined her, her body would not be covered in livid marks, emblematic of continuous beatings. By now Gwynne had exchanged the cup of tea for a bowl of soup and was feeding Ally spoonful by spoonful. The child's eyes were already brighter in recognition of the much-needed sustenance. She continued to cough, and Lucas wondered at the state of her lungs, but he could tell that the food was having a welcome effect on the child's demeanour and health. They needed to examine her, talk to her, bathe her, and put her in dry clothing. She had not come in with a parent and that worried him. Did it mean that she was totally on her own without any means by which to sustain herself?

Phillip came to tell him that the fire was satisfactorily sending its heat out into the examination room. Lucas nodded and touched the boy on his head. He felt that he had been lucky to have found this child who was so ready to share his recent happiness with everyone. They had found each other, really. He, Lucas, had been in dire straits just like Phillip. It had been a fortuitous moment for the both of them. As they exchanged a look, Lucas hoped he was conveying his confidence that he *could* be like a father to him. It was a good feeling.

Phillip smiled in response. "Shall I push 'er into the surgery now?"

Gwynne stood up from her seated position where she had been feeding Ally and answered him, although Phillip had directed his question at Lucas. "Yes, I think Ally is ready for us, Phillip. Go ahead." Phillip manoeuvred the push-chair around the table and across the short distance into the examining room. Lucas and Gwynne followed him. Inside the room, they lifted the girl off the chair and placed her gently on the bed. Phillip rolled the chair out of the room and closed the door behind him.

Chapter XVII

The next week had brought so many new little patients into their establishment that Gwynne and Lucas had had barely a moment to breathe, let alone talk to Phillip about his mother. Fortunately, all these new children, six of them, had come in with their mothers, and these concerned women were even able to help, at least with the bathing and the dressing and undressing. One even mopped the bathroom floor while her child was being examined. Another offered to knit some socks for the children if the wool were provided, seeing as her son was going to spend days and nights in the hospital, and she could be of use while he spent time recuperating from a bad beating by a street thug. Gwynne thought that this was an excellent way for the mothers to offer something for the services provided to them and not feel beholden to Lucas or herself for the rest of their lives. She understood their need to feel useful. These were women who had never had to ask for help before. They had always done everything for themselves. That was the nature of their lives. But in dire circumstances, they had to turn to a healer of some sort, like herself previously. Only this time they were not asked to pay anything. Indeed, they felt lucky and grateful. It was also in their nature to demonstrate gratitude. Why not clean the floor in the charity hospital? Why not wash a child or an infant? Why not knit a pair of socks if one had the time? Phillip was dispatched to buy wool and knitting needles and more nightshirts in various sizes from the used clothing store. Perhaps in time they could hire someone to sew nightshirts and even uniforms for herself and Jane. This last had been Lucas's suggestion. He had hired someone to paint a sign with the hospital's name on it over the front entrance downstairs—East End Charity Hospital for Children—as well as one with an arrow to be placed above the staircase and another for over the inner door. Soon all would be official, and what was more official than nurses' uniforms? She remembered the ugly, often dirty uniforms she and the other nurses wore in the Barracks Hospital in Scutari during the War. Hopefully they would be able to change into clean ones more often. Lucas would certainly approve of several uniforms for both her and Jane. Even though Jane was not officially a nurse, she was an employee of the hospital and as such deserved a uniform. He had suggested that the woman, who came by every day to take the soiled linen for washing, could also wash their clothes, once made. Jane had said she knew of a good seamstress, someone who sometimes worked in the theatres of Soho. Robert was thus tasked with contacting her and bringing her by the hospital as soon as possible.

Things were running smoothly. Was this due partly to the sympathy she and Lucas felt for each other, to the almost instant understanding they had when communicating non-verbally and to some extent to the desire on everyone's part to make the hospital a welcoming and comfortable place, to make a success of Lucas's dream? She supposed both of these reasons were plausible. And Charles and Selina just seemed to be a part of it all, everyone else taking turns at lending a hand in attending to their needs. Their new patient Ally, an orphan of fourteen, as soon as she was on the mend, since fortunately there had been no damage to her lungs from exposure to the elements, had taken to following Gwynne around, trying to be of help to her and trying to learn as much as possible from her. Gwynne had the feeling that she could become a good little nurse, and the hospital was certainly in need of more able hands. At some point they were all going to require time off. No one could keep going at such a pace forever. And substitutes would then become a necessity.

After their patients had been fed their lunch, all of the staff had time to sit down and share a meal, usually prepared by Jane. They customarily discussed the state of health of their charges and other matters relating to the hospital, but fortunately it was also a time for them to just relax, and relax they did. Work on the plumbing was going to begin in February when the weather would be getting warmer. There might be a bit more chaos in that period, but she felt that they could deal with it, especially because they all were getting closer to one another, and were really beginning to work as a team, or even a family.

She and Lucas had just finished setting the broken hand of a six-year-old boy who had fallen from a first-story window. How does one fall out of a window? She had the distinct impression that someone had pushed him. A parent? A brother? Some bully? But the child was not talking, the idea of squealing on an acquaintance or family member obviously horrifying to him, worse than his injury, and perhaps even grounds for a more serious beating. He was in pain and Lucas was loath to send him back out into the warzone that was the boy's life. The boy reluctantly agreed to stay at least for one night, and Jane took him off to be bathed before allowing him to get into a clean bed. He was young enough not to mind being looked after by a motherly woman such as Jane. Perhaps there was no motherly woman in his life. They instructed him to keep his splinted hand out of the water and off he and Jane went. Ally had been in the room with them, watching, learning, and responding to orders. She had a gentle touch and Gwynne felt that her small hands and fingers might prove useful in the days to come. Lucas seemed to agree because he never discouraged the child from these lessons. If she was going to stay with them—and she had nowhere to go—she might as well be useful. But it was more than that. Gwynne was beginning to sense that Ally was becoming attached especially to her, but also to Lucas, almost as if she was yearning for parental figures in her life, or maybe just a modicum of love. And why not provide it if they could?

Phillip had just entered the consulting-room.

"Could Ally 'elp me bring up some buckets o' water?" he asked.

Lucas was washing his hands and Gwynne was putting their tools in order. "A good idea," said Lucas. "Four hands are better than two." He chuckled and then added, "Soon it won't be necessary. By summer's end we should have water coming straight out of taps."

Phillip smiled and their two young dependents went off together to haul water. When they left, and the busyness of the previous hour was definitely gone, and the sense that night was coming on, and the day's work done, a kind of stillness took over in the room. Gwynne suddenly felt very tired, so she dropped into one of the chairs. Perhaps she would have five minutes before Charles called to her and needed her. The place was quiet—the patients in their beds, the parents of some of them gone home, Jane in the bathing room with their new little convalescent, Jonathan off on an errand for supplies, and Robert playing with his little sister and Charles before the fire in the big hearth in the central room. Soup was simmering on the stove and Robert was also keeping an eye on that. He was such a responsible lad. He seemed much older than his years.

Gwynne closed her eyes. She was about to rest her head and arms on Lucas's desk, when she heard him walk over to the door and gently close it. She sat unmoving but did not open her eyes. She heard him drag a chair in front of hers and sit down.

"Gwynne, if you're tired, why don't you go home and lie down? I will take care of Charles until he is ready to go to bed."

With her eyes still closed, she smiled at him. She felt his head lean closer to hers. She felt as if she could sit here forever, barely moving, just inhaling, and exhaling, with this man so close to her, doing the same. Was it possible to have a conversation without words, just the sounds of breathing? She put her elbow up on the desk and rested her head on her hand. Now this was comfort. How long would they have until her little son would cry out for her?

"I wish we could sit like this, just the two of us, every day," Lucas broke the silence.

"The peace is most welcome."

"It is more than that, Gwynne, much more."

At this Gwynne opened her eyes. Lucas took her free hand in his. He played with her fingers. She was accustomed now to this bit of intimacy between them. She had known Lucas for over a month, perhaps less if you counted the days he had been away in Kent. But it was no longer a shock to her senses to have her hand in his. There was a warmth and a tenderness and a feeling of well-being. She had not imagined such collusion with a man, not after Edmund. She certainly had never willed it to happen. She had not pictured it happening to her. The only act of association with a male that she had participated in had been one of pain and horror, and giving her consent to another man had seemed impossible. Not anymore. She smiled again and lifted her head off her hand. She needed to listen with both ears to what was about to come from Lucas's lips. Maybe it was not going to be a declaration of his affection. Maybe it was only going to be a plea for a daily meeting between them, just as the entire staff met every day at mealtimes to discuss hospital matters. But maybe not. She waited.

At first, he hung his head for a moment, and then he took a deep breath. Finally, his eyes met hers. She liked his face, especially when he was happy, when he picked up Charles or Selina and danced with them around the room, or when he was solemn and concentrated, examining the children who came to receive his gentleness and his care. In fact, it could be said that she loved his face, even when expressing pain, and she had seen those moments. He was not in the habit of keeping a beard, but at the end of the day, like now, she could make out the wispy blonde hairs around his chin. It would be lovely to know what they felt like beneath her fingertips. She was about to lift her hand to touch them when Lucas cleared his throat and began to speak.

"There is something I have to admit to you, dear Gwynne." A short beat. A moment's hesitation. He swallowed, then continued. "Although I fear to some extent your reaction to this admission, I know that I must be brave and not hold back on you.

Perhaps you have already noticed my unwillingness to leave your side when it is definitely time for me to go home and leave you to go to bed." Again, he sucked air and lowered his gaze to their locked fingers. "The truth is, I never want to leave you. I feel that my place is here next to you...always...not just by day. I have no use for the luxuries of my home in Chelsea, for the encounters with my social and economic peers. I would give up everything for the chance to be not just your colleague but your husband." And then he slipped off his chair and went down on one knee just like any gentleman of old wooing the gentle lady of his dreams. Gwynne knew for certain she did not want Lucas beneath her. She did not want him "begging" for her hand in marriage. So, she, too, went down to the floor on both knees, propriety forcing her to keep her knees locked, although she would have been much more comfortable on one. She took both his hands in hers. Did she detect a certain amount of surprise in his face as she boldly imitated him?

"Oh Lucas, I don't want you to plead for my hand. We are equals, remember?" And he nodded.

"Will you marry me, then, as my equal? Marry me any way you like, just please marry me."

Gwynne laughed now, feeling happy. "I must tell you something, Lucas, before I answer you." Was she really going to say this to him, reveal such a startling thing about her past experience? "Despite the fact," she began hesitantly, "despite the fact that I have borne a child and been subjected to male desire on two occasions, you must know that I...I...have never...actually...been...kissed by a man. I have never allowed a man to come near my lips with his own...I am just saying this because I would like..." but Lucas never gave her the chance to complete her sentence, interpreting her words as a direct entreaty to have him be the one, the first one to accomplish this task. He dropped the other knee to the ground. He pulled her closer to him by means of their clasped hands. He bent his head down to hers. His face drew nearer and nearer and finally his lips succumbed to the force of gravity or love and they were upon hers, cautious at first, testing her readiness, with infinitesimal lunges like soft dew drops on a beautiful morning. She had not realized how parched she had really been, how deeply she had yearned for this contact. She had told him of her innocence in this oh so human exchange, because with him honesty just seemed to flow from her veins, and sometimes she spoke aloud things to him that she had never spoken to herself.

His uncertainty soon yielded to boldness. He was forgetting himself, forgetting the guilt that she had conjured in him for the cruelty of another man of his class. He was being himself. And then, he said it into her mouth, as if he were feeding her: "I love you, Gwynne. I have loved you from the first time I set eyes on your face." And she took his words and his sentiment and his love and she breathed in his lips. And it *was* a conversation. Never had she given her soul to anyone. But now she finally had, as she had known all along that she would.

*

Lucas heard two little fists pounding on the door. He reluctantly separated his lips from Gwynne's and leaned his forehead against hers. He had almost forgotten when, where, and how they were, so engaged was he in that ardent dialogue between the forces that had propelled them to merge. Was there anything more intimate than a kiss? He heard Robert's voice speak to Charles. "Your Ma and your Da will open the door soon. They 'ave to finish up their work."

Gwynne and he laughed softly at Robert's words. So, the others had all bought the notion that he was Charles' father. So be it. He could make that a reality, too. He just had to tell his solicitor that he was and fill in his name on Charles' birth certificate under father, if such a document existed.

It was time to get up from the floor. Lucas stood first and helped his beloved—how musical the sound of that word—to rise as well. But before he could relinquish himself to the outside world, he needed to embrace this woman tightly. He wrapped his arms around her, and she sighed into his chest. Then she lifted her face up to him and said what he had always wanted to hear: "I love you, Lucas." He smiled and placed his hands on either side of her head. How he desired to kiss her again, but the little fists were becoming more insistent. Gwynne broke from him and swiftly went to open the door to her determined little son.

Chapter XVIII

Lucas walked through the streets of Whitechapel in the early morning hours. The sun was out after weeks of cold rain. The air still had a winter chill in it, but spring would be here soon. Workers were already at the Hospital fitting pipes into newly formed holes in the floors of the various rooms. Finally, the apartment on the other side, similar to Gwynne's, had become available, and Jonathan and Robert were preparing it to become attached to the main rooms in the centre. Jonathan and Robert had extended all the windows at the back of their Hospital, all the way up to the ceiling, and light was pouring into the bathing-room. It was beautiful and exhilarating. They were starting to do the same to the windows of the new ward. Yesterday evening during his official transactions with Gaunt, the landlord, he had been informed that the large storage area on the main floor, directly beneath the Hospital, could be space that they could use, and converted into anything they might need. It would be necessary to discuss with everyone involved how best to implement it. Could it become some kind of home to all of the staff, a place where they could rest or sleep? Could it become a new consulting-room?

But the question most pressing to him was still the matter of his possible marriage to Gwynne. Days had passed since that declaration of their mutual love and there had been no follow-up. They hadn't had any time! There was so much to do, and the days ended in utter exhaustion especially for Gwynne, who was often disturbed in the middle of the night by some needy child. As soon as the newly installed bell rang, Phillip ran to allow the prospective patient to enter the building, set him or her up before the welcome hearth, and then went to awaken Gwynne, who had managed so far to deal with the emergencies without his own intervention, until the following morning when he arrived. Ally was learning quickly but was in no way ready to take over

Gwynne's work and give her a much-needed day of rest. Gwynne could make medical decisions, but Ally could only follow orders at the moment. They needed another nurse or another doctor for sure, or perhaps both.

The other important reason why marriage had not yet become a serious topic of discussion between them was the very reason behind his excursion this morning. They had finally been able to confront Phillip on the subject of his mother. When Gwynne had finally got the opportunity to ask him about this mother of whom he never spoke, Lucas saw how the brave little boy could barely keep his emotions in check. He held back tears until he blurted out: "I miss 'er somethin' awful." After that there was no reason to prop up the floodgates of withheld misery. Gwynne wrapped the child in her arms as long as his outpouring lasted. Lucas was bewildered. Why had Phillip not approached him? Why the reticence? Did he not trust him to understand his plight?

"But why have you never told me of your need to be reunited, Phillip?"

Phillip's chest heaved as he attempted to answer Lucas's blunt question. Fortunately, they were all in Gwynne's flat, where Phillip had come to bring Gwynne a few necessary buckets of water. She had never asked him to do this. But Phillip had anticipated her needs early on and never shirked what he considered his duty towards her. This action alone should have persuaded Lucas that Phillip's mother must have somehow engrained in her son a modicum of ethical behaviour. Lucas stretched out his hand to caress the boy's head.

"Ye've been so kind to me...." Phillip could not continue right away. His breathing was in difficulty from all the previous sobbing. Lucas placed both hands on either shoulder and urged the boy to relax and take deep breaths.

"Take your time, Phillip. This is not an interrogation. I just want to understand."

Phillip heaved a sigh and went on. "I jist couldn't tell ye. I donna want this to ever end. I was afraid...."

"Afraid that you would hurt me by remaining loyal to your mother? That would never happen. If you need your mother, and it is only natural, let's do something about it."

But Phillip was shaking his head. "Afraid ye'd think I was an ingrate. 'Ow could I want me mother if'n I 'ave the both of ye?" And then the tears began to flow again. Lucas looked over at Gwynne, whose own tears were beginning to fall as well.

And that is why a few mornings later, he was on the street walking to the Workhouse to meet Phillip's mother, see if she was suited to the work she might have to do for them, and then see to her permanent removal from the Workhouse. He was a little daunted by the task at hand and would have preferred Gwynne to be with him. She was just so much more familiar with the ins and outs of Whitechapel culture, but in truth, only he would have the authority to seek to employ the woman. It had made Gwynne slightly bitter to admit this, of course. As far as he was concerned, she had as much authority, but the actual authorities would never agree with him. They could not go together, as one of them had to be on the premises of the Hospital at all times. And so here he was, about to ring the bell at the big wooden door that blocked his way, at the entrance to that dreaded place. Gwynne had even been called here on a few occasions to treat some sickly inmates, whose condition had already reached such dire straits that she barely had had the time to pronounce them dead. Obviously saving money was more important than saving lives in the workhouse business. He should not be surprised. His sister had often railed against the lack of charity in the English system. His sister! Tonight, he vowed to go home for dinner to Chelsea and speak with her about coming to the Hospital to teach the orphans. He had also planned to ask permission from his aunt to bring some of his patients, who were on the mend, to Kent to spend a few days in the luxuriously healthy air of the countryside, when spring was really and truly here at last. On that occasion, if possible, Gwynne, he hoped, could accompany him. They had to find another doctor or student willing to run the operation for a few days. Perhaps he could go to the University and ask if his Hospital could be a place where students could train in the art of treating children. Why not?

Thinking of his sister as he walked through the twisting streets of this disadvantaged London neighbourhood, and greeting the children and mothers that already knew him, he summoned up an ancient memory of when he was a lad on the point of entering the university. His all-important meeting with his friend Rupert had not yet taken place, but his growing unease with the male representatives of his class was already becoming more than apparent. He had spent the morning with his uncle in town—the others in his family, his aunt and sister, were still in Kent—and now he was sitting in his uncle's gentleman's club in London near the Parliament buildings. His uncle was in conversation with a few other members that he knew well, seated on comfortable armchairs and settees around a small table, most of the men smoking cigars or pipes. He was getting impatient, since he was not at all interested in the political discussion the men were having. The smell of tobacco was annoying him. Feigning shivers from the cold outdoors from which he and his uncle had just removed themselves, he got up and went over to the large hearth at one end of the grand room. He stood in front of the fire, his arms outstretched towards the warmth crackling upwards, and rubbed his hands. He heard the men around his uncle laugh about something. He wondered what they thought so funny about a taxation bill before the Senate. Was he remembering this now because he was beginning to understand that the people of East London, poor and uneducated though they may be, seemed so individual and interesting to him today—no longer a conglomerate mass of people known as "the poor"? He had come to know truly intelligent and unusual characters among these lower classes. And the men in that room in his Uncle Graham's club had seemed somehow less singular and less worthy of notice to his eighteen- or nineteen-year-old self. While he stood by the fire, a middle-aged man took a chair and drew it towards the fireplace. He coughed, then addressed Lucas.

"You are Lacey's boy, aren't you, young man?"

Lucas turned around towards the deep voice. He placed one hand on the rich mahogany mantel and partially leaned his weight on it. The slight man had a dark red beard and moustache, looked pleasant enough, and was probably the age of his uncle. He was smoking a pipe and drinking an amber-coloured liquid from a cognac glass. Besides talking politics, smoking and drinking seemed the most common pastime among these gentlemen. Lucas cleared his throat and answered, "Yes, I am."

"I knew your father well, and Graham, too, before they married, in fact. The name is Somers." He reached his hand towards Lucas, who took it in his and shook it as was the ritual between men meeting for the first time. Somers smiled up at Lucas and Lucas returned the smile. He remembered wondering why the man wanted to speak to him of all people. "You do not frequent your uncle's favourite club very often, do you?"

"Hardly at all. We came here to eat luncheon, is all. But Uncle Graham seems to be enjoying himself with his colleagues over there. I wonder what they find so fascinating to talk about." Not really wishing to continue conversing with this man Somers, but not exactly certain why this was the case, Lucas sat down in a chair about a foot away from the man in question. He pulled out of the inside pocket of his frock coat a small volume of contemporary poetry that his sister had encouraged him to read. Throughout the volume there were paper markers, obviously placed there to indicate to Lucas which poems Isa thought especially important. There was a poem by a seventeen-year-old called Christina Rossetti that she particularly wanted him to peruse. But this occupation was interrupted by the man seated to his right.

"So, you are a studious lad. Your father was, too, certainly more than I was at your age. I was more interested in the ladies." He laughed easily as he uttered these words. "What is it you are reading?"

Lucas closed the volume and turned to the man, a little more curiously now since he had mentioned his father twice. "It is a book of poems that my sister has urged me to read."

"I see there are markers all over the place. Are those your sister's suggestions, too?"

Lucas nodded.

"The lovely Isabel Lacey..."

"You have met her?"

"Well, everyone knows about your beautiful sister."

"What do you mean 'everyone'? Isabel is but fifteen years old. She has not even made her debut in society!"

"And what a debut that will be. She will certainly be turning heads."

Lucas recalled that his blood began to rise during this outrageous conversation. "My sister is much more than a pretty face, I'll have you know. Much more!"

"To be sure. To be sure." And then Somers chuckled.

"I don't understand. Isabel may be exceedingly young, but she will be...no...she *is* a great intellect," Lucas added in defence of his younger sibling.

Somers turned to him, looking rather astonished at Lucas's vehemence. "You are an unusual lad. What do you do for fun? What do you do with your friends on a Saturday night, for instance?"

Lucas realized that, in truth, he spent most of his free time, when not studying, with Isabel. He just preferred her company. Either Isabel or riding his horse. The other boys he knew from school could not hold a candle to her ability to stimulate him. "My good sir, don't you enjoy the company of an intelligent woman, someone who could even advise and inspire you to be better?" was Lucas's response to the man's query.

"I have a wife who dispenses her advice most freely. That's for sure!" He slapped his knee with his hand and laughed heartily.

For some reason everything about this man was beginning to provoke the anger of Lucas the younger. His sarcasm was most definitely unappealing. Looking back, Lucas felt again the discomfort that the man's humiliating interaction with him had aroused. Somers had been mocking him. Lucas recollected that at this juncture he stood up. Gwynne had been definitely right about that. When he felt threatened, he naturally wanted to be on his feet in order to feel less like a helpless victim. The noise in the room had been getting louder. There was certainly more laughter. It was as if they were laughing at him *and* at the inferior position of his poor sister. It was as if men regarded women in terms of one thing only—their appearance. He could tolerate this man's opprobrious comments no longer.

"You have shown great disrespect towards women, and more precisely my sister. I cannot believe that my father was a friend to you. There is nothing to recommend your shameful attitude!" With that Lucas stormed away from the man towards his uncle. He stopped when he reached the smoky huddle that the men were creating. His Uncle Graham looked up at him.

"I think my nephew is exceedingly hungry. I will take my leave of you all now and go to luncheon with him." The other men nodded as his uncle stood up, made his way over to Lucas, and put his arm on his back. Lucas was seething. He knew that he would never return to this place again. He did not like the exclusive company of 'gentlemen'. Today, a decade older than that boy at his uncle's club, he still felt the same way. There was something irritating about the way that gentlemen conversed with each other when women were not around. Who were these 'gentlemen' really? Were they barbarians or were they the seemingly polite, well-educated, and well-mannered members of the aristocracy?

Lucas stood and waited for someone to answer his ringing of the bell to the Workhouse. A small window opened in the centre of the thick door. A woman stuck her head through the space and asked what he wanted. What did he want? He wanted to meet and talk with Phillip's mother. He hadn't told Phillip that he was coming here today. What if she made a terrible impression on him? Did that matter? Wasn't his sole responsibility in all this the welfare of Phillip?

"I am sorry to disturb you. My name is Dr. Lucas Lacey—"

"—the doctor o' the 'Ospital fer Children? Yes, I 'eard of ye."

Well, that was interesting. She had heard of him. Was that a good thing?

"'Ave ye been called to see sumun'?"

"Ah, no, not exactly, but there is someone I *would* like to see."

"That'd be Mr. Osborne. 'E's in charge. Step inside then," she ordered him, as she began to unlock the locks and pull in the creaky old door. As he heard the sound of the hinges, he had a sudden recollection of an occasion spent with his father in Maidstone, when he was about five years old. His mother had probably been at home with the baby. The two of them had taken the coach to this town on a beautiful summer's morning. He was not sure why his father had brought him along, perhaps to be out of his mother's hair? At any rate, he remembered walking through the town with his father and feeling very hungry, but his father had insisted that first they had to do something. At some point they turned down the corner of a main street, and within minutes they were in a sort of deserted courtyard. His father rang the bell of a large painted green door. There was a plaque on the wall explaining what place they were visiting, but he was not tall enough to carefully decipher the words. He had begun to read by this time and was pulling on his father's sleeve to lift him up. He just wanted to read anything and everything that presented itself to him. Reading had become the most exciting part of his life. There was no time however because a woman had, just as this one had, pushed aside the wooden cover of the small opening at the centre of the door. His father identified himself. He had been expected, and the strange woman let them in. Eventually he learned that they had been to the County Workhouse in order to visit the father of one of the servants. His father, too, had found it in himself to release the poor elderly man from his horrible existence and take him back to their estate to live the remainder of his days, in relative comfort, with his son in a recently vacated cottage. The servant had happened to mention to Lucas's mother that his father was not long for the world, and his mother, being the kindly person that she was, had entreated her husband to reunite the old man with his son. And that was the purpose of that particular visit to a Workhouse. His memory did not include the exploration of the innards of that place. He only recalled that the old man actually lived quite a few years after coming to their estate. It had taken the turning of the key in the lock of this door, here in East London, to remind him of that journey to Maidstone, where he had spent such an important moment with his father. How fitting that his father had also made such an expedition on behalf of a fellow human, one in his employ. Although it disturbed him that his father had been friends with the indelicate and boorish Mr. Somers, the fact that he had considered the happiness of an old man made Lucas proud. He smiled as he was led into the office of the venerable Mr. Osborne, a portly red-faced fellow who seemed surprised as his underling announced Lucas's name. Perhaps Lucas's spontaneous smile, induced by that rather happy memory from his childhood before the demise of his parents, had a winning effect, because this gentleman of considerable proportions removed himself from his seated position with an alacrity that did not somehow fit his size, and extended his hand to be shaken.

"I've heard much about you, Doctor. I am pleased to make your acquaintance." He heartily grasped Lucas's hand, and then added, "But I do not seem to recall having—"

"—No, no I have come of my own accord. I was uh...wondering if I could have a colloquy with one of your inmates."

"Oh, yes? And who might that be, Dr. Lacey?" Mr. Osborne was a little taken aback by this request and screwed up one eye, in his attempt to make sense of this anomaly in his life.

"Well, I would like to see Mrs. Sylvia Macadam, if I may, the mother of—"

"—of little Phillip, the coal-monger's boy?"

"Why yes, although he...never mind." Lucas suddenly thought better of revealing where Phillip had ended up. "You remember the names of all your inmates so readily?"

Mr. Osborne shook his head. "Why, no, not really, but Sylvia is the head of our laundry here in the Workhouse."

"The head of your laundry?"

"Why, that's right and it is a very important job. Are you thinking of sending your laundry, by any chance, here to our premises for washing? For we are ready and willing to take on any new customer as important as yourself." Mr. Osborne eyed him hopefully.

"Actually, I wished to speak of her son with her, if I may?"

"Is he sick?"

Lucas quickly allayed the man of his fears. "Oh no, he is thriving. May I see her, then, on her own?" Mr. Osborne looked suspicious but seemed willing enough in the end to make it happen.

"Helen! Where are you?" Helen, the door-minder, appeared at the threshold of the office. "Take the Doctor here to see old Syl. They can talk in the courtyard...not for long, mind you. She has important work to do." And with that he went back to his desk and ushered Lucas out with a wave of his hand. Clearly the initial goodwill had been all used up by their short chat. At least, thought Lucas, he was much better than Housman. In fact, he actually seemed to value "old Syl." Surely, she could not be that old. Or maybe it was a term of affection? Following the swinging skirts of Helen, Lucas made his way through the dingy smelly corridors of the infamous Whitechapel Workhouse to the laundry on the other side of a courtyard.

So, Phillip's mother had it in her to run a laundry? Lucas felt buoyed up by this new revelation.

Chapter XIX

Lucas had left for the Workhouse on his quest to find Phillip's mother. Gwynne had understood his nervousness. In the hospital, around the children, and the other members of the staff, he felt confident, despite his lack of experience with the ways of Whitechapel. But on the outside, he was still, and maybe would always be, an "outsider". It was a feeling no one liked, but he had sufficiently grasped the importance of his mission to swallow his fear of being made uncomfortable and to press on, in the hope of bringing happiness to a very dear person. Gwynne smiled to herself. Not just Phillip was growing up. So was Lucas.

The hospital was humming along this morning, the routine becoming second nature to everyone, despite the banging and booming of the plumbers at work on the new pipes. Jane and Ally were bathing some children. Robert was fitting a new door onto its hinges. Malcolm and Phillip were playing on the newly waxed floor of the central room, not only with Selina and Charles, but with two other little toddler patients who were finally getting better after a narrow escape from a fire, but still covered in bandages after being burned on their arms and legs. Fortunately, they were no longer in too much pain. They had treated the burns of the drunken father who had allowed the fire to happen in the first place, but had sent him home to deal with the damage days ago. The mother, dishevelled and worn-out as she was, still came every day to see her offspring, and in fact, it was this woman herself who had waxed and polished the wooden floor upon which her children now amused themselves with the toys at their disposal. Gwynne was relieved that, despite the husband's tendency to drink himself into a stupor on occasion, there seemed to be love in this family. It was not always the case.

Although feeling pleased with the so far smooth functioning of this hospital project commandeered by herself and Lucas,

Gwynne was beginning to experience something close to exhaustion. No one had had a day off since the beginning. There would come a time in the not-too-distant future when one or all of them would collapse. And where was the promised introduction of Isabel, Lucas's sister, into the mix? They could use her to engage the children on the mend, who needed something with which to occupy their minds. The staff, such as it was, had so many things to think about every day. The fact of having food in their bellies and a blazing fire to keep them warm was not enough to propel them through their days of labour without some days of rest.

Gwynne heard the ring of the doorbell, summoning Phillip to the task of seeing who their next needy urchin would be. She was sitting in the examining-room, waiting precisely for this event to unfold, feeling slightly worn out, but not unprepared. She rose up from her chair, thinking that it had been days since she and Lucas had kissed and confessed their love for each other in this very room, surrounded by the paraphernalia of their trade. It had been a momentous occasion in both their lives, but most certainly in hers. She would never have expected such a thing to happen to her—contemplating attaching herself to a man—not after Edmund's grotesque intrusion into her life. She had had her son, and she had supposed that would have been enough to sustain her forever. But apparently not. Here she was—actually in love!

She shook her head and moved towards the entrance to greet the new patient, but instead she found Phillip in conversation with a handsome and well-dressed young gentleman of approximately Lucas's age. He was quite tall, as tall as Lucas, with wavy dark hair in contrast to her beloved's blonde locks, but with a disarming smile and a gentle demeanour, engaging their young doorman with every respect due to him. They both turned to her as she neared them.

"And this is our Nurse Gwynne," was Phillip's introduction. Phillip extended his arm towards her, and Gwynne came forward.

The stranger had already removed his hat and gloves. He took a few steps in her direction and bowed rather ceremoniously.

"I hope I am not disturbing your work. I came to see my good friend Dr. Lacey, without prior warning, only to discover that he is out at this hour. My name is Dr. Rupert Keynes. I am pleased to meet you, Nurse Gwynne."

"It is an honour to meet a friend of Dr. Lacey," Gwynne replied quietly, realizing that Lucas had never mentioned this man, but she did like the look of him. She was usually so wary around gentlemen, never trusting their intentions, but obviously she was changing, and becoming more ready to accept them at face value.

"Since Lucas is not here, would you and your young man, Phillip, be able to show me around your hospital? I have come precisely for this reason. I have delayed this visit for far too long. I think what you are doing here is astonishing and important and supremely admirable." He stopped his complimentary speech momentarily to look around at the surroundings, taking in Malcolm, Selina, Charles, and the little boys playing on the floor, Robert at work in his corner of the room, the hearth beating out its colourful warmth, the sounds of splashing and laughter in the bathing-room behind a closed door, a glimpse of the ward on his right where several children were lying in their special beds-on-wheels constructed by Robert and his father, as well as the room she had just exited, where it was obvious she and Lucas did their examining of the youngsters in their care. Although he would not have known that she and Lucas fully shared this job, despite her not being a doctor.

Gwynne smiled and nodded at him. "Of course," she replied, glad that the noise of the plumbers had stopped while they took a small tea break from their work of attaching pipes and breaking walls and floors, and generally making a racket.

"Shall I make us some tea, Nurse Gwynne?" asked Phillip. "I expect Ally and Jane might be thirsty, too, after them two monsters in there with 'em—" he cocked his head to the side to point at the noise coming from the bathroom. "Are finished making summat of a mess."

Gwynne replied with a nod to Phillip, and looked up at Lucas's friend, who also seemed pleased with the offer of tea. "Let us start with the examining-room, which contains all of the equipment from Lucas's father's office, and more, at this point." She beckoned him to enter, and he followed her in. It was the first time that another adult, other than the ones working in the hospital, had entered the special space where she and Lucas did their diagnostic communing, in gestures sometimes more than words. It was also the space where they had recently communed in a more intimate way. She wasn't sure if this crossing of the threshold into *their* domain by a stranger was troubling to her. She chided herself for being so proprietary. *Come, Gwynne, it's not as if you own the place, or Lucas for that matter.* Would she become one of those women who could not even share her man with a friend?

This Dr. Keynes was now looking at her curiously. Had she somehow conveyed her uneasiness? "But how did Lucas get into doing this sort of thing? Where did the idea come from? It's not as if either of us was that passionate about medicine in the first place. And I daresay it would take a good deal of passion to undertake such a commitment!" So, he did know of Lucas's dilemma in terms of his profession. Did he know, though, of Lucas's special bond with children?

"Well, I think that Lucas's hesitations and reluctance to set up a practice for adults, yes, has always been there, but you must know that around children, Lucas...well...he thrives around children. They bring out the best in him, the genius in him, if I may say so." Had she said too much? Was she allowed to speak of these things? Did she have the right to claim to know Lucas? Dr Keynes was listening to her words with great attention. He began to nod in a pensive, lost-in-thought sort of way.

"Perhaps I do not know Lucas as well as I think I do, or as well as I should. Perhaps he was not as forthcoming with me as he has been with you...I...I...mean as a colleague. You see, we went to university together, but it was outside of our studies that we were drawn into each other's orbit. We really had no time for medicine when we were together. We talked of so many other things...or at least...now that I think of it...*I* talked of those other...." His voice trailed off here as he journeyed back in time to when he and Lucas enjoyed each other's company. He looked a little embarrassed.

"When was the last time you spoke with Lucas?" Did this young man know of Lucas's descent into despair, or had they been friends before that life-altering event? Her question made him look even more embarrassed.

"Well, I...I...don't exactly remember. It was after graduation, for sure...." He gave a deep sigh and turned to her. "The truth is we've lost touch. I'm not sure why. We travelled through France and Italy for an entire summer when we were students. We experienced momentous moments together, or at least I think so, and then...and then...it seemed as if neither of us could make a decision about our futures...and..." He shrugged. Gwynne was wondering if now an awkward moment of silence would ensue, but instead this Rupert Keynes gave her a big smile and said, "But now Lucas has changed his life around and become the talk of the town. How I admire him!"

As they emerged from the room, another ring at the door urgently called Phillip back into action. Gwynne turned to Lucas's friend and said, "I may have to deal with this next emergency..." but she could not finish her sentence as the youngest son of a neighbourhood coster-monger, the meat-pie seller to be exact, burst onto the scene before Phillip had even reached the door. As soon as Henry, the child, saw her, he ran by Phillip and began an incomprehensible explanation of why he was there. She gathered that his elder brother, fourteen-year-old William, was having trouble breathing. She tried to get him to describe the symptoms. Had he swallowed something too large to pass down his throat? Was there something William couldn't eat? But she could not get anything intelligible out of the boy, except that there was no way that William could come to the hospital. All Henry kept saying after a while was: "'E's dyin'!"

After a few moments, Dr. Keynes asked her, "Does Lucas have a tracheostomy tube here? I have brought my doctor's bag. I left it in the entrance, but we may need one of those, if his airway is completely blocked. Do you know what that is?"

Gwynne nodded and returned into their examining room to fetch it. When she came out with it, Dr. Keynes was already dressed for the outdoors, bag in hand. He nodded at her, and at that moment she made the decision to go with him to the home of the ailing child. "I will come with you. I have never performed the procedure...."

"Neither have I," he responded truthfully, "but I have seen it done, and I may need your help." He turned to Phillip. "When we are gone, should another child come along in need of care, could you come and fetch Nurse Gwynne?"

"O' course, Dr. Keynes, but Ally knows summat about some such stuff. An' maybe Dr. Lacey'll come back by then."

Gwynne pulled her wrap over her shoulders and followed Henry and Dr. Keynes out the door. What a relief to know that someone with skills she did not possess would be there with her. She did not want this child to die because of her incompetence. She had much to learn about medicine yet.

*

On his way back to the hospital with Sylvia, who had impressed him no end with her quiet and calm demeanour, as well as her skills in leading a workforce of ten other women, who washed, hung to dry, and folded the linen of various establishments around town, in the laundry of the Workhouse itself, Lucas felt such a need to be with and talk to Gwynne. He was excited about the reunion of mother and child certainly. But having just had a completely new experience for him, that of being inside a workhouse, one which Gwynne had had before him on certain occasions, and one which could have actually become her own fate, had he not arrived in such a timely manner to intervene in and circumvent that progression towards utter poverty, he was almost desperate to share all his thoughts about it. He and Sylvia had even discussed the possibility of starting their own small laundry on the premises, just for their own use, in fact, in that large storage room under the stairs that Gaunt had offered him. Perhaps Ellen the washerwoman who now provided the service for them out of her residence, could actually come and work with Sylvia, because the business would require more hands. And when he told her of the fact that in a few months, they would have piped-in water, she seemed to demonstrate the keenness of her attitude towards real employment in an even more profuse way. "Piped-in water right on t' premises! I ne'er seen t' likes o' that! An' that's where me boy works, too, with a gentleman such as yoursel' and a gentle lady such as Nurse Gwynne!"

Lucas had to smile at her enthusiasm. "Perhaps, the room may be large enough to also accommodate sleeping quarters and a small parlour for you and Phillip. That way in the evening you can enjoy some private moments. But there is one thing I have to tell you that may surprise you about your son. A while ago, around Christmastime, a young lad came to us, terribly emaciated, on the verge of death, in fact, from starvation. He is doing well now, partly due to the fact that he is surrounded by warmth, and partly to the fact that he is being well fed, but mostly because Phillip has become like a brother to him. Phillip is our night watchman and sleeps in his own little room with Malcolm, who will never leave the hospital, because he has nowhere to go. He is part of our family now, and I am warning you that he might become part of yours as well. Do you understand me?"

"O' course I do. Me boy is a darlin' child is what ye're tellin' me and I can believe it. I am e'er so proud. An' if'n it means I 'ave two sons, so be it." Sylvia smiled up at him, and Lucas wondered at how he could have possibly questioned the suitability of Phillip's mother for their enterprise. Why, she was as endearing as her son himself.

When they entered the premises of the hospital, there was a great deal of commotion already, but when Phillip saw his mother for the first time, it felt like pandemonium had broken out. The encounter was probably one of the happiest moments Lucas had ever witnessed. He almost cried along with the boy and his mother. But he had no time to participate in the joy of that moment because Ally was calling to him from the examining-room. Where was Gwynne?

"I need you, Dr. Lacey. Nurse Gwynne was called out to an emergency!"

"What emergency?"

"A young boy on the verge o' death. He canna' breathe. She went with t'other doctor, your frien', an' they took a special istrument wi' 'em."

"What friend?"

Phillip caught the end of this dialogue and chimed in, "Your friend Dr. Keynes."

"What?! Rupert Keynes, here?"

"Yessir," replied Phillip, nodding emphatically before he went back to hugging his long-lost mother.

"But, Dr. Lacey, I need you in 'ere immediately. This 'ere patient is about to 'ave a baby," Ally urged him.

"A baby?"

"Yes, an' she's not much older 'n me."

"Have you ever delivered a baby, or helped at a birth, Ally?"

Ally shook her head.

"Where's Jane?" At that moment, Jane came forth from the bathing-room, wiping her hands on a towel.

"I'm 'ere, Lucas. I've come to 'elp."

Then Sylvia piped in. "I've been at several births in the Workhouse, sir. I can 'elp, too, if'n your Nurse Gwynne is out at t' moment."

"Well, then, let us all wash up. Phillip, boil water. Let us see to this young mother-to-be."

Chapter XX

"I can't believe that so much has happened today," commented Lucas to Gwynne, both alone at last in her quarters, with Charles sound asleep in his little crib. The rest of the day had proceeded swiftly after Gwynne and Rupert had returned from their impromptu surgery, performed in the less-than-ideal circumstances of the cramped home of the pie-seller and her three children. Tomorrow, they had all decided they would transport the boy, William, to the hospital in Rupert's personal carriage. He had come in a hansom cab in the morning, but tomorrow he would use his carriage. They would have preferred bringing the ailing child to the hospital today, so he could be constantly monitored, despite the success of the tracheostomy procedure, but they were too afraid to move him in his fragile state. Rupert had already returned to William's house on his way home to check that the boy was breathing through the tube without difficulty. He had not come back to the hospital, so Lucas and Gwynne assumed that all was well.

The child Sophie, for she was but fourteen, was recovering well from the birth of her little boy, which Ally declared they should call Rupert, since on that day he had saved William's life by being available to replace Lucas. Sophie was not averse to the name at all, thinking it had a very gentlemanly ring to it. She did not know who her own father was, and she certainly did not want to name her son after the brute responsible for her pregnancy in the first place.

She and Ally were cohabiting the second ward, at the moment, together with the baby. Robert and Jonathan had completed the joining of the once-separate apartment to the rest of the hospital. It would become the wing where the female patients would stay, and the first ward would be the exclusive home of the live-in male patients. As soon as Sylvia, Phillip, and Malcolm would be installed downstairs, the small bedroom that Phillip and Malcolm had once shared would become Ally's sleeping quarters. She had been staying with Gwynne, but now that the new ward was ready, she had moved in there for the time being. Sophie, though exhausted, had been telling them that she had nowhere to go once she would be on her feet again. She had no desire to return to the home of her baby's father.

"I been workin' in 'is house as a cook and servant. 'Is wife 'ates me, although she 'as no idea 'er 'usband is the father of me baby." The woman in question just assumed the worst about Sophie. Sophie offered up her services as the cook of their establishment, and Jane had remarked that it would be a relief to have one less job to do. Heating water on the stove and constantly transporting it in pails to the room where she bathed the children was an endless task, although it was Phillip who descended the stairs to fetch the water.

Of course, Lucas wanted to get to know Sophie a little better before making such a hasty decision, but he could see that Gwynne had no desire to throw the girl out, and certainly not with a baby in tow. He would have to go, finally, as planned, to Chelsea tonight, and speak with his sister about coming to the hospital and taking on the task of teaching at least the children under their care, if not some of the adults. Both he and Gwynne agreed that she was urgently needed. It was no longer about helping her find an outlet for her intellectual talents; it was about adding a new dimension to the functionality of the hospital as a home, as well, for destitute and orphaned children.

And the other great piece of luck was the apparition of Rupert in their midst precisely when a second doctor had been absolutely essential! Gwynne more than approved of him. She was genuinely impressed by his performance today, and that was saying a great deal, she being the most experienced caregiver among them, and Lucas had made it abundantly clear to his once-estranged friend that Gwynne was an equal in all things, despite the fact that her education did not match theirs, and that she was paid by the charity his family had set up to sustain the hospital. Rupert had also pledged his willingness to work in the hospital, not just when he or Gwynne needed a break, but on a regular basis. He seemed really enthusiastic about the endeavour and ready to prove himself as a healer to children. His work as a medical researcher ebbed and flowed, and he did not feel as desperately required to perform those services as the ones necessary to preserve the young lives of the needy children of East London. He had declared that saving the boy's life today had been one of the most exhilarating experiences of his life. He would never have thought to undertake the establishment of a charity hospital, never have demonstrated such resourcefulness and creativity, but he was more than well-disposed to the idea of adding himself to the roster of able-bodied nurturers in Lucas's and Gwynne's institution.

"I so wanted to tell Rupert about us, Gwynne, about how we really are together, but I could not bring myself to." Gwynne brought him a cup of tea and sat beside him at the table. Once she was seated, Lucas took both her hands in his and kissed them. "I missed you today. I know we were not parted for that long, but all I wanted was to be alone with you so I could share my thoughts and feelings with you. It is as if I have not lived something unless I have described the minutiae of the experience to you. Only then does it all become real." Gwynne nodded and gave him that smile of hers that expressed her embrace of his total self. He basked in it. Her simple acknowledgement could sustain him through life. Now she just had to marry him.

"I had the impression that you and Rupert were once very close, and yet you couldn't tell him of our bond?"

"It is not because we have been parted for so long. It is not because our friendship lacked something essential. It is only because I feel that I must tell my family first—especially my aunt. She has the right to know...first."

Gwynne nodded meditatively. For a while they just sat and drank their tea in comfortable silence. Then Lucas began to slowly paint his impressions of the Workhouse and, for them, its most important inhabitant. And although work on a laundry would not begin until the plumbers had finished with the pipes, Sylvia would definitely be a help to Jane and the rest of them. She would have to be fitted for a set of uniforms just like her, Ally, and Jane.

When Lucas finished his tea, he reluctantly stood up to go. It was getting late, and he wanted to speak with his sister before dinner in the Lacey household was terminated. As soon as Gwynne rose, he put his arms around her and held her tightly to him. There had been no physical intimacy between them in the evening hours, since Ally had been sharing Gwynne's room and her bed at night. Now that Lucas knew she would not be bursting in on them, he consummated his overwhelming desire to eliminate any space between their two bodies. He longed to share the bed that Ally had so lately vacated. The need to join in that quintessential marital coupling was becoming more and more prominent and more and more difficult to ignore. He must advise his aunt as soon as possible of his decision to marry Gwynne. He did not know how much longer he could contain his yearning for her. His nights were feverish and oppressive as his imagination swirled with the form and figure of his beloved. He wanted her with him. He wanted to transport her and her son into his lodging now and begin their union now.

"Do you have to go?" murmured Gwynne. "Tomorrow morning Rupert will be here bright and early with William. You could visit Isabel then, Lucas." Gwynne wrapped her arms more tightly around him. In answer, he placed a finger under her chin, raised it, and bent his mouth to hers. His lips enclosed hers and the world outside them grew dim and silent. He focussed on nothing but the sensations inside his mouth. And then suddenly it was as if they were dancing, Gwynne leading him, pressing his body ever so slightly but insistently towards her bed. What was happening? Where were they going? To what conclusion was she drawing him? Then he lifted her off the ground and pirouetted with her in his arms, her lips detaching from his, and her face raised upwards towards the ceiling. He almost laughed. And then Gwynne laughed, so he joined her in her mirth. When he put her down, their legs bumped the side of her bed. She looked seriously into his eyes. What was she saying? What was she declaring to him? That she was ready for the next step whatever it would be? He did not know what to do, so he sank his face into her chest, kissing her exposed skin, speaking nonsense into her flesh, but telling her that he desired her with all of himself, that he would always want her, that he would always need her, and love her.

She whispered in his ear: "It is time, Lucas. It is time for us to be one."

"Now?" he asked in astonishment. "Before our marriage?"

"I *am* married to you, aren't I? Are you not married to me?" Lucas gazed at her in wonderment.

"Without benefit of church or state?"

"Yes," she simply responded. And he knew she meant it. She was just being her unclothed self with him, as they had always been with each other. *He* was the one that had slipped into dishonesty by not declaring how much he desired her with every fibre of his being. *He* was the one who had pulled the strings of society around them, imprisoning the authentic, candid couple that they really were.

"It is a little frightening to defy my upbringing, my family, my..."

"Class?"

Lucas nodded, ashamed, but willing to expose his weakness.

Gwynne smiled at him. "My dear Lucas, you have already defied every aspect of your class. You are a citizen of East London and the man I love." Then she simply sat down on the bed, looked up at him, and offered him her hand. When he took it, she gave a slight tug, and he was sitting at her side. "Be my husband, Lucas. Marry me right now."

"Are you sure?" he gasped, wanting desperately to succumb to the urgency of the tumult inside him, wanting to be absolutely united to this miracle of a woman. Surely there was no woman like her, a woman so rapturously honest and real and courageous.

She just gazed into his eyes, the smile still adorning her lips, and he knew he had no choice but to be as forthright, brave, and loving as she was. He realized that he was not terrified anymore. He knew what she wanted. He knew what he wanted. He was meant to be right here, right now. He placed his hands on her shoulders and drew her lips to his. He remembered the electricity between them the first time he had touched her, and he felt it again, a heat that rose through his fingers from the touch of her skin to somewhere deep inside him, thawing the pain of the past and the deathly cold of his time before Gwynne, before her life-giving presence in his existence on earth. He leaned into her and allowed his weight to make her fall backwards. It was as if they both sighed in unison as they gave themselves up to the body's call to join with the other. His mind went dark as they fumbled with clothing. He and she would be their naked selves, unburdened by laws and society and anything that was superfluous to the essence of their physical merging.

*

It was as she had always known—that she would experience her troth to this man in an unconventional way. Since society—the niceties and ceremonies of society—had betrayed her in the shape of a corrupt gentleman, she had had no use for any social conventions. She loved Lucas and he loved her. She had already been robbed of innocence. She had already created a child. She was free of the grip of the orthodox trappings of her country's culture. And Lucas, little by little, had freed himself as well. She had told him the truth. She wanted to be with him now, awaken in the morning with him by her side. No one else in their little community doubted that this was happening on a regular basis anyway. They all assumed that Charles was Lucas's son, and that for a certain period of time he had abandoned her for who knows what reasons, only to reappear in a particularly unfortunate period in her life. And she had taken him back. Did she really care what anyone thought about this? She only wanted them to respect her as a nurse and a healer of children. Her relationship to Lucas, with or without the blessing of church and state, belonged only to her—as it should. She was willing to pay the consequences, and the way that Lucas was striking out into unknown territory, that of her body, showed that he, too, was willing to pay the consequences.

At first, they had both been timid, frightened by their passion. But why should they be? His touch on her skin, in places she had never known were there for her to feel joy, was like a thrilling rush of self-knowledge, one yes-moment after another, beckoning her to surrender to the physical reality of friction, the stroking and caressing of two emotionally- and electrically-charged humans, obeying the commands of their bodies. And she gave in, gasping and moaning in unison with Lucas, needing, craving, seeking the gratification of every impulse, always wanting more, touching whatever she wished to touch, exploring her partner's sensitivities, discovering her own, never withdrawing, pursuing and being pursued, until that final shriek passed her lips, and her husband, yes, her husband discharged into her what she had engendered through the force of her will and desire. She did not know what this was called. Was it love? That love that girls fantasize in the secrecy of their poetic imaginations? Whatever it was, she had longed for it, she had generated it, and she had received it. She was breathless with its result. Edmund had spoiled nothing for her. She could not divine what he had extracted from their violent encounter, except perhaps the pleasure of inflicting pain. But she could not believe that he had had anything like the elation she was now feeling, Lucas panting in her ear, channelling his arms around her, tighter, ever tighter, pulling her to him with all his strength, as if she were not already glued to him. And suddenly he rolled over, heaving her on top of him, wrapping his legs around hers, as if he could not let go of her. She could feel his heart pounding, communicating his union with her, his human need for her.

"I'm here, Lucas. I'm here. Do you want to tell me something?" She was kissing his head, stroking his hair. "Do you want *me* to say something? Tell me, Lucas. Tell me what you need." Was he reliving his childhood terror? Was he locked in an embrace with the only survivor of that tragedy? "I love you, Lucas. I am with you. I am real. Look at me, Lucas." She lifted her head from his. She brushed her fingers over his cheek. She kissed the tears from beneath his closed eyelids. His heartbeat began to return to normal. He eased his grip on her back. And finally, he opened his eyes. He brought his hands up to either side of her face and held it before him. He searched her eyes.

"What are you asking me, Lucas?"

"Never leave me, Gwynne."

She smiled at him. "Is that all? Lucas, I pushed you here so that you could know how much *I* wanted to fulfil my promise to you, that nothing could keep me from you any longer, nothing could prevent our coupling. How could I ever leave you? Haven't I shown you that I will cleave to you despite everything? It is certainly not the idea of marriage that has brought you to my bed. It is you, just you, and you alone. This was my promise to you." And then she lay her head on his chest. She felt his lips press against the top of her head. She heard him sigh in relief.

Chapter XXI

It was morning–just. The light was pale, but he recognized immediately his surroundings. He remembered everything of the night before with the most distinct clarity, the joy, the sudden fear of loss of something, someone so precious, and then the reassurance. He was the luckiest of men, for he was lying here with the wisest of women, the most honest of women. His back was to her, so he turned around towards her, reaching out his hand to touch her, but she was not there. He sat up in surprise, and there she was pouring some hot water into the tub by the stove. She was going to perform her morning ablutions. Her back was to him, and he did not utter her name. He just watched, entranced by the curve of her back, her dark long hair falling around her. She was wearing a coat but had removed her shoes. Obviously, she had visited the privy downstairs in the courtyard first, but the water had been set upon the stove earlier to heat. When she stood up, she removed her coat and nightdress and hung them over a chair. Then she went back to the basin and dipped a sponge into the water, lifting one foot onto the rim and began to wash herself. His noisy intake of breath, his astonishment at her beauty on display for no one but him, attracted her attention, and she lifted the side of her head towards him and offered him, her husband of one night, that smile of complete and total recognition and acceptance. He felt his heart miss a beat and all of himself strain towards her. He would have liked his hand to be the one caressing her inner thigh. She nodded to him.

"Come, Lucas. Come and have a wash before the day begins."

At home, Peter would have already filled his bath with heated water. He would have stepped in and luxuriated in the warm suds with no thought to the work that had produced the luxury. He understood after the months spent here in East London how much energy was expended in the bathing of their little patients, but when he was in his own rooms, he took his endless pleasures for granted. But now he knew that this moment was better, because he was with the woman who had made life, his life, feel worth living. He got up to fulfil her summons.

"If you need, you may use the chamber pot under the bed, instead of descending to the privy. I did not use it because I did not want to disturb your sleep."

She was certainly right. He felt the call to relieve himself, but here, in this room, with her eyes on him? Could he do it? She knew every inch of his body now. She had always known his weaknesses and failures. She had never rejected a single part of him. As he reached under the bed to draw out the chamber pot, he remembered the intimacy experienced on the Continent with Rupert. They had shared the same quarters, used the same chamber pot, never once balking at the exposure. Rupert had felt like a brother, and he had enjoyed the familiarity. In his own family everyone was rather fastidious and private about everything, except with the servants perhaps who went freely everywhere without actually being seen. How unfair that reality was. Now that he knew well so many members of the lower classes, people whom he considered brothers and sisters, he saw the ugliness, on the part of his class, in the lack of awareness of their presence. Yes, his family treated the servants well, but that did not mean that they considered them as people like themselves. He had always known that his sister's relationship with the servants was different, but could she ever think of them as people of equal standing, of equal significance? He would have to ask her.

With his back to his beloved, he relieved himself. Gwynne had emptied countless chamber pots in her life both in the Crimea and in England. She had no fears of reality and she treated everyone as equals. And this particular bodily necessity that he once lived only in private he now shared with her. When he turned to her, she was still intent on her washing. She was standing in the tub now soaping, then rinsing her abdomen. Everything about the morning was so natural and harmonious and delectable. Its simplicity was disarming. But now the urge to apply the sponge himself to his dear wife was overpowering. He stepped into the bath in front of her, and delicately removed the moistened instrument of pleasure. He first turned her around and stroked her back and her buttocks, kneeling behind her as he washed her calves. When she about faced, his head, no, his lips were exactly at the height of her dark triangle of hair. Without thinking he pressed his mouth against it. He wrapped his arms around her and pulled her closer and closer. He drank in every sensation of the totality of that place on the map of her body—the softness, the wetness, the interwoven fabric of its make-up. Did other men do this? Did they kiss that other set of female lips with as much abandon, as if slaking their thirst at the fountain of femininity? He could not stop himself. He arched his neck backwards and rammed his mouth as far under and deep as he could possibly go. Gwynne was whimpering, her hands now on his head, her legs more apart, her knees sinking forward, as if she wished him to assail her more forcefully. So he responded, both of them opening themselves up to the other. The primness of the earlier moment when he had risen from bed had been utterly banished. He was a new man, enthralled to his woman, held spellbound to her need for him and his for her. His grinding mouth lapped up every savoury ripple and taste of her. He felt mighty and huge and more human than ever before. He belonged somewhere at last, at the very centre of this woman in upheaval, this woman groaning from pleasure. She finally let out a loud sigh, bending forward over him, her hands sliding to his shoulders. She breathed deeply and noisily for a while, then she, too, dropped to her knees. They hugged each other. He started to laugh, feeling a joy that could not be contained.

"What was that, Lucas?"

"I have no idea, but it was delicious and exciting, and I hope to spend my life doing it." He laughed some more and so did she. His desire to enter inside that centre of femaleness with his own centre of maleness was quashed by the rupture of their enclosed circle of two by the wail from the no longer sleeping Charles. He groaned in disappointment as Gwynne got up to see to her toddler, standing up and shaking the top bar of his crib. He felt her hand on his head.

"I'm sorry, Lucas. Tonight. It will happen tonight. I am yours tonight."

"I can't wait," he said, smiling, as Gwynne pulled on her nightdress, more from the chill of the air than propriety. She smiled back at him.

"Finish washing yourself. I will heat up some milk for Charles and we can have some tea before you go to Chelsea."

Lucas nodded.

*

Lucas had just left her room with her son in his arms. He declared that before going to Chelsea, he would check in on everyone in the wards, and together with Rupert examine William, perhaps see to the removal of the tube. He had told her to rest for the morning, maybe even the entire day. If no one summoned her because she was absolutely needed next door, she could have a well-earned break from all her toil of the last months. He would see to the care of Charles, even take him to visit his family, since he was already a member of that family.

No one had worked harder than Gwynne from the beginning. She had been there even in the dead of night, if a child was desperate for her abilities to heal them, whereas he had always gone home in the evening, not returning until the morning after was well in progress. He had never had to take care of his own necessities—the accoutrements of personal hygiene, clean and pressed clothes, breakfast, etc. He administered to Charles sometimes, once he was in the hospital, often feeding him if Charles so wished it, as all the staff ate around the central dining table and discussed the urgencies and tasks of the day for each one of them. But he understood that there was a much longer list of Charles's quotidian requirements that he was not called upon to fulfil. So, he had urged her to have a lie-in, perhaps go out and take a walk through the neighbourhood later, think exclusively about herself. She deserved it. He had kissed her fervently on her lips as he put her back to bed. He had stroked her face and told her they would be married as soon as possible, and he would take her to live with him in his rooms under the care and supervision of Peter and Susan, so that she would have less to do and think about. It was important for her to keep up her strength. "What if we made a child last night?" he had even asked.

She had smiled at his protectiveness, recalling how much harder her life as a nurse had been during the war in the Barracks Hospital, never having enough to eat, never feeling warm enough in the winter, always exhausted by the long hours, overwhelmed by the gruesomeness of the conditions, and the suffering of the soldiers. She had assured him that she was not as fragile as he supposed, but she was very willing to spend some restful moments in bed with no one calling to her. He had reminded her that he would call to her that night, that he was already yearning for their physical intimacy, that he would be imagining her naked self all through the day. They had laughed at this and then he had rushed out, swooping up Charles on the way to the door, not giving the boy a second to realize that he was being separated from his mother.

Gwynne lay in her bed, recalling the heat-filled moments of the previous night and morning. Lucas continued to be a revolution in her life, surprising her time and time again by his very nature and by her never-before-imagined response to it. All the pleasurable sensations that had overtaken her in the last ten hours had been so riotously and radically astounding! It was as if upheaval in her small life had become the norm. Would she ever get used to this love? Did she want to? Oddly enough, as she lay in her bed, she, too, began to fantasize about the night to come in Lucas's arms.

However, the whole idea of marriage, and marriage to an aristocrat at that, was something she found troubling. What would she lose? The gentlemen of this era owned everything, wives and children included. The thought of yielding herself to someone else's ownership, of turning into her browbeaten mother, who had never received a word of praise for anything she had accomplished in life, held a kind of threat for her. The present, this secret intermingling, integration, and fusion of all their personal, and yet male and female attributes, too, with society and morays thrown out with the bath water, was so appealing. With Lucas, now, she was just herself, but more fulfilled than she had ever been. Could they not stay like this? And if she were to have another child, because physical intercourse was now and would always be a part of their association, so what? No one in the next room would judge her. In fact, several days ago, when she found herself alone with Jane, in a moment of relaxation, drinking tea, all the children in their care, including Selina and Charles, either asleep or on their way, she had asked Jane to describe her wedding day.

The first thing Jane had said was: "So, our favourite Lord an' doctor 'as finally asked ye to marry 'im! 'Bout time, too! 'E'll ne'er find a better 'un 'n you." Jane had placed her hand on hers in solidarity. "An' why would ye be interested in me wedding day? Yours 'll be nothin' like, I'm sure."

"Just tell me how you felt, Jane. Were you scared? It's like handing yourself over to a great big conglomerate of laws and customs and forms of behaviour you may not want to be mixed up with. Were you ever afraid to lose yourself? Men are part of a...a...club, an exclusive men's club where women have no rights, no freedoms. Once married, you become part of the baggage of that man, one piece of his possessions. I...I..."

"Me dear, dear Gwynne, surely ye know that your man in't ne'er goin' to be like that. 'E listens to you. 'E respec's you. 'E looks to you for guidance. 'E loves you!" Gwynne had been surprised that Jane had noticed all those things. But she also knew that it was true.

"But what about everyone else...his family...Jane? Lucas is an Earl. His uncle sits in the House of Lords. I am a lowly...Will the others respect me, too? I like being me. Do I really want to become Mrs. Lacey?"

"Gwynne, it doesna matter what they call ye, Miss Littleford or Mrs. Lacey. Ye are an' always will be Nurse Gwynne. You tell 'im and the rest of 'em that you inten' to stay Nurse Gwynne fore'er. An' it's us ye will be seein' everyday, not them Lords an' Ladies. An' we don' give a fig 'bout them Lords an' Ladies, do we?" Gwynne had had to laugh. No, she did not give a fig about them. She knew that Lucas's desire for marriage had everything to do with pleasing his aunt and uncle. After all, they had sacrificed so much for himself and his sister. He felt, and rightly so, that they deserved to feel at peace where he was concerned, and being settled in marriage, albeit to the daughter of a wheelwright, represented for them a form of peace.

Chapter XXII

As soon as Lucas walked through the hospital door, he made swiftly to his examining room, nodding curtly to anyone in his path. He leaned forward to put Charles down and the toddler jumped out of his arms and ran towards Malcolm, who was playing with the healthier children under the dining-table. Lucas took his eyes from him momentarily and pulled off his surgeon's smock from the hook inside the door of the room. He did not want the others to see that he was still in yesterday's clothing, although there was no reason to believe that anyone would be startled by the fact that he had not gone home last night. They probably thought that it routinely happened anyway. Still, he was what he was, a member of the upper classes, and he was used to having impeccable clothes. He took off his jacket and put the white coat on over his shirt and vest. Now he felt less transparent to the others. Rupert might notice when he arrived, but it was also possible that Rupert might think that he had remained all night because the patients could not be left alone. Did it matter? He and Gwynne would be married sooner than later. No one in his family would or could object to the woman who had changed his life and had made him so much happier. He even imagined his aunt furious with him when he showed up with a baby that he had failed to legitimize! That Gwynne was from a different class would matter to some degree, but they would be able to ascertain, once she opened her mouth, how educated and genteel she was. And since she would rarely, if ever, be seen in the drawing-rooms of the aristocracy, who could possibly care about the poverty of her dress? Nothing would change in his life: he and Gwynne would live and continue to work in the warrens of East London, and never set foot in the grand homes of the rich and worldly.

As he finished buttoning up his coat, there was a commotion at the doorway. Phillip ran to answer the bell. Rupert, with

William in his arms, entered first, followed by the boy's mother, Bonnie, her younger son, Henry, and her six-year-old daughter, Maggie. It reminded Lucas how important his sister could be to this community, and to all the children he had come to know in it, if she would agree to install herself here to teach them, at least to read and write and add and subtract. He caught a sign from Rupert as he lay William onto the reclining push-chair that Phillip had immediately provided. Lucas nodded and opened the door to the examining-room wider, in order to allow this essential means of locomotion to be wheeled into the surgery.

"Is Gwynne about?" asked Rupert immediately.

Lucas blushed and looked down at William. "No, not this morning. I told her l-l-last night that she could have some time off today," Lucas stammered out his response.

"That makes two absences," Phillip chimed in. "Me mom told Jane to stay at 'ome, too, today, that she would take over all 'er duties."

"Well, Phillip," Lucas added with a smile, "they both deserve it, and we will have to think about a day off for you, as well."

"Oh, I'm jus' fine. No need to worry none 'bout me."

"Listen to Dr. Lacey, Phillip," his mother interjected into the boy's recital of bravado. "We don't want ye takin' to the beds o' the sick. Do we, doctor?"

"No, Sylvia. Your young man is too valuable."

*

After Bonnie had given her boy a thorough scrubbing in one of the baths in the bathroom, all the while declaring in astonishment at the fact that the grey water went down a drain pipe, especially hooked up to flow down to the large cesspit in the earth below the building, and after he was towelled down, Lucas brought William a clean night shirt, lifted him into the push-chair, propelled him into the boys' ward, and hoisted him onto a bed.

He wondered how William's mother would behave when the taps would be flowing with water *into* the place, not just out of it—an event scheduled to take place at any moment. The plumbers were to install in the bathroom a cistern that would gather up and store water, since the water company supplied water to homes only about two to three hours a day. This way they would have it in continual supply. Stone sinks had already been provided to the bathroom, the kitchen, and Gwynne's apartment. The stove in the former apartment on the other side, now the girls' ward, had been moved into the bathroom so the heating of water could take place directly in the room where so much of it was used. When all this work would be completed, in the blink of an eye, water would come pouring out of the faucets. That would mean so much less back-breaking work. Then the next step would be the fitting up of the laundry room, in some ways easier and less time-consuming, because it was on the main floor, and the engineering feat of the travelling upwards of water would no longer be an issue.

Lucas urged William to rest and told him that Ally would come and help him take some liquid nourishment in the form of soup in a few hours' time. When he bent down to pull the blanket over the boy, he felt his frail arms encircle him. So moved was Lucas by this gratitude, so freely given, that he sat down by the child and hugged him as well. What an astonishing moment! There was nothing like the sincerity of children, or of these children, at any rate, children who grew up with so little. He was not sure of the offspring of the Lords and Ladies of England. And as a boy, the only being that *he* had ever hugged with so much fervour was a horse.

Just as he stood up to take leave of William, Phillip ran into the ward. He came up beside him and pulled him by his coat sleeve, "Dr. Lacey, you'll ne'er believe this. There be a Lady at our door, t' most beautiful Lady I 'ave ever laid eyes on—a Princess, an' she wishes to speak to you."

Lucas almost laughed. Who could this Princess be that had so impressed Phillip? Someone who wanted to make a contribution to the charity? "Is Dr. Keynes talking with her now, Phillip?"

"Yes, 'e is, but it be you she be lookin' fer."

"I am coming, then, Phillip. Let us see who this veritable Princess is."

When he reached the doorway, stood on the threshold and looked across the room at the person in the entrance talking quite naturally to Rupert, he actually had to laugh. Phillip looked up at him curiously. He put his hand on the boy's head and said, "Why, Phillip, it is no Princess. She is none other than my very own beloved sister, Isabel, come to visit us when it had been my intention today of going to visit her! What a pleasant surprise! Come and let me introduce you to one of the kindest creatures in the universe!"

As he walked towards his sister, he could not fail to notice that, in a way, she did look like a Princess, for she was rather unsuitably attired for this place with her voluminous skirts and perfectly coiffed hair. She certainly was beautiful, her blonde hair made, painstakingly he might add, by her lady's maid, to perfectly fit the shape and shading of her facial features. He had a perverse notion at that moment that, being who she was, one of the most intelligent and well-informed women on earth, as well as kind, as he had mentioned to Phillip, she just might be the only type of Lady of the drawing-room that Rupert could possibly fall in love with, since she was so glaringly different than all the others he was sure Rupert had been introduced to. Again, Lucas chuckled. How absurd his thoughts were this morning. He was definitely thinking about love, having recently experienced the great benefits of love in the flat next door. What a wonderful thought, though, it was—Rupert and Isabel—his two favourite people who had peopled his life before the advent of Gwynne. Why had he never thought of it before when he and Rupert were university friends? Because, he supposed, at that time he had had no such thing on his mind, no consideration for love whatsoever. He moved quickly towards his sister, feeling a great burst of affection and goodwill welling up inside his chest.

When he reached her, she smiled at him, and he wrapped his arms around her, slightly lifting her off her feet. He was so happy to see her here, not in their home in Chelsea, for it was here that he wanted her to be, here that he wanted her to find the real and honest and satisfying employment of her gifts.

"Oh, Isabel, I am just so happy to see you!" It was a sentiment that was obvious to anyone in the vicinity. He kissed his sister on both cheeks. She was a little startled at his ardour, but he could sense that she, too, was happy to see him. "I was just about to come and visit you in Chelsea. I have much to tell you and ask you!" Even Rupert seemed a little taken aback now. It was time to introduce her to everyone, show her all there was to see, and then maybe take her next door to discuss with Gwynne their idea of a school on the premises. Would she embrace their intention as much as he needed her to?

"Were you really keen on seeing me today, Lucas? It has been so long. *I* needed to see you and where you worked, so I took the carriage, telling our aunt as little as possible about where I was going unaccompanied. I do not know if she would have let me venture here by myself, and somehow, I wanted to do this on my own, without her as a chaperone." Isabel turned to Rupert and said, "You do know, I am sure, how protected and coddled we women are today, as if malefactors are everywhere lying in wait for us to appear." Lucas glanced at Rupert. Rupert seemed absolutely enchanted by Isabel's forthrightness. He nodded vigorously in agreement. And again, Lucas had to chuckle at all that was transpiring today. It was as if he and Gwynne had created this chain of events, as if attraction or chemistry or love itself, and not a potential baby, was what their act had spawned.

"My dear Lucas, you *are* in an ebullient mood today," Isabel commented. "I have not seen you like this in—"

"—years," he interrupted.

"That is because, Miss Lacey, Lucas and Gwynne are doing something glorious here, and I, for one, am so proud to have become a part of it as recently as yesterday."

"Well, if you have come to familiarize yourself with our little institution here, you should meet everyone involved," pronounced Lucas, taking his sister by the arm and making his way, with Rupert, on her other side, around the premises. Everyone, including the children, not in their beds, came to see the beautiful Princess. Each one, Ally, Sylvia, Bonnie and her children, Malcolm, and the other patients were formally introduced, and Isabel, in perfect form, gave them all a little curtsey. Sylvia explained the absence of Jane and her family. At a certain moment, Charles came bounding out from under the table, to see what all the fuss was about, and began to pull on Lucas's trouser leg. Lucas bent down to pick up the toddler and when he did, Charles began to slap the sides of his cheeks, staring into his face, and crying, "Da, da, da, da, da." All and sundry began to laugh, and Lucas couldn't help but wonder what was going through Isabel's mind at that moment. His eyes were completely on Charles at the time, and he could not see either Rupert's or Isabel's reaction. But react they must have, even if they might think that Charles said that word to any adult male in the room, but of course there was no other, besides Rupert, Jonathan being downstairs working on the laundry with his son Robert, and the affection that passed between himself and the boy was ever so entirely evident. Lucas lifted the little one onto his shoulders, and marched on, going from room to room, pointing out anything essential, determined not to stumble after any perceived embarrassment at the child's utterances.

Phillip had not yet been introduced. He seemed a little shy at the apparition of such a grand personage in their midst. With one hand holding onto Charles above him, he brought Phillip over with the other and proclaimed to his sister: "And this is Phillip, my right-hand man, possibly the most important person in this entire establishment. He runs this hospital. He takes note of everything we need, everything we don't have, like coal, wood, food, utensils, and bedding...everything. He makes sure that we acquire these things. And he answers the bell, takes care of newcomers, sees to the fires in the stoves and the hearths, and last but not least he hauls up all the buckets of water for the cooking, bathing, and cleaning. He basically sees to the smoothly running efficiency of the place, and he does a damn good job of it. We would be nowhere without him!"

Phillip looked ever so proud of himself after hearing Lucas's list of his skills and accomplishments, but after Isabel curtsied and he gave his most distinguished bow, he said sincerely, "I am afraid, miss, that Dr. Lacey's mistaken as to me importance 'ere. The mos' important person 'ere is by far Nurse Gwynne 'erself, an' she 'as been takin' care of us folks 'ere in Whitechapel for a very long time." Everyone murmured in agreement, and it almost brought tears to Lucas's eyes, for this was his woman, the woman he loved.

"And where is this spirit of the place, the inimitable Nurse Gwynne?" asked Isabel finally. Before anyone could answer there was a ring of the bell and Phillip went to answer it. The seamstress, tasked with sewing uniforms for the women and night dresses and shirts in all sizes for the patients, was at the door with a bundle of clothing. Lucas left Isabel in the capable hands of Rupert, lifted Charles off his shoulders, held him instead in his arms, and went to deal with her. She had been making the night clothes for their residents very regularly, because they were urgently needed, but now it seemed that she had completed the three sets of uniforms each for Ally, Jane, and Gwynne. She placed them on the large dining-table, and he asked her to measure a uniform for Sylvia. He asked her to wait for him while he went next door to get Nurse Gwynne, and then they would settle the bill. The woman was only too happy to have more work to do. She and Sylvia went into the little room where she and her son and Malcolm slept, and Lucas called to Isabel and said he would return shortly.

He took Gwynne's uniforms with him, placed them under one arm, and with Charles sitting comfortably in the crook of the other, he proceeded to her quarters next door.

He knocked at her door and waited a few seconds for her to open it. When she did, she looked surprised to see him, for he was supposed to be going to Chelsea.

"You'll never guess what has happened, Gwynne. My sister has come to us! She is next door being escorted by everyone around the hospital. She just wanted to see the place for herself and me included."

"But have you spoken to her yet about our idea of a school?"

"Not yet. Not without you. So put on your new uniform," he said, and he handed the bundle of uniforms to her as he entered and turned to close the door. "And I will bring her over here to meet you and discuss our proposal. What do you think?"

"You seem very excited," commented Gwynne with a smile. She took Charles from him and brought the child over to his cot to change his wet nappy.

"Shouldn't I be, my love? If she says yes, then everything we have dreamed of could be coming true, not to mention the fact that Rupert seems smitten with her. I feel sure that he will be advocating in our favour just to get a glimpse of her every day." At that, Gwynne started to laugh, and so did he. As she bent over to deal with her baby, Lucas came behind her, placed his hands on her shoulders, and kissed the top of her head. "I also think we had better tell her of our plans to marry in the immediate future, the very immediate future."

Gwynne left Charles to himself and turned around to face Lucas. They embraced each other, Gwynne leaning her head against his chest. "I will go back next door now and bring my sister and Rupert over here momentarily. Phillip can come and get me or Rupert if there is a new emergency." He slightly pulled away from her and lifted her chin up. "Are you ready for this declaration?"

"The declaration of our love, or of our impending marriage?"

"Well, of both."

"Because I am not feeling as confident as you about my acceptance into your family. What will they think of *my* family, a father who is a wheelwright, and a mother who is a governess? I think they must have been expecting you to marry nothing less than royalty."

Lucas was shaking his head. "No, no, no. I don't agree. I think that my aunt will be overjoyed that I have found someone and that you make me so happy. Please, Gwynne, give them an opportunity to prove themselves in your eyes. I believe in them."

Chapter XXIII

The four of them were all sitting in her apartment drinking some tea, Rupert and Isabel on one side of the table, herself and Lucas on the other. Gwynne had managed to feed Charles some soup and put on her uniform before the others entered her dwelling. Charles, although excited at first by all the newness this day had brought, had finally settled down for a nap in his cot. She had not managed to pin up her hair underneath the little cap that the seamstress had provided, so it was freely hanging beneath her shoulders. Luckily, she was not at work with the children. Her hair would not have done in that case.

The uniform itself was made up of three parts—a pale blue blouse, a dark blue skirt, and a white apron with the name: East London Charity Hospital for Children neatly embroidered in red thread across the front. It fit well and made her feel very professional. Lucas had commented on how well it looked on her and that pleased her. It was probably the best thing for her to wear to meet Lucas's sister, since she had no clothes in her wardrobe that could match that of a lady.

Isabel was a great deal like Lucas himself. Certainly, they looked like siblings. They were both tall and blonde and gentle. Isabel perhaps did not create as much intimacy around her when she engaged in conversation. Well, that was maybe because Lucas focused so much attention on herself when they were together, but he was also like that when in the company of the children under their care. There was an attentiveness that he bestowed on his interlocutors that was just part and parcel of who he was. But Isabel was much like Lucas had described—a woman of great intellect and passion as well, locked up like some princess in her tower. Here she was, however, in her own humble abode, taking these unusual surroundings, for a Lady such as herself at any rate, in her stride. Gwynne wondered if Isabel could ever be made to feel uncomfortable. She had an ease about her that she could not remember even the great Lady Ridgely, Edmund's mother, ever possessing. Of course, Isabel was so much younger than that austere Lady, but it seemed that Isabel, like her brother, was not that closely linked to her title; her self-worth was based not on outward appearance but on inner strength. She had strength of character, no doubt about it, more than Lucas possibly, because she had not suffered in the same way after the loss of her parents. For Isabel, her real parents were in fact her aunt and uncle. She probably had no memory at all of the ones responsible for her birth.

Gwynne found herself liking Isabel indeed. She remembered that at one time she had been rather afraid to meet her, since she worried that Lucas's relationship with his sister might diminish the strong attachment growing between themselves. That fear had now dissipated. Lucas's body beside hers was radiating a current so powerful between them, (or perhaps it was her current flowing through him and back to her?) that she did not fear that his love for his sister could extinguish anything of their bond. She felt relaxed and happy. Also, Isabel was responding most positively, even enthusiastically, without any prodding from Rupert, to their proposal. It seemed she was ready to start tomorrow. She just had to collect the accoutrements necessary to teach—primers, slates, chalk, papers, and pencils for such an enterprise.

"So, I could not be here first thing in the morning, but later sometime in the afternoon. But I am most willing to try. What an admirable idea! I am so pleased you thought of me," Isabel offered.

"We will have to find a suitable place for you to work. Initially," Lucas continued, "I had thought of setting the school up right in the central room next door, where everything happens, but now I am thinking that there is too much commotion in there. Perhaps downstairs," and here Lucas turned to Gwynne, "perhaps there is enough space to have a laundry, Sylvia's quarters, *and* a classroom on the main floor. What do you think, Gwynne?"

"We just have to ask Jonathan. But until that possibility comes to fruition, Isabel could start her school in here while I am working."

"And what about Charles? Where does he spend his day?" Isabel asked.

"He just spends it with us. Malcolm, who once was a patient but now lives here, has been playing with Selina, Jane's three-year-old and Charles and the other children, well enough to be out of bed. Phillip also entertains Charles when he is free. It has not been too complicated so far, but when Malcolm will be engaged with his studies with you, it will obviously be much more difficult." Gwynne looked at Lucas inquiringly as she finished this explanation. Obviously, they had not thought about this problem before. If she and Jane and Lucas were all taken with patients, who *would* take care of Charles and Selina?

"What about Sophie? Since she will be staying on with us, with her own baby, perhaps she can also mind Selina and Charles," Lucas offered.

"But she will also be cooking for us now. Of course, Sylvia will not be starting up the laundry for a few weeks. She represents an extra pair of hands. She seems very capable of doing many things," Gwynne responded.

Lucas nodded. "However, we may have a problem in the future. When the children, our very very useful children, are at their lessons, including Robert, they are not fulfilling their other duties. Who knew how valuable children could be?" He turned to Isabel and Rupert now. "We were never that useful as children, were we? Besides studying, we did what we wanted. No one really needed us," mused Lucas.

Gwynne was prompted to say something about the upper classes, but considering that she was surrounded by representatives of that milieu, kept her tongue. Isabel and Lucas reminisced a little about the freedom of their childhood, with Rupert adding commentary about his own. She sat back for a moment, leaning into her chair. Lucas was aware of her withdrawal and took her hand in his. He clasped hers on top of the table, and the gesture was therefore visible to the other two. It was a declaration of sorts. A gentleman would not hold the hand of a woman unless he was engaged to her, thought Gwynne, would he? She could feel the attention now from both Isabel and Rupert. Surely, it was time to stop talking of childhood and to start talking of adult things. Lucas took a deep breath.

"There was another reason why I was coming today to speak with you, Isabel. I intended to tell both you and Aunt Edith of our intention to be married...that is, mine and Gwynne's...and as soon as possible, too."

Isabel laid her hand on top of theirs. "I knew at Christmas, my dear brother, that there was more to your relationship with Gwynne than that of medical colleagues." Isabel looked straight at Gwynne now. "I just knew he was in love. It was the way he spoke of you. But I did not know whether *he* knew it at the time, so I did not say anything." Isabel smiled now at her. Gwynne sensed that she more than approved of her brother's choice of partner.

"Oh, I knew all right, but I was not saying it to myself just then. It was overwhelming. I had never expected such a thing ever to happen to me," responded Lucas.

"I am so happy for you both," said Isabel.

"And I second that," chimed in Rupert. "You lucky man. It finally happened to you." Rupert turned now to Gwynne. "This man is like a brother to me, Nurse Gwynne. Please accept my offer thus to be a brother, as well, to you." Gwynne felt moved by this offer from someone she barely knew, although with whom she had treated a sick child. He would be a caring brother if his concern for William was an indication of the kind of man he was.

"I accept your offer, Dr. Keynes," she replied with a smile.

"No, no, you must now call me Rupert if we are to be kin." After a second, Rupert proceeded with a question. "And when would this proposed marriage take place?"

Lucas answered immediately. "I would like it to take place tomorrow, but certainly within a week or so. If this room is going to be utilized as a classroom, I think that Charles and Gwynne should come as soon as possible to live in my rooms." Both Rupert and Isabel looked a little shocked. Isabel removed her hand from the betrothed couple's and at first brought it to her mouth. Then she placed it back on the table and spoke.

"But how can Aunt Edith and Uncle Graham prepare a wedding in such a short time, Lucas? You are asking too much of them. A wedding is a great undertaking," said Isabel, looking almost horrified.

"But we are not going to have that kind of a wedding. We are going to be married, yes." Lucas put his arm around Gwynne as he said this, claiming solidarity with her against the customs of his class. "But there is not going to be any kind of spectacle." Isabel was frowning. Gwynne could see how puzzled she was. Lucas continued. "It is imperative as well that there be no announcement in the society pages of the newspaper. We are consummating our love before God, but not before the members of the aristocracy. Gwynne and I do not live there, in that world. We are not a part of it and will never be a part of it."

Isabel and Rupert seemed a little stunned at first, especially Isabel. "Do you not think that Aunt Edith and Uncle Graham may be a little hurt by your lack of consideration for them and their position in—"

"Actually, I do," interrupted Lucas in the middle of his sister's question, "I have pondered on that very thing, and yet I can see no way around it. Gwynne and I are a working couple. We will never have time for 'society' and I...I...can never go back to living a lie." Gwynne saw how stricken Lucas was when he uttered these words to Isabel. She understood that hurting his sister was a possibility that he would find quite unbearable. And, in truth, it was she herself who had more or less engineered this situation, by emphasizing her unwillingness to climb the rungs of the established social order. Isabel was still silent. You could see in her face the complicated twists and turns of her thought processes.

"And where would this marriage take place?" was Isabel's next question.

"Why, right here, I think, in our hospital," responded her brother.

"Here?" This response was enunciated in unison by those two specimens of the upper echelons of society, sitting across from Gwynne and Lucas. But surely these two would understand, thought Gwynne, if they were as enlightened as Lucas claimed they were.

"You mean you don't wish to be married in our church in Kent, the church where every member of our family has been married since time immemorial?"

Lucas bent his body over the table, trying to shrink the distance between his sister and himself as much as possible. "It has nothing to do with what I want, dear Isabel, but everything to do with this place and the people who work here. Think about it. If we get married in Kent, then Rupert, here," Lucas pointed to his friend as he mentioned his name, "could not be present at the wedding. He would have to be here to take care of things while we were in Kent. Hospitals can never close down—not even for weddings. And then there's Jane...I cannot imagine that Gwynne would be happy getting married if Jane were not at her side." He looked at Gwynne at that moment, and once he perceived her tiny smile, he turned his gaze on Rupert. Rupert responded immediately to Lucas's plea.

"Of course! If you are asking me to be your best man, then, I heartily accept, Lucas. Don't you see, Isabel, this all makes sense." Rupert turned his body to face Isabel. "Gwynne and Lucas need their comrades here to be present at their wedding. All these people working here are their community now. This is where your brother has come alive. It is his way of honouring that. And if an emergency comes up, we will postpone the wedding, for as long as the emergency takes to get solved." Rupert began to chuckle. "It might take an entire day before all the vows get pronounced, and we'd have to find a vicar ready to put up with such a preposterous style of wedding...but, in the end, it could be quite...quite...thrilling!" Rupert's smile and enthusiasm was quite infectious.

"I don't care if, besides Aunt Edith and Uncle Graham, you and Rupert, there are no Lords and Ladies present, Isabel."

Gwynne could see that Lucas was finally beginning to relax. He withdrew from his position across the centre of the table and leaned back in his chair. It seemed that he was still a little worried about Isabel, but he had made his claim, and it was her turn to reveal her true nature.

It was apparent that Isabel was absorbing all the emotion, as well as the principles, behind her brother's choice. Finally, she took a deep breath, and then uttered the truth of what she was experiencing in the moment.

"How I envy you your freedom, Lucas," she ruefully stated.

"Me, too," declared Rupert. After the enunciation of this short statement, Rupert slightly turned his head and stared directly into Isabel's eyes.

Chapter XXIV

So much had happened since Lucas's declaration to his sister and Rupert the day before. Gwynne felt as if a whirlwind had swept through their lives. To be perfectly honest, when Lucas had exhorted her to take the day off and remain alone in her chambers, she had only wanted to concentrate on and absorb the stirrings in her body that the previous night and morning had evoked. The intimacy, long-awaited between herself and Lucas, had caused a different kind of turbulence, to be sure, within her. The pleasure it had afforded had thoroughly astounded her. And now, the day after, she must prepare to be married by the end of the week, for Rupert had found a vicar, actually a distant friend of theirs from university, who accepted to preside at the rather unusual wedding in a rather unusual setting, one completely in abeyance to the whims of the state of health of the children of East London. After all, who knew who could come calling in the midst of the ceremony?

She was going to meet her betrothed's guardians, and how would that turn out? Just because it had gone quite well with Isabel did not mean that she would fare so well with such an august aristocratic couple. And she had been totally terrified of the idea of marriage in the first place. Would she be forced to succumb to the laws of society even though she would not participate in its ceremonies and splendours? Would she remain simple Nurse Gwynne forevermore? Jane declared that she would, but today was not yesterday. Today was bringing her closer and closer to reality.

Lucas had decided to bring Charles with him when he and Isabel went back to Chelsea to confront their Aunt Edith with the overwhelming news. He insisted that she would not really be able to relax if she had the responsibility of taking care of their energetic toddler. It was to be a true day of freedom for her. It was also a great deal for his aunt to swallow—an unorthodox wedding to an unorthodox woman with a child. But apparently, she had risen to the occasion, and Lucas was quite ecstatic. The fact that he was finally happy in life was all that his aunt wanted. Isabel had sung her praises and had assured their aunt that Nurse Gwynne would meet all her expectations for a daughter-in-law. As long as Isabel, herself, when the time came, provided fair warning, so that a spectacular wedding could finally be performed on their estate in Kent, Aunt Edith was willing to forego some pomp and circumstance for the wedding of her elder brother. Gwynne wondered how Isabel had really felt about that promise to her aunt, for she seemed to truly crave her brother's liberty, his immunity from the pull of aristocracy's noose. Gwynne was happy that she and Lucas could at least provide for Isabel the opportunity to express herself, her creativity, her willingness to work for the good of others. Perhaps she would finally have a sense of accomplishment. Isabel deserved it.

Despite all this good will towards her on the part of Lucas's family and Rupert, it was however apparent to Gwynne that Isabel was still quite mystified by the rushed nature of the forthcoming wedding. Telling her that her schoolroom would have to be set up here, in her personal chambers, and that therefore she and Charles would have to move into Lucas's rooms as soon as possible, could not have possibly satisfied her. She was too intelligent to swallow such a flimsy explanation. She could imagine Isabel's imagination, not to mention that of her aunt and uncle, spinning out of control.

Isabel was still about, although she had finished teaching for the day, her very first day. She was downstairs speaking with Jonathan and Robert and Sylvia about the proposed set-up of the three new interiors destined to occupy the space that Mr. Gaunt, the landlord, had made available to them. Gwynne herself was having a quiet moment in her flat with her son, after a long day next door. New children had shown up on their doorstep today, and all of them had been required to remain in the hospital for further treatment. It was a good thing that Sophie, the child-mother, and Sylvia were now part of the permanent staff. There was ever so much to do. And then, for several hours, Malcolm, Phillip, and Robert had begun their lessons along with several other recovering children. This meant that looking after Selina and Charles fell to one of the adults, not actually engaged with administering to a sickly child. It had worked out today mainly because a mother of one of the newcomers had been only too willing to attend to the needs of their own children, while everyone else was seeing to hers. But what about tomorrow, and the days after?

There was a knock at her door. With Charles sleepily tucked into his crib, but not yet asleep, Gwynne went to her door, almost hoping it was not Phillip or Malcolm telling her that she was needed by either Rupert or Lucas. She felt that she needed this peaceful moment to digest all of the happenings of the last few days, as well as the ones of the future.

She opened the door to Isabel, who had presumably finished her colloquy with their builders. "May I come in? I thought I should tidy up your room before I head home for the day...but I can see that you have already done that. I don't know where you get so much energy to do so many things in one day." Isabel smiled, and Gwynne could tell that there was admiration in her words.

"Would you like to come in and have a cup of tea, Isabel? You can tell me what all of you have decided about downstairs. I think that my son is just about to fall asleep and perhaps we can steal a few moments of peace and quiet together—"

"—in such a hectic place," Isabel finished Gwynne's sentence for her. "That would be a lovely idea. I do so wish to get to know you better." Isabel entered and Gwynne went over to the stove to fill the kettle and place it on the fire. Then they both sat down at her table, taking the same places that each had assumed the previous day, facing each other. At first, Isabel did her best to describe how Jonathan would divide the space in the most beneficial way possible. While Gwynne filled their cups with tea, Isabel took paper and pen from the stockpile necessary for her teaching. She proved to be admirably able to draw the configuration of the rooms. Gwynne was impressed by Isabel's skill at rendering the look of each and every detail within the laundry, Sylvia's family room, and her own classroom. How well women of the aristocracy were taught to do such things, and yet they were never asked to put those skills to use.

"I am sure that Jonathan could utilize these gifts of yours to display all the things he is capable of doing for others after he has finished with us and our hospital."

"I would be happy to do drawings of this type as a way for him to promote himself," replied Isabel to Gwynne's remark. "But do you think," she asked with a broad grin on her face, "that you will ever be finished with him? Lucas wants him to put in several flush toilets now in the courtyard where the privy stands, for the use of at least the members of the staff. Who knows how long that will take him?" Isabel blushed a little as she remarked on her brother's new proposals. Gwynne had not been aware of Lucas's intention of making their lives even better, but she smiled inwardly as she reflected on his thoughtfulness. What a wonderful idea! She could see that East London had changed him in that he could speak of such things directly to Isabel. East London was taking the aristocrat out of an aristocrat and turning him into a man of the people. Would his sister be able to keep up? However, other than blushing, she had introduced the subject herself. That was a good sign.

"Do you think that Rupert and Lucas will be long now? Have they almost finished up for the day?"

"Yes, I think that with the help of Ally, our young nurse-in-training, they will be able to take care of the last little patients that came in today. I am so thankful to that girl. She is such a dear child and so willing to learn. Everything she learns, she accomplishes with care and concentration. I have much confidence in her." Isabel nodded and then asked her about her own teacher, a woman they obviously both admired. Gwynne reminisced for a while, but she could see that Isabel was becoming anxious.

"Is there something you want to tell your brother before you leave today? If so, I can pass on whatever it is, if it is your wish to go home now."

"Oh, that will not be necessary because I have convinced him to stay with the family in Chelsea tonight, and I believe that Rupert will be coming with him to dine with us." Lucas had not informed her of his intention to do so. They had not had a moment to themselves today. She felt a sense of loss at the thought that he would not be sharing her bed tonight. They had managed to do so last night, and the desire to repeat those pleasures, to discard their clothes, and embrace each other's nakedness was uppermost on her mind, as the day was drawing to a close.

"I hope you do not feel left out in any way, Gwynne. The invitation is extended to you, as well. My aunt and uncle do so want to meet you, but I understand that on occasion you may be summoned at night to deal with some emergency. The hospital cannot function without a caregiver at night. I am sorry that it is always you. Now that you will be leaving the premises, what is going to happen?"

Gwynne felt the sincerity of Isabel's words and was glad that her sister-in-law-to-be did not notice the disappointment on her face at the thought of Lucas abandoning her tonight. Or maybe she did but took it to mean that she felt isolated in some way from the festivities. Gwynne drank some tea and then answered: "I think that Lucas intends to speak to the medical faculty of the university and try to persuade them to allow students to intern in our little hospital. Maybe other aspiring doctors will have the urge to specialize in the treatment of children. And since this hospital is the only place in which to do that, hopefully Lucas and the professors can reach some agreement. Perhaps we can acquire one practitioner-in-training during the day, and one during the night. Once Sylvia, Phillip, and Malcolm move downstairs, such an individual can either sleep in their small room, or even here...I hadn't really thought about sleeping arrangements...." In truth, she hadn't really thought much about those details because she had been so much more absorbed by her own physical adventures in the bedroom. Sometimes, when she and Lucas were administering to some little patient, she felt overcome by a desire to remove everyone from her surroundings and remain alone with him. She kept imagining him embracing her. Her fantasies often went beyond those embraces. What was happening to her? She almost felt as if she no longer knew herself. She had once been such a self-contained human-being. But since the advent of Lucas into her life, the barriers of protection that she had so carefully built around her had been starting to crumble into dust. Isabel broke into her reverie.

"What a splendid idea!" remarked Isabel, for an instant looking so much like her brother. Gwynne smiled to herself, wondering if that was what she liked most about the young woman. "I hope that will free up your evenings to do other things besides work and provide for your child."

Did Isabel think that she and Lucas, after a hard day's work, would want to attend some ball or evening extravaganza? "What do you mean, Isabel?" Gwynne drank some more tea as she ordered her thoughts before speaking. "I think that after a few weeks of working here...I mean teaching..." and now she hesitated. She did not want to insult Isabel or her life as a lady of leisure, but she did feel obliged to offer a sense of reality to the rather innocent woman. "I think you, too, may experience a great deal of weariness at the end of the day. You may only want to go home and sleep." Gwynne hoped that she had not overstepped the bounds of familiarity between sisters-to-be.

But Isabel was able to react good-humouredly. Gwynne had forgotten just how socially dexterous the woman really was. "Of course. Of course. What was I thinking? At least, however, you will not have to wake up in the middle of the night to treat some sorry urchin, and you and Lucas can come home to a well-cooked meal...and...be taken care of by the servants. This will make you so much more ready to take on the next day of work with all the strength necessary to carry out your duties." Isabel was so well-meaning that Gwynne had to smile. In fact, she hadn't thought of those things. She hadn't thought of the servants who took care of Lucas, his daily needs, the cleaning of his clothes, his surroundings. It hit her that she would no longer have to carry out the daily tasks of a woman who did not have a myriad of servants (and how many would there be?) once she moved into those mysterious rooms of a gentleman. Would she actually like it, giving up domination of her own tiny world?

"And you could possibly leave Charles in the care of a nanny, at least for certain things, on certain days. How does that strike you?" Gwynne was startled. She must have revealed her shock, because Isabel hurriedly continued speaking. "All this must be somewhat bewildering to you, my dear Gwynne." Isabel stretched a hand across the table and touched the other woman's arm. "I don't mean to revolutionize your life, but you are marrying a gentleman, a rather unusual one, but nevertheless a man of means, who is very capable of making your life a great deal easier. Is that such a bad thing? Surely you can see that you can devote greater attention to your little charges if you have fewer responsibilities."

She did see that. She was beginning to comprehend the magnitude of adjustment that marriage would bring to her life. The question was definitely: is that such a bad thing? Part of her wished to revolt, and say that yes, it was, if it changed who she was. But would it be that bad, really? Was Isabel, to some degree, correct? "I guess I may feel less tired all the time." She paused after uttering these words, unsure what else to say.

"My dear Gwynne, I can see that no one could possibly accuse you of scheming your way into our, mine and Lucas's, world of ease and comfort. I do believe that you had hardly thought about it!"

"No, I have had so many other things to...uh...think about."

"But then, my dear, why are you rushing headlong into marriage at this exhilaratingly rapid pace? You could slow down...unless...unless..." Isabel did not finish her sentence, leaving the weighty question to hover in the air between them.

Gwynne shook her head. It suddenly came to her why Lucas wished to marry so quickly. She understood his urgency. It was who he was. He had already undergone so much change in the last few months. He had taken leaps into a thoroughly unknown world, guided essentially only by his feelings for her, and the instinctive knowledge that it would save him. She herself was not in any way ashamed of the intermingling that they had experienced in this very room, without the permission of some representative of God. She had little experience of the representatives of God. She had learned to live, as had her fellow humans here in the warrens of East London, without the guidance of any clergyman. And she had never pondered the sinfulness of their lustful loving. Nor had she pondered the sinfulness of seeking to provide for her child in the only way available to her on that bleak day in December. She did not think that hers were punishable offences. She was not afraid of God's judgement. Truth be told, Edmund had much more to fear. She had only acted out of love. Lucas, however, needed marriage. He needed to follow in the footsteps of his own beloved parents. He needed to show them not only that he was capable of living well and creating good in this world with their hospital, but that he was also capable of giving himself to a woman, of giving himself up to love, in the way that they, his parents, had. He was a member of his class, and she had to understand that, and so she was doing this, this marriage for him. She was no longer uncertain as she had been a week ago, a day ago, even an hour ago. She owed Lucas this, this somewhat neat package. After all, his gift to her had possibly been even greater.

"Unless...there is some other reason...I'm sorry...I shouldn't even be thinking such things...but yesterday when Lucas showed up with Charles in tow, as loving as any father...I know it crossed the mind of my aunt, and when my uncle came home...I could see that he was bursting with questions...such a precipitous marriage...but Lucas offered no substantial reason...I know he loves you...but I also know that everyone in this place believes that he is the father of your son...." And now for the first time, Gwynne could see the discomfort of this supremely comfortable woman. A line had been crossed. She was no longer in the confines of her confined world, where the rules were all laid out and well-understood. She was in another territory. She could almost hear Isabel's thoughts. *Unless...unless Lucas was just doing his duty, finally, after having committed some youthful indiscretion several years before. He probably had never been informed of the outcome of his folly, but then he met her again, and had to do the gentlemanly thing this time, being the good man that he was. Probably he had always loved her long ago, but now he was ready for marriage and the responsibilities of fatherhood and so it would all work out.* Poor Isabel. If she could just tell her that little lie, then everything would be alright. But she couldn't. She couldn't start this ever so important relationship with a lie. So, she shook her head again. She smiled, sadly, at first, because she was about to destroy the convenient storyline that the family had all concocted.

"No, Isabel, I cannot simply tell you that Charles is Lucas's child. How nice that would be!" And she meant it too. "Someday I may tell you *that* story, but it is not for today. It is too painful. The people here, the ones I work with, just assume that Lucas is

Charles's father, because it is not unusual. Gentlemen often impregnate women of the lower classes. And my friends do not judge. And they are happy for me. At any rate, I am an educated woman in their minds, and not so much lower than Lucas." Gwynne took a deep breath. Isabel was nodding, her eyes and ears focussed on everything she, her sister-in-law-to-be, was transmitting. Even so, how much more could she tell her?

"Then why, dear Gwynne, is my brother so anxious to forego all formality, and cause such confusion and disruption to the state of mind of our most wonderful guardians, who have so selflessly dedicated themselves to our happiness? Why can't he give this little bit of joy to them and have a proper wedding?"

"Because, Isabel," Gwynne carefully began, "your brother is not as free as you think he is." She sighed. Had she divulged too much, too little? Would Isabel understand? What did this exquisite, pampered, intelligent, and good woman know of the world? Could she take this thought to its logical conclusion? Could she forgive her brother his "precipitous" marriage because he had already consummated his love, was sinfully enjoying the pleasures of the flesh, and therefore needed to absolve himself through the religious rite of marriage as soon as possible? Isabel sat. She puzzled. She weighed. She struggled. Gwynne watched and prayed for her to comprehend. She realized that she wanted this woman's approval, although not sure why. But she wanted it. Then she saw on Isabel's face the recognition of the truth, the surprise, the discomfort, the reluctance to accept. Isabel stared long and hard at her, trying to grasp...what?...her lack of embarrassment at having performed an act exclusively the right of the properly married?

"But, do you mean, that for you, there is no need for actual marriage, but for my brother, less free than you, there is?" Isabel looked pained. It was so much to take in.

"Yes," she answered. "I am your brother's wife, whether we take vows or not before a minister of the Lord. I love him completely."

There followed after this admission a quick intake of breath from Isabel, who then responded. "I know. I know you love each other. But why, why do something reprehensible? It isn't necessary."

"But it *was* necessary...to us." Now Gwynne lowered her eyes. She could not bear the weight of Isabel's shock. She had gone too far. The lie would have been better. "I'm sorry, Isabel. I should have lied to you. Everyone else thinks that Charles is Lucas's. I let them think that. He behaves like Charles's father, so what difference would it make?" She had made a grave error in judgement. Between herself and Lucas there had never been any subterfuge. There had always been only the naked truth. But she could not presume that his sister would accept this truth. Tears sprang to her eyes. She had hurt Lucas's sister, a person he loved and admired. Yes, she had gone too far. Lucas, so like his sister in many ways, was different. He had been hurt by life and the wounds could only be healed by the truth. But Isabel had not been thrown from a carriage hurtling into the abyss. She had not witnessed the demise of her parents. She had never felt unworthy. Despite her expanded intellect, she lived in a proscribed environment. She accepted the rules of society, even though she felt burdened by them. Gwynne lifted her tear-stained face to Isabel. They looked at each other across that great social divide.

Finally, Isabel spoke. "I...I...could not ever be like you. I do not know what has happened to you to make you be the way you are. But I accept that your past has made you this way and mine has made me be the way I am. It is possible that even in time I will never be able to fully comprehend why you and Lucas have chosen this path." Now her voice grew quieter. "But I admire your courage, the courage to tell me the truth. You could so easily have lied. It's true. But you didn't. I think you are a remarkable person.

I have never encountered anyone like you. You must give me time to digest all that I have learned from you." Isabel looked bereft, almost lost, as if what had moored her to the earth had forsaken her, and she felt as if she were going to topple over. Instead, she stood up. Did she want to extricate herself from this place, the contaminated witness to her brother's sordid attachment to a woman without honour? Had her brother's chosen bride just destroyed her imperfect but controllable universe? Gwynne waited for whatever judgement would rain down upon her. Surely Isabel had more to say than that she was a remarkable person. Gwynne did not rise. She only raised her eyes. She felt as if she were about to be punished.

Isabel's chest heaved, but she looked at Gwynne with something like warmth in her eyes. "What is so baffling to me is that I see you as a good and morally upright woman. And yet," here she shook her head in desperation, "and yet, no good and morally upright woman of my acquaintance, of my former acquaintance, would ever do what you have done. Do you understand my bewilderment? The situation is all so unacceptable, but *you* are not!" Isabel spoke these last words in a much louder voice and used her arms and hands to express her total frustration.

And now Gwynne had to stand up, too. She had to insist upon her equality with this ambassador of her lofty social class. She was not a dishonourable woman and Isabel had made that clear. "Perhaps, Isabel, though you may think now that the deed is ignominious—although, as you say, the female perpetrator of that deed is not—perhaps the deed itself is not what you judge it to be. Every deed enacted must be judged through the people who perform it. Lying with a man does not exist in and of itself without any distinctiveness. When a man takes from a woman what she is not willing to give, then, yes, that deed represents an act of evil." Gwynne almost faltered at this point. She stared down at her hands as they pressed against the top of the table, as if trying to gain strength from its solidity. This moment of pause in her forceful defence of herself was enough to allow Isabel to continue the thought she was proposing.

"And so, you are saying that when a man and a woman truly love each other, and...and...are not taking anything away from each other...the act itself must be viewed differently. What you and my brother are doing together, by mutual agreement..." Here Gwynne nodded, because it was by mutual agreement, although perhaps initiated by herself...for it had been the right time, and she had not discouraged her impulse to seek fruition to a promise delivered so many months before..."...should be considered as right and good because no one is being hurt...but...but don't we have commandments for a reason? What kind of society would we be without our commandments, which we must uphold in order to preserve...to preserve..." Isabel's hands searched the air for that conclusive word, and it was Gwynne who finally provided it.

"Civilization?" Isabel nodded. "What civilization would that be, Isabel? The civilization that engaged in a devastating, senseless war in the Crimea? Do you know how many were maimed, were killed, or died of starvation and cholera? Can you not imagine how uncivilized those hospital wards would seem to you if you had had the opportunity to step inside one? You would have lost your belief in civilization in seconds. You would have seen instantly that there is only one commandment: Do not hurt a fellow human. That and only that. I am afraid there is no civilization without adherence to this commandment. And the fact that your brother and I lie with each other, without the sanction of the Church, has no impact on our morality as humans, on our ability to create a civilized environment for humans." She had said it. She had finally vocalized the lessons learned in war. She had needed to say these things for a long time, but she had not considered to whom she was delivering these statements of belief. Had she been unthinking? Had she hurt a fellow human being, not just anyone, but the woman who would be a sister, in order to find release from the pain of her own nightmare, of her own dreadful awakening to the truth of the world's sorry state of affairs? She looked guiltily into the eyes of her interlocutor. Isabel seemed ready to cry. She had pushed Isabel too soon and too far into the muck and mire of reality. "Forgive me, Isabel. You do not deserve my preaching. I have gone too far in my desire to defend what can only seem to you as sins. Perhaps now we can never be friends, something that your dear brother has always wanted. It is my fault. If you hate me—"

"—hate you? How can I hate you? Never has anyone ever been so honest and forthright with me! Never has anyone so eloquently put me in my place. I am a spoiled princess whose first real taste of reality has taken place right here in your very flat. I have so much to learn from you." Her voice broke. Despite her avowal to the contrary, to the fact that she did not hate her, Isabel could not prevent the tears from falling. Gwynne went around the table to be at the poor woman's side. Should she take her in her arms? She hesitated momentarily, and then she finally did. Isabel sobbed and Gwynne knew that she had let the princess out of her cage. Isabel sobbed for her own stilted youth, for the artificiality and artifice of her upbringing. Lucas had been right. His sister *was* capable of making the intellectual leap. Only being a woman had prevented her from escape.

When Isabel finally pulled away from Gwynne and her breathing began to slow, she looked straight into Gwynne's eyes. "I do not really know if I can fully fathom...yet...what I have heard in here today. But I know that I am able to concentrate my thoughts on the positive outcome of my brother's good fortune in finding you." She shook her head slowly, sagely even. Yes, she had learned much today. "Perhaps one day, I will have such good fortune, too."

"My dear Isabel, fortune is staring straight in your face." There was a knock at the door. Rupert called to both of them, and Isabel turned round and reached for the door handle, twisted it, and let fortune into the room.

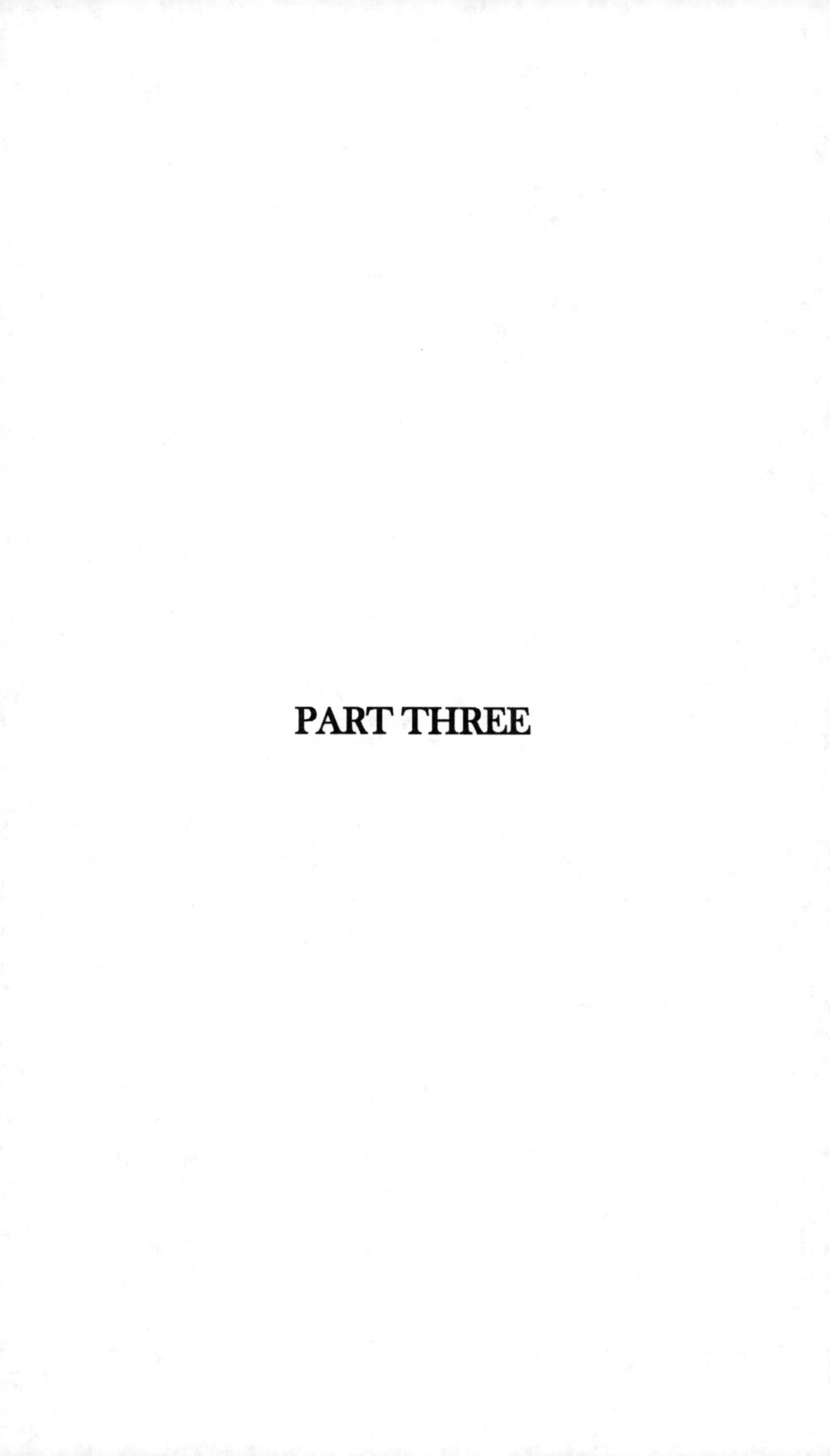

PART THREE

Chapter XXV

Winter was upon them again, although the end of the previous year had been so much colder. As Gwynne went about the girls' ward and the boys' ward, now full of children on the mend in their beds, floating in and out of necessary sleep, or playing on the floor with some toy—they were quite well-stocked these days in the matter of toys—or using crayons to fill paper with their imaginative renderings of what they saw and felt, she remembered those weeks of snow, spreading over the streets that usually seemed so dark and damp in this neighbourhood. It was warmer, and rainier, and the air in the narrow passageways was certainly quite foul, but the presence of their little hospital lightened the atmosphere considerably. She smiled at her memories, all her memories of the past year. Life had certainly changed for her. The rhythm of this life was gratifying and continuously brought new and exciting challenges, not just for her, but for her incredible family—her fellow workers, brothers and sisters all of them, as well as the more intimate constituents of her family, Lucas and Charles. Today, in fact, she had remarked to Lucas that a new member of their family would be joining them at the end of next summer. He had embraced her, lifted her off the ground, and literally danced for joy. She was feeling strong, stronger than the last time. She had worked quite solidly almost right up until Charles was born, and knew that, barring some sudden misfortune, she was capable of continuing to work by Lucas's side through the coming months. She had had to convince him that this was perfectly suitable in the world of the poor and less fortunate, although socially superior females kept to their confinement during this period. Truth be told, he didn't give her much argument, because he was barely paying attention to such matters, so consumed was he by the happiness of the moment. Since their at-home servants Susan and Peter also had a baby now, they had created a little nursery in their rented rooms, and often Charles stayed there as well during the working day. Selina, too, at least a few days a week, came and played with Charles in their home under the supervision of a nanny. Eventually a teacher was to be hired when the children would be of an age to begin their learning. Lucas's aunt Edith was seriously considering taking in all the orphans that had made their way to the hospital and had since been cured of whatever had ailed them. She wanted to bring them to live in the healthful air of Kent. There were one or two buildings on their estate that could be used to house the children. This would probably happen sometime in the New Year after Lucas's uncle retired from the House of Lords and would spend most of his time in the country with his wife. Both of them seemed rather excited by the new undertaking they were considering. What generous people they were! Gwynne was truly fortunate to have them as her parents through marriage. And they never forced her to take a prominent role as the wife of their nephew in society. They understood the seriousness of her vocation and all the stamina that it demanded. She was not even sure how many of their acquaintances were actually aware of the kind of marriage Lucas had contracted. At any rate all the excitement at the moment was being generated by the "official" coming marriage of Rupert and Isabel. After she and Lucas had been happily married months ago at the very centre of their work environment, it had not taken Rupert very long before he admitted his love for Isabel. He had proposed marriage within weeks of their own, and naturally, Isabel had gleefully accepted. The marriage of course would take place in Kent and Rupert and Isabel would most probably live in the Chelsea house. Gwynne herself had never had any desire to go and live there. Lucas had offered but she was perfectly delighted to remain where they were with fewer servants always about the place. She was the daughter of a wheelwright and a governess and had grown up in a small country cottage. Yes, she had been privileged in her education, but she was never one for a massive mansion consuming her energies in its overwhelming management. She was content to have fewer tasks to accomplish because of the addition of a few servants in her life, to have a day of freedom to spend with her husband and son, and not to be plagued by having to make an inordinate amount of daily decisions in the running of an enormous household. If Isabel wished to do that, she could, yet she suspected that the energy needed to run her school, expanding as it was with new students from Whitechapel's poverty-stricken streets, would only be enough to accomplish that singular goal, and a competent housekeeper would definitely be necessary to maintain the Chelsea establishment.

Gwynne's friendship with Isabel had developed slowly but surely. She supposed that the very fact of her marriage to her brother had made Isabel's relationship with her easier. She and Lucas were no longer living in sin. But Gwynne never expressed less than the truth to her sister-in-law, no matter how difficult to swallow. She sincerely believed that Isabel was grateful for this. And anyway, spending so much of her time in East London had rubbed off on this supremely elegant lady. She was more real, less vague, as Lucas would say. Lucas had told her that the more coiffed and comely his sister became according to society's strict rules of fashion, the less vivid and vibrant she also became. Now Isabel, like Gwynne and the other female employees of the hospital, wore the simple uniform, and she was proud of it, too. She was a worker and a woman, no longer an overindulged princess. She no longer needed the approval of society. Isabel was on the road to defining her identity for herself and by herself. It was quite an achievement and she and Lucas had had much to do with this transformation. A great deal had been achieved in the last year by all of them. To think of her starving self in the weeks before Christmas last year, ready to throw herself into the arms of any male willing to pay her! What a horrendous thought! And yet, here she was a year later, an accomplished nurse running a hospital together with her husband, respected by all, and viewed as an equal. Even the great Miss Nightingale had not actually been able to realize such a feat. It had been more like a dream for her. Lucas was pressing her lately about taking the plunge and going together with Rupert and Isabel to meet this august and consummate health practitioner, to talk about what they had achieved so far, and about what might be embarked upon in the future. Yes, this possible encounter was something that she could now ponder and make come true.

While she was changing the dressing of a five-year-old girl whose arm had been severely cut, probably wilfully, by an angry older brother, Gwynne heard a commotion going on at the front door of the hospital. It was not necessary for her to check on whatever was taking place, because both Rupert and Lucas were about. The boys, Phillip, Malcolm, and Robert were downstairs at their lessons with Isabel. In a short while, the school was to be moved up to the floor above the hospital because as soon as a tenant left, Gaunt was eager to rent the premises to them, and physical expansion was definitely necessary. Eventually, she supposed they would take over the entire building. When Jonathan and his son would be finished renovating the room upstairs and Isabel transferred the tables and desks up there, the classroom on the ground floor would become the home of Ally, Sophie, and her baby. This was necessary because Rupert needed his own surgery at this point in time, and what was first Phillip's and Malcolm's quarters and eventually that of Ally and Sophie would now serve to house all of Rupert's equipment. Her own little apartment next door was being used for diverse purposes although it still looked like her place. The student doctors who now were an essential part of the establishment often slept there at night. Sophie did much of the cooking there and the staff often ate there as well. Too much happened at the heart of the hospital with patients and parents waiting to be seen and people moving in and out of the examining room, the bathing room, and the wards. Commotion was the norm and that is why Gwynne did not stop what she was doing to check on the new event. She expected to hear Lucas's voice calming some parent and then the door to the examining room closing. But the noise continued. Something was definitely wrong. Perhaps some child was on the verge of death? Gwynne quickly finished with the little girl and put her into her bed, pulling the blanket up to the child's neck. She kissed her on the forehead and walked over to the door of the ward to see if she was urgently needed.

There were so many people about it was hard to see the state of health of the newcomer. It was Robert and Phillip who seemed to be carrying someone. Isabel was following them. There were also two plumbers at the entrance. They had come to install some new tubs in the bathing room. Lucas and Rupert were running out of the surgery to the aid of the patient. When the plumbers moved aside, Gwynne saw the blood pouring from lacerations all over the body of the female victim of some enraged perpetrator. It was impossible to tell whether she could be saved after so much loss of blood. And yet she had saved many a soldier with multiple wounds in the Crimean War and knew that a sea of red was not any reason at all to give up. Lucas turned and directly looked at her. It was a sign that he wanted her by his side. She quickly approached the group as Phillip went to get the push-chair in which to lay the patient, and Rupert took his place to support the almost lifeless body. At this moment one of the plumbers made a very loud comment.

"You canna try to save 'er! She's not a child! She be a woman of the streets an' this be a children's hospital! Do ye intend to treat any ailin' whore that makes 'er way 'ere?! She should ha' known better than to come 'ere!"

As soon as he spoke everyone stopped in their tracks. Rupert and Lucas just stared at each other, not knowing how to proceed. To be sure they were a children's hospital, but the woman was dying, and painted face or not, she deserved medical attention in a room full of capable people. Gwynne pushed her way through to her.

"We may be a children's hospital, but I am still Nurse Gwynne and I have never turned anyone in need away from my door. Phillip, if this hospital does not have the legal right to treat her, then place her in the chair and take her to my old room next door!"

"I will assist you, Gwynne," Isabel immediately spoke up. As Robert and Rupert gently lay the patient onto the push-chair, Lucas immediately came to life.

"Dr. Keynes, how old do you think this patient is? She doesn't look more than fifteen to me."

"You're absolutely right, Dr. Lacey. Her face may be gaudy, but she is probably just a girl."

"Right," Lucas reconfirmed his colleague's affirmation. "Phillip, bring her into the examining room immediately. We will all treat this 'child' together. Nurse Gwynne, your skills on the battlefield will be paramount." Lucas nodded at her and all of them followed Phillip, pushing the patient into the surgery.

Gwynne turned around to look at Isabel. "I think more hands are necessary, and Ally is not at work today. Jane is running an errand, and Sylvia and the other washer women are in the laundry. Sophie is nursing her baby next door. I will take you up on your offer of assistance." Isabel nodded vigorously and strode stalwartly into the surgery. Her complexion was a little pale. She may have been scared at her own instantaneous overture to help, but Gwynne knew she would never back down now and who knew how useful all her years of needlework in the drawing-room could prove when faced with sewing up the cuts and wounds wreaked on this poor girl of the streets? She had confidence in Isabel. She would rather Isabel at her side as a nurse than a hundred other ladies. As they entered the operating theatre, she placed a hand on Isabel's arm and gave it a small squeeze. Isabel turned to her, and Gwynne smiled.

"You will do fine. I will tell you exactly what I need." Isabel took a deep breath and turned her gaze back on the patient being laid by the men onto the bed.

*

Rupert and Lucas were the only ones left in the surgery. It looked as if a war had been fought in the room. There was blood on the floor, bloody towels and bandages covering tables, the bed, and the counters. The utensils used in their attempt to save the woman from bleeding to death were heaped helter-skelter on all the surfaces the room had to offer. Rupert and Lucas were sitting on two chairs beneath the window. To Lucas, Rupert looked dazed and drained of all energy. Not that he, too, felt any different. The women, however, were still at work. They were making the patient as comfortable as possible on the ward. Jane had returned and was lending a hand. He had never seen so many cuts on a person's body in his life! The man who owned her was a savage. All of a sudden, Rupert, on the same wavelength as himself, came to life.

"I think he wanted to make her die a slow death. He could easily have stabbed her and killed her outright. Instead, he just slashed her wherever he could." Rupert took a deep breath. "Did you notice he didn't touch her face at all? Almost as if he considered that he might want to use her again for his nefarious purposes." Rupert shook his head. He was trying to fathom something unfathomable.

Lucas stretched his legs out in front of him and leaned his head back until it hit the top of the chair. His hands lay on his thighs. He had no words either. There was no way to understand such brutality. It was beyond him. He almost felt like crying. And yet Gwynne and Isabel were carrying on, doing their nurturing, their caring, their comforting. "Do you think women are stronger than men, Rupert?"

Rupert leaned forward and placed his elbows on his knees, dropping his head into his hands. After a few seconds, he raised himself up and looked squarely at his friend. "I do believe that *our* women are, at any rate. Gwynne is unbelievable. And Isabel! She can sew, I mean suture, like any well-trained surgical nurse. Their hands were moving like the wind. *They* staunched the bloodletting. *They* saved that woman's life, or at least I hope so. We won't know for a while, but still, their effort was valiant." He stopped his flood of praise momentarily, and then added, "Have you ever heard Gwynne talking with the children...no...I mean, have you ever seen her listening to them tell her their horror stories? They talk and then they get better. She's like a magician drawing out their innermost feelings. Sometimes they whisper. Sometimes they cry. Sometimes the telling comes out in a rush, sometimes little by little, interspersed with sighs or whimpers. What kind of medicine is she administering, Lucas? How does she do it?"

Lucas smiled, happy that his friend was beginning to realize the uncanny merits of his beloved. "I have no idea, Rupert, but I can tell you that I have been the recipient of her tenderness. She has saved my life."

"I was under the impression," Rupert responded, looking inquiringly at Lucas, "that you had saved hers from the wolves of destitution."

Lucas shook his head. Again, he felt the urge to cry. A year ago, he might have died had he not met with Gwynne's benevolence. He sighed deeply and moved to rise from his chair. It would be better to start tidying up and restore some order to the surgery. He was not ready for Rupert to see the tears begin to well up in his eyes.

Rupert said nothing as Lucas began to pick up the discarded blood-soaked bandages from the floor. Finally, from his seated position, he commented on the task that Lucas was trying to complete, weary though he was. "Perhaps we can let our student,

Doctor Powell, do this work. He loves to clean. He is the neatest person I have ever seen...and unbelievably thorough. He will move a scalpel a fraction of an inch over if the distance between it and the one beside it is not equal to the distances between the other instruments." Rupert chuckled and Lucas joined him after this humorous description of their favourite helper. Rupert added, "But he will make a decent doctor. Of this, I am sure." Lucas nodded in agreement.

Jane came into the room at this point. "Why don't ye two go next door to Gwynne's ol' place and 'ave a cuppa tea? Sophie's baby is fast asleep. She can 'elp me. Gwynne an' Isabel can join you later when they's finished." Rupert and Lucas were only too willing to escape the scene of carnage. They removed their sullied surgical aprons, threw them into the basket, which would be taken down to the laundry, and exited.

Lucas put the kettle onto the stove and lit the fire. He filled the pot with tea. Rupert was already sitting at the table. When the water had boiled, he poured it into the pot and then placed the pot in front of Rupert. He got the cups from the cupboard and then the milk that was sitting in a jug on the outdoor landing outside the back door. It was quite chilly outside, enough to keep the milk from going bad. When he sat and gazed at his friend opposite him, he distinctly felt that Rupert looked uncomfortable, as if he were pondering something difficult to say. When he didn't speak, Lucas filled the bottoms of the cups with some milk and passed the sugar bowl to his brother-in-arms, soon to be brother-in-law. What was bothering him? Lucas decided to pour the tea and wait. They both drank for a while, thankful for the warmth and the sustenance. Then he began the conversation. "You know...today...we...uh...learned a great deal from our women. That plumber stymied us, made us irresolute in our duties...but Gwynne and Isabel did not hesitate. That girl..." Here he pointed towards their hospital next door as he mentioned the last patient.

"Is in their debt...and...and so are we. We behaved like fools, don't you think? Is that what is bothering you?"

Rupert squirmed uncomfortably in his chair. He drank some more tea and then placed the cup back on the table. He sighed. "I hope it won't make Isabel change her mind about me. She is so much better than me. Lucas, I am utterly and completely in love with her."

"I know." Lucas smiled broadly. "My sister is like no other. I have always felt that way. I didn't...and don't deserve her as a sister. But don't worry." Lucas gently slapped Rupert's arm. "She loves you, too. You make a great pair—my sister and my best friend. There is no other for you but her."

Rupert leaned away from Lucas but stared directly into his eyes. "You know, Isabel and I were talking about this for the last several days." He stopped and swallowed before he continued. "Lucas, how long have we known each other?"

Lucas was rather startled at this question. Where was this conversation going? "Why, a decade, I think. From when we started university and we are both thirty, now."

Rupert began nodding. "Do you think you know me well?"

"What's wrong, Rupert?"

"Answer me, please."

"Yes, I think so."

"And do you think you knew me, uh...almost as well, when we were students, considering we travelled together and spent so much time together."

Lucas felt suddenly uneasy about the trajectory of this strange dialogue. "Tell me, Rupert, what is bothering you? I don't understand."

"Well, I think I divulged a great deal of information to you about myself, about the things I loved, about the things I wanted in my life. I was very open with you. Was I not?"

"Yes, Rupert, yes, yes, you were." Rupert was very still as he spoke, but Lucas was getting more agitated. His last rejoinder was accompanied by the movement of both his hands. He was definitely revealing his frustration with these questions.

Rupert drew his body even more backwards, his hands trailing along the table, following this movement, until they reached the edge. Then he brought his upper body forward and gripped the end of the table, almost as if he were ready to spring up and pounce. But he didn't. He waited and took several breaths before speaking. The words came out slowly and were well-enunciated, as if he were somehow containing his anger. "Your sister and I were wondering, Lucas, why you never considered introducing us earlier. Surely if you were so close to your beloved sister, and you were in possession of so much knowledge of my character, you might have come to the conclusion years ago that 'there was no other for me but her' as you have just so eloquently expressed."

His friend's words stabbed him with the force of a hurricane. He would not bleed from these words as the girl-prostitute had from the knife wielded by her tormentor, but it was certainly true that he had never before felt such a powerful sting of anger from a person he loved. And in fact, he was mostly stunned by the truth of Rupert's statement. His lack of real connection to his sister and his friend in the last decade was obvious. He had been so consumed by his own tortured thoughts that he had had no room in his heart for the two most important people in his life at the time. How could they even have tolerated him? What feat of prophecy had Gwynne managed to pull from her nurse's bag of tricks to enable her to have any faith in his eventual transformation into a functional human being? She had waved her wand and produced a miracle. How unworthy he had been of Isabel and Rupert's love. Lucas slumped in his chair, hollowed out by this new awareness of his perfidy. Could he actually tell Rupert of his state of mind in the years leading up to his arrival in this very setting, the setting that had been witness to his metamorphosis? He took a deep breath. He let the tears fall. And then he spoke.

"Rupert, I have never been honest with you...or...or Isabel, for that matter, about all that I was...was...going through in those years, in the years before I met Gwynne." He swallowed noisily. He wiped a shirtsleeve across his face. He did not look at Rupert. He stared at the table. Rupert was not a stranger, as Gwynne had been. Rupert was a person that he had failed. "I did not think of you. I did not think of Isabel in those years. I had no thought of your happiness. I was totally engulfed by my own malaise." He glanced quickly at Rupert's face, but just as suddenly dropped his gaze downward. He wished to see his friend's reaction, but he just as much did not want to be faced with the truth. In that flash of sight, he had only noticed that Rupert was listening intently, totally focussed on his words and what they meant. Lucas went on. "Being sick in mind is not an excuse. Carrying the burden of a guilt so great as to make one little more than a mindless and heartless machine, functioning barely and mostly through force of habit, is not an excuse. I have no excuse for being so totally self-involved as to not be able to imagine the possibility of shared happiness in others. Love was the furthest thing from my mind. And the truth is, had I not met Gwynne at the precise moment in which I did, I would not be sitting in front of you now. I would have thrown myself off some bridge into the Thames!"

"And drowned as your parents had."

Another stunning bolt of truth from the mouth of the man he had wronged. Now Lucas lifted his head and really looked at the face of his interlocutor. Rupert had made all of the necessary mental leaps. He had instantly understood. So, Lucas just nodded. There was no other response. And besides, he felt drained of all words. His tears had stopped by now. In a short space of time all had been squeezed out of him. Should he add an apology? But strangely enough, the apology was not coming from his own lips. It was coming from the lips of the person who had been his companion all those years ago.

"Lucas, I am sorry for not having been mindful of your predicament. Of course, I knew how you had lost your parents and when it happened, but you had a family, and your relationship to your aunt and uncle seemed so much like a regular son-parent connection, so much like my own with my parents that I hardly imagined that you could still be suffering from the loss of your real ones. It never occurred to me." Here Rupert pointed at his chest. "*I* was the selfish one. That lack of imagination or...or concern on my part prevented me from being able to help you." There was a pause in his flow of words. It appeared that Rupert was deep in thought. Then finally he shaped that thought. "Surely you do not believe that you were somehow at fault for the accident that killed them. That's preposterous. You were six years old. Is that the guilt of which you are speaking?"

Again, Lucas could do nothing but nod.

"I see. And Isabel never knew this."

Lucas shook his head.

"And so, you waited until it got so bad that you just had to tell someone, someone whom you instantly trusted would take that sense of guilt and reshape it into something else. Am I right?"

Had he thought that Gwynne would refashion his narrative differently? Or had he just poured out his heart to her because he could not help himself? He really didn't know. Perhaps she would know. He would have to ask her. "I don't know Rupert. I don't know precisely what I was thinking. I only wanted what she had to offer. I wanted to wrap myself up in her...in the aura of her...in her arms...in her intensity."

"She did save you, after all, my dear Lucas."

"Yes, she did."

"And I am utterly grateful," pronounced Rupert ever so solemnly.

Chapter XXVI

"Lucas, we have to get that girl out of the hospital, out of East London. She isn't safe. Next time, her keeper will kill her. He has beaten her with his belt so many times, her back is constantly blue. She is fifteen years old, and she is forced sometimes to be with twelve different men in a night. And when she goes out during the day, she is always followed. Once when she tried to run away during the day, some urchin notified a police constable, and she was caught and brought to the station, where she would have been charged for theft of the clothes on her back. Instead, the keeper came and paid off the sergeant, took her back, and kept her in the brothel half-naked, so she could not go out into the streets. She brings in a great deal of money but gets none of it. They practically starve her. And when they have completely used her up, they will throw her into the streets with the swill!" Gwynne was passionately making her plea to Lucas for the saving of the child-prostitute, Claire. They were at home and preparing to go to bed after a hectic day at the hospital. Lucas shook his head in wonder. London was home to so much horror, of the kind that only humans could make. He, on the other hand, was in a clean, well-heated room, his stomach full, and getting into a comfortable bed with a woman who would lovingly nurture his body and soul even further than the generous luxuries he had always known.

"The problem is that we don't know what that miserable plumber could say to his mates in the pub. And what if someone overhears him, someone close to that brothel-keeper, or that villain himself? We don't have guards at the hospital. We don't have policemen protecting the premises from men with malice in their hearts. Claire is not safe," Gwynne repeated. She got into bed and pulled the quilt to her chin. She lay her head on the pillow but faced Lucas, who was also turned towards her. He wanted to stroke her face and calm her with soothing words. But that was not what Gwynne wanted. She wanted him to offer up a solution. So he did.

"Let us take her to Kent when we go down there for Christmas. She can become a kitchen maid or...or...she can be the first orphan in my aunt's orphanage and help take care of the smaller children."

"But, Lucas, we aren't going for another week. Her keeper could come at any time. He owns her and her enslavement enriches him." Although Lucas refrained from touching her, Gwynne stretched her hand to his face and caressed his cheek and then his hair. "She needs a chance to live, not like a plaything for the pleasure of men, but like a human being of value." Gwynne almost choked on these last words. Her eyes began to glisten with tears. "We can't let her die before she has even begun to live. She is really just a child." Lucas moved closer and wrapped his arms around Gwynne. She lay her head on his chest and began to cry.

"We could bring her here to convalesce from her wounds. She really is still quite frail." Lucas hesitated for a moment. "Or better still, tomorrow morning we could take her to the Chelsea house and Isabel could take care of her there. She has stopped teaching for the Christmas season. In a few days, she can take Claire with her to Kent. I will urge Rupert to go with them. He and Isabel are meant to stay for some days in Kent and then go to his parents' estate in Somerset. Isabel would never say no. Claire means a great deal to her."

"But Lucas, what if something happens to her tonight?"

"Both the students, Drs. Powell and Bainbridge, are there tonight...but...if you want, I can go back there now and bring her home." He stirred and sat up, pulling Gwynne into a seated position as well. "Is that what you wish?" He placed a finger under her chin and raised her head. Not that he really looked forward to getting up and getting dressed and heading out into the cold, but Gwynne was beside herself. Clearly, she felt the responsibility of a sister to this girl who had been punished by the evil of men. Who could blame her? She herself could have suffered a similar fate had not her mother been able to give her that introduction to Miss Nightingale when she was but sixteen. Gwynne had not escaped pain, but she had certainly escaped the dire circumstances of this particular child, and then she had ultimately learned a skill that could sustain her through life, one that had given her something to live for.

"I should have spoken up earlier, before we left the hospital. It was only the sight of that plumber finishing up his work in the bathing-room that made me imagine the worst. I hadn't thought about her safety before that. And it wasn't until this afternoon that she revealed to me the horror of her life." Gwynne shook her head in frustration. "I wasn't thinking straight when we left work. I was thinking about *her* and her plight, but not about her owner's greed and possible willingness to assail the hospital in order to get his property back. Oh, Lucas, that is all she is to him. Doesn't she deserve better?" This last question came out in a wail.

Lucas drew Gwynne closer to him and embraced her as vigorously as possible. He was willing to believe that some of her tears were for herself. His wife was always so strong for everyone, but he—and he considered this his good fortune—got to see another side of her, when she felt overcome by all the cruelty that existed in the world. He had wanted to broach the subject that Rupert had brought up the day before—whether she believed that in some way, when he had confided to her his extreme sense of guilt for the tragedy that had befallen his family that what he had wanted was in fact what he got—a whole other interpretation of events. Was it just possible that somewhere inside of him he was prepared to accept an alternate version, as if he had unconsciously understood that he was not responsible for the death of his parents? Because hadn't he embraced her rendering readily, leaping at it in fact, ingesting it voraciously, and allowing it to transform his vision of life itself? But such a conversation was not going to take place tonight. He had been learning in these months following their marriage or more accurately their cohabitation, that there was a back and forth in the fulfilling of each of their needs. Sometimes it wasn't his turn. And tonight, it wasn't. And although it would be onerous to tear himself from the warmth of her body, he knew that he had to in order to alleviate his wife's burden of guilt towards the girl. If Gwynne thought that she should have known better than to leave Claire in East London at the mercy of the whims of her owner's pitiless heart, then who was he to contest her?

"Fortunately, the Lacey household carriage is here tonight and not in Chelsea. I can harness the horses myself without having to wake any of the servants. Do you think that Claire can walk down the stairs herself or will I have to carry her?"

"Oh, Lucas, thank you. I will come with you and help in whatever way I can." Gwynne held his head in her hands and proceeded to kiss his lips, his cheeks, and his forehead.

"It is not necessary for you to disturb yourself. Stay at home and go to sleep."

But Gwynne got out of bed. "I will never be able to sleep. If I come, we will be faster and back here more quickly."

Lucas did not challenge her.

*

Thankfully Gwynne's premonition that Claire's depraved brothel keeper would be storming the gates did not come true. Lucas did not want to imagine the havoc that such a man could wreak on their establishment had he discovered his precious possession in their midst. He could still devise a means to retaliate if he came to know that Claire had been sheltered in their hospital. He would caution all of the staff to plead ignorance of her whereabouts after she had been treated. They could just say that she had been discharged and that vile man would have to scour the streets himself to find her. Hopefully that would be the end of it. But in some way the plumber may have been right. What they had done—and he was not sorry they had done it—might lead to more prostitutes in need showing up on their doorstep. Claire's brothel was within walking distance. This was something they would all have to discuss. Gwynne had treated prostitutes before when she was simply Nurse Gwynne and everyone in the neighbourhood knew that she would help anyone who required medical assistance. If it was not the keepers themselves, it could be the men who bought them that injured these women, and they deserved to be treated if not saved from a violent death.

When they were finally back in their warm bedroom, and Claire tucked safely away in a guest room, Lucas, although exhausted, brought up his misgivings about the outcome of their decision to treat Claire. He was seated, his back resting against the wall at the head of the bed. Gwynne was still undressing, and Lucas was hoping she would choose not to put on a nightdress even though it was winter. How he loved lying beside her nakedness all night long. He never wanted anything, not even a simple piece of cloth, to act as a barrier between them. That she was with child was not discernible in any way yet, would not be for a few months, and she was not feeling any discomfort. There was no caution against their intermingling. That would stop when she told him it was no longer possible because it was too hard for her. But her unclothed body would always be a delight. Seeking completion was not the only pleasure that two bodies could provide each other. This part of their life was the best reward he could ever have for choosing to live and not to die in that far-off time one year ago. It felt like aeons ago.

"What if I paid a visit to the bawdy house myself, and told the man in charge, this Mr. Frederick, as she calls him, that we will willingly seek to alleviate any illness or injury contracted by their girls? We cannot ultimately take in all of them, save them from their lives, I mean...and we have no idea anyway that this is what they would choose...but at least we could endeavour to keep them alive, and keep Frederick from setting fire to our establishment out of revenge. We thus keep him on our side."

"And allow him to continue thrashing them and starving them," commented Gwynne. Lucas happily noted that she did not seek out her nightshirt. She slid naked into bed beside him, brushing the skin of her legs along his.

"Yes, I suppose so," he answered as dejectedly as he knew she felt. "We cannot solve the problem of prostitution and the unwarranted punishments these women are constantly being subjected to. We can only be doctors and nurses."

"That man Frederick once brought me a girl who was dying. Her lungs were infected and beyond treatment. You may offer him whatever you like, but his instinct is not to save them. His instinct is to replace the sick ones with healthier specimens."

Lucas sighed. What she said was possibly, probably true. Gwynne lay her head on his chest, and he lifted his arm around her, letting his hand slide up and down her arm from shoulder to elbow. With his other hand he caressed her hair and face. Finally, he offered up his view of the situation. "I just want to make sure he is not an enemy. We cannot defend ourselves from the likes of him and his minions. He probably has thugs that do his dirty work for him. He has his business, and we have ours, but I don't want to get in his way, for the sake of our hospital. We can treat his girls when he allows them to come the best way we know how. It is possible that sometimes they may die from illness, disease, malnutrition, and the blows reigned down upon them, but if they come in time, then maybe we can save some of them. And perhaps he won't set fire to our precious hospital."

He could feel Gwynne's head nodding over the skin of his chest, and then she spoke. "We can wait a few days, see if he has somehow found out that we treated Claire. Maybe after we come back from Kent, you can do your negotiating with him. Right now, I am just relieved that Claire is with us and no longer prey to that hunter." And then Gwynne, who never ceased to amaze him, lifted herself up, placed one leg over his body, thereby straddling him for all intents and purposes, and brought her face above his own. She gently eased herself down and placed her lips upon his. He circled his arms around her back and yielded his mouth to hers. How did she intuit so completely what it was that he wished? How was it that he did not have to ask or speak of his desire for her? Where did she acquire that knack of understanding? And then she was whispering in his ear, answering his unspoken questions.

"I hope you don't mind my boldness, Lucas, but sometimes I just feel that I must wrap myself around you..." Her breathing was becoming more pronounced as he entered her and allowed her to encompass him. So, it was not that she knew so well what *he* wanted. It was better. It was that she wanted it, too, precisely at the moment that their joining was paramount in his mind.

*

When Gwynne, with a sigh, slipped out of his embrace, after their expenditure of passion, and lay down by his side, her arm sliding over his abdomen, leaving her hand to rest there, so the coolness of her departure was slightly less perceptible to him, Lucas also turned on his side and with his hand sought out the wet warmth between her legs. She let him delicately slip his finger inside and fondle the soft swelling that their commingling had created. He loved doing this, certainly before he plunged into her, but also after, not wanting to lose one drop of that moisture, not ever wanting to forget the anatomy of their love, this time, for all time. It was a way of remembering, of retaining, of acknowledging gratitude for his having stayed alive, for not having committed the sin of abandoning life before he had really experienced its essence and purpose. Ultimately, however, he withdrew his finger and lay back, his head against the pillow. There was something he had to say.

"Gwynne?"

"Yes."

"How...how did you know that I needed...your...your version of my history...I mean when we first met?" He was going to ask her then, wasn't he? The question was just coming out of him, as if...as if he could not stop it, now that he was thinking it. "Did you sense that I was...was seeking not just your absolution, but also that I...I...was open to reinterpretation?" Even if he stammered on every single word, he was going to ask her. "Did I confess to you because I could no longer hold it in, or because...because somehow, I...I...saw in you someone who would simply say: enough is enough. What you think happened did not happen. Here, instead, is what really happened."

Gwynne put her hands on either side of his face, and looked deep into his eyes. "Why are you asking me this...now, my love?"

"Because...because that is what Rupert immediately understood, when I told him about how you saved me. He understood that I was ready for a change in my faulty childish narrative."

"You told him?"

"Yes. I had to."

"Had to?"

"Yes. After we finished treating Claire and you, Isabel, and Jane were settling her into bed. Rupert and I went to have some tea. And he asked me point-blank how come I had never introduced him to Isabel all those years ago when we were students. He had a right to know that I was guilty of never having had a thought for them or their happiness. I had been completely remiss. And so, I told him why."

"You told him of the accident and the aftermath."

"Well, yes, but mostly about you and how you prevented me from throwing my life away. I would have...You know it. But I don't know if I told you everything that day because, as Rupert says, I was waiting for the perfect someone to show me the error of my self-judgement, or...or...just because I could no longer stop the outflow. It just had to come out."

"But why, Lucas, does it have to be 'either-or'?" Gwynne drew closer to his face and kissed him tenderly on his forehead and then on his lips. When she drew away, she smiled at him, and for Lucas, it was as if the air her lips had moved as she spread them, passed directly through his intake of breath and channelled down through his entire body to his toes. It was a sensation like no other. It connected him to her, soul to soul, perhaps not as triumphantly as body to body, the action so recently and memorably consummated. It was too subtle to compete with that, but it was not in any way fragile. It was as real and unforgettable. Lucas smiled back. He closed his eyes.

Chapter XXVII

Ally and Doctor Powell were treating a sickly infant in Lucas's examining room. Gwynne had sent them off with the mother to do both the diagnosis and treatment without her, because if they were going to be left alone for the next five days, what with Rupert and Lucas and herself away in Kent for Christmas, it was time for them to get as much practice as possible. It was not so much a question of skill, for they both had that as well as knowledge. It was a question of confidence. Their two medical students and Ally were ready for the challenge, and anxious to prove themselves. Gwynne imagined that it must have been hard for the two young men to tell their families that they would be working over the Christmas season, but the rewards were substantially greater than the losses. As for Ally, who had no other family than her co-workers in the hospital, she would be well taken care of by Jane and Jonathan. Gwynne felt guilty, mostly towards Ally, who was like a little sister to her. Young as she was, it was time for her to grow up, and become the reliable, competent mistress of her profession that she so obviously could.

This morning Lucas was seeing accountants and solicitors to do with the charity. Malcolm was off ordering supplies. Sophie was cooking next door, baby Rupert asleep in Charles's old crib. Charles and Selina and Peter and Susan's child were out with the nanny in the park. Jonathan and Robert were working on the new wing on the floor above her. Sylvia and her staff were in the laundry. Jane was bathing children, and so only Phillip was with her in the main space of the hospital. After putting more logs on the fire, Phillip was sitting at *his* desk, newly acquired for the purpose of writing down information about each patient. Phillip had discovered after all the months of learning with Isabel that he loved keeping neat written records, even of the money disbursed by the hospital. Malcolm was happy to make the journeys around town, talk to shopkeepers and the children and parents he knew in the streets. He had become a rather gregarious, good-humoured child. He had a loving surrogate mother in Sylvia, and a responsible older brother in Phillip. Phillip, on the other hand, had become wiser, more mature and serious. Gwynne realized that she truly loved him even though he had been reunited with his mother. She did not compete with Sylvia for his filial affection. There was no need for that. He knew she loved him in her way, and he certainly loved her back.

Gwynne's hands were busy—collecting and sorting dirty clothing and sheets to be brought down to the laundry, folding blankets and towels, washing floors—but her mind was keeping columns much as Phillip was with his pen, perhaps just in more detail, a detail that concerned the evolution and progress of her hospital and the people that made it what it was. She knew that others would have to join them soon, more nurses for her to teach, more cleaners to maintain the high standards of hygiene, when the upstairs floor became fully functional. Jane, too, would begin to delegate responsibilities to others and have less to do with the physical up-keep herself. Transformation of their once tiny hospital was in the offing, and nostalgic as she could be for the way things once were, she would have to accept the inevitable. And anyway, she was expecting a baby and would have to devote her energies to that new life.

The calm and quiet of the morning was broken by the ringing of the front doorbell. Phillip immediately rose to see if he was needed to help some child climb the stairs. He pushed the glass door to the entrance open and walked to the head of the stairs and peered down. Gwynne could hear what was presumably an adult trudging upwards towards their landing. Phillip stepped backwards through the open door into the entrance to the hospital. A large, well-dressed man with a scowl on his face filled the doorframe, looking beyond the boy and directly at Gwynne. Phillip moved out of his way, obviously intimidated by the glowering unfriendly figure before him, perhaps reminding him of his own previous master. Gwynne immediately came forward, wishing to somehow protect Phillip from harm.

"Mr. Frederick, how do you do? It has been a while since I have seen you. I hope you are well," she said rather formally, although knowing that a ruthless man such as the brothel keeper did not deserve such niceties.

"No chit-chat, Nurse Gwynne. You know why I am here."

"I believe I do. Would you please come in? Phillip and I were just about to have a cup of tea." She nodded at Phillip, who immediately went to the stove to prepare the drink. "You may join us, for I can see we have business to discuss."

"Business? You call kidnapping one of my girls 'business'?"

"Please sit down, Mr. Frederick." Gwynne pointed to the first chair at the large table where the staff often ate and drank. She herself went around to the other side and sat down.

The man finally entered the room, his hostility glaring in every step he took. But he did sit down. Gwynne's polite demeanour had had its effect. "Well, speak up, Nurse Gwynne," he uttered in frustration at her stalling.

"What can I say, Mr. Frederick? We did stitch Claire up as best as we could. We hope she will live. That is all I can say as her nurse, but I do speak for the doctors as well in this hospital. If by 'kidnapping' you mean that we kept her here to recuperate a few days after treatment, we had no choice. She was too weak to leave immediately. If you mean that now she is not capable of fulfilling her duties to you in as satisfactory a manner as before, surely you cannot blame us. We did not cause her injuries—"

"—Wh-what are you talking about? Do you mean to tell me she is no longer here!?" Frederick interrupted her.

"Yes, we let her go, presumably back to you, although she did not exactly say." Gwynne held her tongue now and watched the reaction to her news spread across the despicable face of this despicable man. Phillip brought two cups and two teaspoons to the table, and then returned with the pot of tea and some milk. The sugar bowl was already on the table. Instead of sitting down with them, he went back to his desk, but he did not take his eyes off the exchange between the two adults. Gwynne put milk into the cups and poured the tea. She pushed a spoon over to Frederick, who responded by picking it up and reaching over to take some sugar. After helping himself to three spoonfuls, he began to stir the tea in a thoughtful manner. Gwynne began to relax. She looked over at Phillip, who was behind Frederick, who could therefore not see Phillip's nod. He smiled at her in appreciation of her delicate performance.

Frederick began to sip his tea. He finally spoke: "I hope you understand the importance of the matter we are discussing, Nurse Gwynne."

Gwynne considered it a triumph that he continued to call her by her name. She believed it showed respect. "Whether a patient lives or dies is of the utmost importance to us, Mr. Frederick. Now, if you wish to discuss the future with me, then by all means, let us have that discussion. We..." She made a circular motion with her finger to indicate everyone in the hospital. "...are willing to aid in any way we can with the health and well-being of the girls who work in your establishment. This is a charity hospital, so no payment is required, but if you ever wish to make a donation, I can inform you of the name of the solicitor in charge of the operation. But there is one requirement, Mr. Frederick."

"And what would that be?" Frederick did not seem to like the sound of that. No one ever gave *him* orders.

"Well, if we deem it necessary for a girl to recuperate on the premises here for several days, I think you should heed our judgement. And perhaps, although this is only a suggestion, you should bring a girl who is feeling poorly here a wee bit sooner than the last time you came to me. The results of our encounter may have proved more fruitful." Was she being too forceful with this man? Could she have gone too far?

But he responded hastily, almost as if he wished to get away from her and her suggestions as soon as possible. "All right. All right. As you wish." He hurriedly finished his cup of tea and stood up. "You're sure she did not tell anyone where she might have gone?"

Gwynne looked up at Phillip. "Phillip knows everything that goes on in this place. Phillip," she addressed the boy in question. "Did Claire say where she was going?"

Frederick looked at the boy, too. Phillip shrugged and said, "She said nuffin', I mean nothing, about where she was goin', I mean going." Gwynne had to smile at Phillip's conscious efforts to improve his spoken English. Isabel would be proud.

Frederick headed toward the door. His mood was not good. Who would he take it out on? Gwynne shuddered to think.

Before he exited, Frederick turned back to Gwynne. Was he going to thank her? Was that too much to ask?

"Next time one of *my* girls shows up here without *my* knowledge, you'd do best to inform *me* immediately. I am a businessman, and *my* property represents *my* business. Do you understand?"

The tough exterior, and most probably interior, of the man was beginning to reassert itself. "To be sure, Mr. Frederick, but I hope in future, on these premises at any rate, you will refrain from calling your workers *property*. They are made of the same sinews, muscles, and organs as we are!"

Frederick slammed the door shut behind him in answer.

After a few moments, when he was sure that Frederick was out the door, Phillip began to laugh. Gwynne, too, could not help herself. They were both just so relieved that the ordeal was over. When their laughter was becoming quite raucous, Jane opened the door to the bathing room to inquire what was happening. Her question only made them laugh even more. Finally, Gwynne spoke. "I think, Phillip, we deserve another cup of tea."

"Right, Nurse Gwynne. Comin', I mean coming, right up!"

Chapter XXVIII

Gwynne seemed to be having several alone moments in these last few days—moments when she took stock of her life and that of her hospital. Dr. Bainbridge was with Ally in Rupert's examining room dealing with an ailing baby, and she had just left Dr. Powell in Lucas's examining room with a boy of twelve who had been seriously injured in an altercation with some grown man he did not yet wish to talk about. Perhaps at some time in the future she would get the child, whose name was Samuel, to be more forthcoming. He seemed a sad little fellow. And there did not appear to be any mother. Phillip was questioning the mother of the baby and taking down the notes in a notebook. He would later transfer the information to his record book. He was good at getting the background story, and he was very good at registering the information. She wondered what profession he might choose in the future, because he certainly had skills, both managerial and organizational.

Gwynne let Phillip know that she was going to her old apartment because Sophie had asked her to take the bread out of the oven at a particular time. She was out on a buying errand for her kitchen. Little Rupert was sleeping in his crib next to Phillip's desk. If he woke and needed his mother and she was not back yet, Phillip could always come next door and get her, but he seemed to know what to do with babies. He had received his experience from Charles. As Gwynne made her way into the hallway to the door of her recently vacated home, she felt a twinge of nostalgia, but maybe, she decided, it was not for the place, but for the fact that Charles had already gone down to Kent with his aunt Isabel. This morning, she and Lucas had not woken up to the boy's entry into their bed. It was the first time that she had been separated from him. Tonight, as well, she would sleep in a house that did not contain him. She wondered how he was doing but surmised that Lucas's aunt Edith was probably taking immensely good care of him. It was the Lady herself that had requested he come down before she and Lucas did, just because she wanted him all to herself for a few days. Gwynne entered the apartment and left the door ajar. Before she gathered the oven mitts and went over to the stove, she went to the sink and turned on the faucet. As she washed her hands, first removing her wedding ring, she thought of her own mother, who had never actually met Charles. She felt regret that she could not go home to see her. She wrote often to her mother, telling her of all the adventures of her little boy, as well as the adventure of marriage. Her mother knew she was with child now, but it was time to invite her parents to London. She and Lucas had been discussing this, and had agreed that they could come anytime in the New Year. There was certainly room in their rented house, even if two families, including that of their servants, lived there. It was quite sprawling. Peter and Susan had recently taken on another female servant to serve her and Lucas better, besides the nanny who had been with them quite a while now. What a task it was taking on a large house and household! Gwynne was grateful that it fell to Susan and not herself. She assumed that Susan liked her absolute freedom in running the place. Some women were much more interfering than she was. Susan need not worry that Gwynne would ever question her decisions. She probably would never give her a single order. At any rate, she hadn't yet. Not that she and Lucas ever entertained. They sometimes had dinner in the Chelsea house with Isabel and Rupert, and Lucas's aunt and uncle when they were in town. Lucas loved Mrs. Blunt's cooking, so why put Susan and Peter through such torture? They seemed to have enough work as it was. And now that they were going to spend three evenings in Kent, it had befallen Susan to alter three different gowns of Isabel's to fit Gwynne, who was slightly smaller. Gwynne had no intention of buying such clothes and Lucas would never have pushed her to do so. But Isabel, understanding how these things worked, was gracious enough to suggest remaking three of her dresses which she no longer wore so that Gwynne would have some measure of well-being in society. Thankfully only Rupert's parents would be there, besides the family...this time. Who knew in the future? Gwynne was really anxious about all the dressing up she had to do this Christmas. She was none too comfortable with the idea of spending time with a roomful of noble ladies and gentlemen. But she knew that both Lucas and Isabel would protect her if need be. She had passed through so many ordeals, not the least of which a bloody war, and yet the coming holiday on a country estate seemed so much more taxing.

After she finished removing the loaves of delicious-smelling bread from the oven—Sophie was a marvel in the kitchen—she went over to the fireplace to put on some more logs. It was a chilly morning. Perhaps it would be better to shut the door and allow the heat to remain inside. She stoked the fire, thinking about the morning that Lucas might be having. He had gone with Jonathan and Robert to see a workshop-storefront with rooms for living in the back. Jonathan needed a place to work in winter. In the warmer months he and Robert often worked in the open space behind the hospital, sometimes in the rooms that had been vacated by previous tenants in the building. But it was really time for him to have his own workshop and display area for other possible customers. It was also convenient to have a place to live behind the shop. The three of them, Jane, Jonathan, and Robert, were earning enough now to leave the horrible rooms the family shared two blocks from the hospital. Gwynne had visited their home on several occasions, and it was just too damp and dingy. They deserved better living quarters. Jane had visited this new place and was ready to move tomorrow, but Jonathan wanted Lucas to see it and approve of it. Lucas's presence would also give confidence to the landlord that Jonathan was a reliable tenant. All in all, it would be a good move for Gwynne's friends and she was happy for them.

Gwynne sat down in front of the hearth and with the long fire iron pushed the burning logs around so that the flames would be more substantial. As she sat there musing on her own and her extended family, there was a knock on the door. She stood up. Before she turned around, Phillip called to her:

"There's a gentleman here to see you, Nurse Gwynne. He says he knows you well." Phillip, then, presumably turned to the mysterious gentleman and told him he could go in. "She's by the fire, sir. I have to get back now to the hospital." Phillip then slipped away and back to his post. Gwynne slowly turned around, wondering who might be facing her and why he had come. What gentlemen did she know?

When she turned around and saw who it was, it took her breath away. She almost screamed. She dropped the iron rod, which fell clattering to the floor. It was true. There was a gentleman that she knew well—too well. She brought her hands up to her face. This was a moment she had been dreading for more than three years. The moment had finally come.

"Wh-what are you doing here, Edmund?"

He was standing in the doorway. He was grinning in his inimitable way. Gwynne never knew if it was a grin of pleasure or of cruelty. Who really knew what made this man happy? He looked older, larger. He was dressed impeccably well in a green wool overcoat, probably of the most recent fashion. She did not think that his larger size was due to some sport he had newly undertaken. She assumed that the sport of eating and drinking exceptionally well contributed to his newfound girth. Not that she would say that he was fat. He was just bulkier. However, she doubted that he was less agile than before. He could cross the room in seconds and pounce upon her as he had previously. Although the fire roared behind her, she shivered at the thought.

"What, no words of joy at seeing a long-lost friend? Where are your manners, *Nurse* Gwynne?" he said with sarcasm embedded in his forceful enunciation of her title. "So, you are a nurse now. Going off on your little sojourn to Crimea paid off, didn't it?" Now Edmund fully entered the room. First he turned and shut the door, and then he removed his top hat and gloves, and placed them along with his ivory-handled walking stick on the large table. Then he proceeded deeper into the room and faced her, leaving a space of several feet between them. Gwynne edged her way backwards, so that she could lay a hand on the wooden chair. If she needed, she could throw it at him, or place it between them somehow. Although Lucas was much taller, he never filled this room the way that Edmund did. Was this perception only her imagination, or did Edmund do that all the time, in whatever room he entered? There was just too much of him. She wanted to call Phillip to come back, but Edmund had shut the door, and presumably Phillip would not hear her. She was trapped. She felt as if she had always been trapped. Had it been folly to think that she could ever escape Edmund? She understood that it would not have been impossible to find her, but why oh why would he want to find her? What more could he take from her? She realized then that she had not returned her wedding ring to her finger. She did not even have that as defence against this foe, the most formidable foe of her life. She wanted to yell at him: *Why do you want to torment me? Haven't you done enough tormenting? Haven't you had an abundance of that particular pleasure?*

"Well, my dear Gwynne, you look ravishing, particularly in that little nurse's cap of yours." He pointed to it as he spoke these words. Gwynne took another slight step backwards as he raised his finger. It was as if she felt it preferable to burn herself rather than be touched by him.

Her mind was racing faster than any train she had ever been on. It was amazing to her that she could be so conscious of her position of weakness in relation to Edmund, and yet have the presence of mind to calculate all of her opportunities of escape. She was weaker than him but not less intelligent, and certainly a great deal wiser than her previous self. She was depending on her survival skills, and she knew there were two men in the next room as well as a boy who would defend her at any cost.

"You look frightened, Gwynne. Do not worry. I am not a ghost. I am very much alive and truly glad to have found you. Aren't you a little glad to see me?"

What was he going on about? She had been running from him practically all of her life. Why would she be glad to see him?

When she did not answer, he sighed deeply. "This is going to be harder than I thought," he began. He slowly undid the buttons of his coat, taking the time, or so it seemed to her, to gather his thoughts. Or was he going to remove the cumbersome garment in order to have more freedom when the time came to ambush her? What were his intentions? Didn't he have better things to do than pursue his childhood prey? But he did not remove the coat. He did, however, take a step closer to her. She felt her chest constrict with anxiety. She would fight him off with all the strength she had in her. If necessary, would she hurt him with the iron poker on the floor by her feet? Was she capable of that? It was a good thing Charles was several hundred miles away. She might have been able to kill Edmund if he threatened to take her son...their son. But her mother had never breathed a word about Charles to anyone, not even her father. When and if they came to London, she could present him to her father as the child of Lucas, or perhaps, like so many others, he would just accept Charles as Lucas's son without any explanation. Her mother would *never* give her secret away unless she expressly gave her permission to do so.

"Shall I tell you why I am here, dear Gwynne, after all these years?" He smiled again. Was he trying to be endearing? This was not the usual sort of behaviour from Edmund. He did not ingratiate himself with her, perhaps with others, from whom he wanted something, but not with her. With her, he just took what he wanted. After all, she was little more than a servant to him, someone of whom it was justifiable to take advantage. "Why so much silence from you?" He spread his arms out, palms opened, beseeching her. Would he get impatient? This was not a good thing. She had to open her mouth, make some little speech, and get him to talk more, so that time would pass and someone would come to her rescue. She deliberately breathed in and out and was just on the point of uttering something when he turned away from her abruptly and started to pace first towards the stove and then towards the new sink. Would he notice the wedding ring? It seemed he did not, for he turned towards the table now, slowly walked around it, and then returned to his original position in front of her. Was he summoning his courage for the onslaught? An onslaught of action or of words? What was happening? He placed his arms behind his back. This was a good sign. He was not intending to lunge at her.

"I have come to make you a proposition." He stopped. He looked at her warily, attempting to interpret her reaction. "You look surprised, my dear."

"A proposition, Edmund? You have something to propose to *me*?" She pointed her index finger at her chest. *Yes, of course, she was surprised! How could she not be surprised? What could she possibly want from him, except to never see or hear from him for the rest of her life?*

"All right then, I will tell you precisely why I have come. I hope it will gratify you in some small way. I hope that my willingness to free you of this...this...bondage...this mundane and ignoble need to work will endear me to you—" He stopped abruptly, almost annoyed with himself. She did not understand what he was talking about, but at least he wasn't about to hurt her. "Why am I talking like this, to *you*, of all people, the one person I do not have to pretend with?" He raised his hands and his eyes upward, as if proclaiming his stupidity to a higher Being. This was so confusing to Gwynne. "Yes, I guess, in truth, that is why I am here...because...there is no pretence with you...and I am oh so weary of pretence." He sighed deeply and looked penetratingly at her.

Was this some kind of truce? Was he discarding his weapons in this battle between them by acknowledging that he had laid himself bare before her, had revealed his true self to her when he had attacked her? And yet...and yet, she believed him capable of doing that with any woman, all women. Surely it was not only she who had brought out his inner demon. Surely there had been other victims. Or was he saying that she was special because he could exhibit all his ugliness to her alone? If so, it was a strange confession. And why would he make it? Did he think she would accept to be his quarry again and again and again just because he was honest about it?

And suddenly he looked sad and dejected. He wanted something, but this time he would have to ask for it. It was obviously not just something that he could take. It was something that she would have to give. And Edmund hated to ask. "I have been behaving badly of late, as my parents would say. *Very* badly, in their eyes. They are disgusted with me. They are ready to disinherit me, the profligate son. Can you believe that?"

"I suppose I can," she replied.

"Yes, I suppose you could, you who have never had anything to squander as I have." Now he looked smug and superior—the real Edmund.

"Edmund, please say what you have come to say." She blurted this out but then wanted to take it back. She could not afford to anger him in any way.

"There is only one way for me to get back into their good graces, one way and one way only." He turned from her now, placed his hands in his coat pockets and walked over to the stove. He did not want her to see his face as he was revealing how he had negotiated with his parents to save face. He was not the powerful male here attacking his prey. No, he was the little boy who had made a pact with his parents so that he could continue to possess the power of money. "I have to marry." He said this without turning to face her.

Gwynne took a sudden intake of breath. Did he want to marry *her* of all people? "Edmund, I still do not understand why you are here. Please tell me why!" And then he did turn around to look at her, and she saw the most helpless look in his eyes. He slowly removed his hands from his pockets. He walked towards her again. Surely, he was not going to get down on one knee! There was no way he would do that. Then something changed in him. A shadow was cast over his face. Anger and ugliness returned. Should she bend down and pick up the iron poker before it was too late?

"Surely, Gwynne, you have not turned into an idiot all this time away from me! Do I have to spell it out for you? If I have to marry, then I can only face marrying you. There! I said it. What more do you want? Do you want me to express undying love? Just be happy that my parents accepted you as my betrothed. They consider you to be a reasonable, no-nonsense kind of girl. And they certainly have never approved of any of the other girls I have...I have...cavorted with over the years, even if they were more suitable from the societal point of view. No, they want to cage me, set boundaries around me, and they think that you, being you, could do that for them." He pointed his hands towards her, not menacingly, mind you, just by way of reference to her suitability from the point of view of his parents. Gwynne almost relaxed at this point, but the situation was too uncomfortable, too painful. How could she disentangle herself from this man without antagonizing him?

"I...I ...am not sure what to say, except that—" Edmund interrupted her.

"Come, come, Gwynne, there can be no pretence between us. I am offering you what can only be described as a fortune in so many ways, not the least of which monetary. You can get out of this hole! You can live the life of every woman's dreams!"

At precisely this point in their colloquy, there was a knock at the door, and after several seconds, Phillip made an entrance. "Sorry to—" and this time Edmund's interruption of another's intended speech was more of a threat.

"—Get out of here, you idiot boy! You are intruding into a private tête-à-tête. Leave this room immediately before I tear you limb from limb!"

"Edmund, do not speak to Phillip in that way! He has every right to come into this room and stay if he so wishes. This is where *he* works and resides. *You* are the intruder!" Gwynne took a deep breath. She would not allow this man to abuse Phillip. And she must at all costs keep Phillip in here with her. And if it took getting Edmund to show his true nature and seek to harm her physically in some way, then having Phillip as a witness, if not a full-bodied protector, was worth whatever would befall her.

Edmund now turned on her. His eyes were enflamed with rage. He spoke carefully, distinctly, enunciating every word with his own special brand of venom, "My family has given you everything. As a child you wanted for nothing, and now you call me an intruder?!" He ceased speaking for a few seconds, breathing noisily, trying to contain himself. "Just give me an answer. Will you or will you not marry me? That is all I wish to hear from you. Know that a 'no' would be the least wise decision you have ever made in your life."

It was Phillip who spoke before she could answer this most absurd of questions. "You canna be...you cannot be marrying our Nurse Gwynne, for she is already married, sir. She already has a little boy and is expecting another child." Phillip stepped further into the room and came closer to them both. Edmund had again shifted his glance from Gwynne to Phillip upon hearing the words coming from the boy's mouth. Gwynne took advantage of Edmund's turning his back and stopping dead in his tracks at Phillip's comment to move quickly to the sink and retrieve her wedding ring. She silently vowed never to remove it again.

"Edmund," she began, when the ring was safely back on her finger. "I am sorry, but Phillip is right. I cannot marry you." She displayed the simple band on her left hand that contained the proof of her marital status. Edmund looked up at her. His face expressed a level of shock that she found hard to describe because it was so tinged with a 'How dare you!' kind of reaction. Indeed, the fact that she had dared to not be available to him for whatever purpose he deemed necessary was beyond him. He needed her as his prey forever and ever, but she was not about to explain this to him. Phillip was also watching Edmund, trying to gauge what such an ill-mannered and overbearing gentleman would do when he was being thwarted by an unchangeable reality, or at least that was what Gwynne thought Phillip might be pondering. She just hoped he would not take it upon himself to exit the room. If need be, she would detain him. And in fact, that is exactly what she did. She walked over to him, her eyes on Edmund all the time, and placed her hand firmly on Phillip's shoulder. The two of them as a unit now faced her hunter in a dramatically adversarial way. Phillip had understood. She silently thanked him.

*

As soon as Lucas returned from his mission to examine Jonathan and Jane's choice of home and workshop, he learned from Ally that Gwynne and Phillip were both next door dealing with some gentleman who had arrived earlier to speak specifically to Gwynne. Who could that have been? He made his way over there to find out. The door was slightly ajar, and he entered the room to witness Gwynne and Phillip standing defiantly before a man in a green coat that he immediately recognized.

"Ridgely! What a surprise to see you here in our very own humble hospital! It has been years, hasn't it, since we were students?" Lucas went over to the man ostensibly to shake his hand, although he had always felt distaste for him, especially because of the deplorable way he had treated his brother. However, he could tell by the look on the man's face that he was not there to make small talk. It looked as if something momentous might have just happened. What could that have been? "I see you have met my wife."

"She's *your* wife, Lacey! Well, well, well. Haven't *you* done well for yourself, Miss Littleford, as was?!" He glared at Gwynne for a moment and then raised his head to the ceiling and began to laugh in a most disagreeable manner. Lucas was startled by the man's boorish behaviour in front of Gwynne, but not completely shocked since he had witnessed his coarseness on many an occasion. And then he reminded himself of the rumours about his disgraceful comportment towards women. What was he doing here in the first place? Surely, he had not come to make a donation. Ridgely did not have a generous bone in his body. "So, to what do I owe your presence here?" he finally asked.

Phillip answered. "He came to ask Gwynne's hand in marriage."

"You what?!"

"Yes, my good man," Edmund said smugly, "Your *wife* and I have had a previous intimate knowledge of each other...or...hadn't she told you?" Edmund added with a nasty snicker. Now he wanted to hurt Gwynne. Lucas rapidly turned his head towards Gwynne, mutely asking her if this was the one. She was white. She seemed to be shivering. Lucas felt invaded by a tidal wave of rage towards his wife's tormentor. He could not hold himself back. He lunged towards his beloved's attacker and grabbed him by his lapels.

His voice came out in a hiss. "Ridgely, I know all about your previous intimate knowledge of each other. I know every horrific detail of your perfidy." From his superior height, he stared down on what he considered the most despicable man in the country. Edmund was no longer smiling. He looked terrified. And then Gwynne was by Lucas's side, her hand gently on his arm.

"Lucas, my love, please do not hurt him." She then spoke directly to her old persecutor. "Edmund, you should go now. You should never come back, either. I have no desire to ever see you again. Our so-called previous intimate knowledge of each other in no way gives you any right to harass me further." Lucas tightened his grip on Edmund's coat. He was burning with loathing, on the one hand, for the detestable creature beneath his gaze and with love, on the other, for the courageous woman facing her oppressor.

"Do what she says, Ridgely. Get out of here. If you don't, Phillip and I would be only too happy to throw you down the stairs!" Phillip stepped up immediately, and faced Edmund, determined to unequivocally reinforce the threat of his employer. Lucas relinquished his hold on Edmund's coat.

Looking depleted and small, Edmund went over to the side of the table where he had left his top hat, gloves, and cane. But the accoutrements of the gentleman did nothing to revive the man's hostile superiority. He was no longer superior. He was just the profligate boy on the verge of being banished from his parental home. His shoulders drooping, he slipped out of the room in search of some other woman to whom he could offer up his wealth and position, as well as his sullied soul.

"Phillip, make sure he descends the stairs. Then leave Nurse Gwynne and myself alone for a while."

"Right, sir," replied Phillip. He closed the door behind him.

Lucas took Gwynne into his arms and hugged her forcefully to him. "He wanted to marry you?! After all he put you through? What? Does he think his past actions represented some form of love?"

"Oh, no, Lucas, I don't think so," Gwynne said, the side of her head against his broad chest, breathing in his strength and steadfast dedication to her. "I dare say the opposite. I am coming to the conclusion that he hates women. I am perhaps the least hateful because he does not need to hide his true nature, his antagonism when he is with me. His parents want him to marry, are forcing him to marry on pain of disinheritance. So he came here to offer me all his worldly goods. Thus, he gets to remain an heir, and at the same time, marry the only woman he could bear to have at his side."

"Some compliment to you, my love!"

Gwynne stood slightly apart from him and looked into his eyes. Lucas noticed the colour had returned to her cheeks. She was no longer shaking. "I was terrified when he showed up. I thought that all was lost, that he would do what he had always done, that he had come to chase me and pin me down. For a moment I thought that he was inescapable, that I had been living an illusion, the illusion that he was actually gone from my life."

"It's not an illusion, Gwynne." Lucas shook his head forcefully. "He *is* gone from your life. This is your life now. Charles, myself, and the new life within you—*we* will hold you and keep you in *this* reality. I promise you."

Gwynne smiled, tears forming beneath her eyes. "Could we go now, Lucas, to Kent? I miss our little boy. I need to be with him."

"Of course." Lucas brushed his hand over her hair. With a finger he gently wiped away the tears falling down her cheeks. Then he placed both his palms on either side of her face and stared at her questioningly. "Didn't he notice the wedding band on your hand before he came out with his outrageous request?"

"Oh, my love," she answered him. "Today I succumbed to folly in thinking that I might save my ring from falling down the drain of the sink when I washed my hands. It has sometimes slipped off, thankfully, only at home, where the basins have no drains. I then unwittingly left it at the side of the sink and went to stir the fire. It was at that moment that Edmund entered the room. I also make you a promise. I will never remove my ring again!"

"If it falls down the drain and into the pipe beneath the sink, we can always call the plumber in to dismantle the pipe and fish out the ring."

"Oh, Lucas, I was hoping that we would never have to set eyes on a plumber again!" Husband and wife laughed.

"Well, actually, my dear Gwynne, they will be coming here again this week, but at least only outside in the courtyard. They are going to install modern flush toilets in the privy!" Gwynne lay her head down again on his chest, but this position did not cover the sound of her groan.

PART FOUR

Chapter XXIX

It was happening. It was truly happening. The four of them, Lucas, herself, Rupert, and Isabel were finally going to have an audience with the great lady, Florence Nightingale herself, in the famed personage's home. Gwynne had penned the letter about a week ago, and Miss Nightingale had given her consent to such a visit to discuss all manner of things related to their hospital, school, and fledgling country orphanage under the auspices of Lucas's aunt Edith. She had actually sounded eager to meet them, having heard all about their endeavour and its success. The woman's eagerness however did not quell Gwynne's anxiety. After all, she had been such an exigent task master to Gwynne. The desire to please her was as great today as it had always been. Gwynne was not even sure if she had ever really pleased her in the past. The lady's encouragement and sometimes praise had only ever been lukewarm at best. She and Lucas were proud of what they had achieved, but who knew how acquainted with the facts Miss Nightingale actually was? It was not as if she had sent spies to uncover how their hospital really functioned. Her knowledge could not even have been second-hand. It had to have come from newspaper reports and the like. Gwynne was sure that her mother and her old mentor did not have an ongoing epistolary relationship.

Their troupe of four was seated in the Lacey carriage on their way to the frightening event. But the others were chattering comfortably amongst themselves. Even Isabel, about to come face-to-face with her heroine, seemed only excited by the prospect, and not nervous in the least. Didn't they realize how difficult and even insurmountable the task ahead of them was? They wished for advice, for approval, for wisdom. Didn't they know that they could just as easily be censured or at least relentlessly quizzed about what they were doing? Part of her just wanted to go home to her newborn baby. Little Eleanora, named after Lucas's mother (as long as she would never be called Lady Nora, for there would only be one of those in Lucas's life), only four weeks alive, had seemed to know this morning that her mother was off on an extremely dangerous mission and might come home battered and bruised from it. She just would not settle in the nanny's arms at all. It was also exceedingly hot today, making the child most uncomfortable. Gwynne was glad that she and Isabel had decided to wear their simple uniforms instead of fancy dresses. That would have been physically unbearable for her, never mind the emotional drama being played out inside her breast. And there was the added problem of her having to be home at a specific hour to feed her baby. She certainly did not want to be leaking milk while in conversation with Miss Nightingale. Fortunately, the added cover of the hospital apron with the embroidered name of the hospital on the front would cover up the unsightly dampness, for a time, anyway. Besides all of that, the thought of her baby going hungry caused her to feel an acute sense of guilt.

Isabel herself was with child, but except for her glowing complexion, making her even more beautiful, she was not showing signs of her state. She seemed to be looking, despite the simplicity of the uniform, even more like the princess that Phillip had declared her to be on the day that she first entered the hospital. Isabel had grown, though, matured into a dedicated working woman. Her students, young and old, loved her. She was not spoiled in any way, even if her hairstyle was always impeccable. Who knew how many hours it took her personal maid to accomplish such an amazing result? Isabel must have to wake up really early to have that particular feat performed on her, thought Gwynne, smiling to herself at the thought of Isabel rising with the sun while Rupert continued to sleep. She was happy for them. They were a happy couple, fully aware of how lucky they were to have found each other, since they were both conventional and most unconventional at the same time. To have found their soulmate among the gentry was quite astounding—for Gwynne, anyway. A part of each of them rebelled against the society they were forced to inhabit. They were the same in that way. And so, each of them satisfied that atypical element of the other's character. Astonishing, really, since they both made their respective parents (or aunt and uncle in the case of Isabel) exceptionally gratified in their choice of mate, and at the same time got what they needed from that unique mate, from the uniqueness of that mate.

The four of them were great friends, but Gwynne would always feel different from them, at least from Rupert and Isabel. She was perhaps more at ease with Jane and Jonathan. Lucas, too, was different. It was safe to say that the trappings of society no longer trapped him at all. He was a total outsider now. Gwynne was certainly thankful for that. Perhaps that is what had kept Edmund away for so long. He had had no idea that Lucas had married her, since their marriage had not been publicized to their peers. She also had to thank Lucas's guardians for that. They had played by their nephew's rules and had only required Isabel to accept to have the glorious, unforgettable, and noble wedding. It had been a rather trying day for her humble self, but Gwynne had survived it. She had only been on display in the church since Isabel had asked her to stand beside her, while Lucas played the role of best man to Rupert. Gwynne was, after all, the sister-in-law, and indeed a friend. Gwynne could not have, nor would she have refused her, however uncomfortable she had known she would be. That small sacrifice had been worth it for having cemented her friendship with Isabel and Rupert. They treated her unequivocally as an equal.

It seemed that the other three riders in the carriage were having a rather heated and interesting discussion while she had been musing on other things. Gwynne now lifted her eyes to her travelling companions and began to take heed. They were conversing about the merits and future of Ally.

"Whenever I quiz our student doctors, who are soon to be graduating, about the diagnosis and prognosis of one or other of our patients," Lucas was saying, "more often than not it is Ally who comes up with the answer, and the correct one, too, before anyone else. That is not to say that Powell and Bainbridge are slow, not at all. It is just that Ally pays greater attention."

"She should become a doctor, in my opinion," Rupert added.

"Do you really mean that, Rupert, my love?" asked his wife.

"Yes, I do," answered Rupert, taking his wife's hand and squeezing it. Gwynne wondered if Rupert might just be saying that in order to ingratiate himself with his wife who had rather strong ideas on the intelligence of women. But he went further to explain his opinion. "I do not know exactly why people have such an aversion to women entering the medical field. Gwynne, here, was treating all and sundry in Whitechapel before Lucas ever came along. Whatever she was lacking in formal studies, she certainly made up for in experience. She was doing as good a job as either Lucas or I could have done with all of our studies and training taken into consideration. Of course, you could say that she had not been exposed to every kind of illness and their individual treatment, but neither had Lucas or I been exposed to everything under the sun. No one ever is. We just have to try and keep learning and accumulate as much knowledge as possible. Why can't women do the same? I certainly agree with Lucas that Ally has whatever it takes to become a doctor. Look at Elizabeth Blackwell. She became a doctor in the United States about ten years ago. Why couldn't Ally do the same?"

"She might just have to go to America, Rupert, to get that degree," answered Isabel. "I doubt whether any university would accept her here in London." Isabel now looked at Gwynne, wondering if she might have an opinion on the matter.

"I agree with Isabel that no matter how intelligent and studious our Ally is, she would be humiliated by her fellow male students. I do not think that England is ready for a female medical student yet. And I am not sure how to change that," said Gwynne.

"Perhaps we could start an all-female medical college," offered Lucas, "in order to avoid the discrimination by all those fearful male students—fearful of women, that is."

"I have noticed, Lucas," Rupert intervened at this point, "that when Ally produces an answer before the other two it is only Bainbridge that winces. He definitely feels threatened by her. But Powell does not. It almost seems that he is proud of her, or at least that he has some measure of admiration for her."

"He is also a little in love," Gwynne smiled as she said this.

"Really?" Both Lucas and Rupert turned to Gwynne in astonishment.

"Hadn't you noticed?" added Gwynne, but obviously they had not.

"And, I might add," Isabel informed them, "that Robert and Sophie are very sweet on each other. But they are moving at a slightly more rapid pace than Ally and her doctor, who are taking it rather slowly. Don't you agree, Gwynne?"

Gwynne nodded, but she didn't expound on her opinion since Robert had spoken to her about his feelings for Sophie in private. He often came to Gwynne to talk about life in general and his life specifically. She would not betray his confidence. Robert's problem had always been his desire to separate himself from his father, from a father not willing at all to support that separation. On any given matter to do with his future, Robert came to Gwynne because he undeniably felt that his father would not understand. He knew his mother would, but Jane, too, would be afraid of upsetting Jonathan. So Robert offered up his confidences to Gwynne. The boy, Samuel, who had come to them as a patient when she was early on in her pregnancy, was now apprenticing with Jonathan. Robert was hoping that his father would start giving the boy more and more responsibility so that he could spend his time studying. Robert really wanted to become a doctor. She and

Robert and Jane were working on a way to break the news to the uncooperative Jonathan.

"Do you think that it might be difficult for our Dr. Powell to contemplate someone like Ally, an orphan of the streets, as a possible future spouse?" asked Rupert. "Since his own family might want him to marry someone of their own class?"

Lucas cleared his throat. "Well, I think that he at least is smart enough to see the ridiculousness of such a requirement, even if his parents are not."

"He also has you as an example of someone who was not afraid to make that leap and marry whoever suited you. Not that you, my dear Gwynne, are beneath anyone, even a royal, in my opinion." Rupert had turned to her as he said this. Was he worried that he had insulted her in some way? Gwynne wished he wouldn't ever think that. No one was actually more complimentary to her than Rupert. Sometimes she thought he positively idealized her when he talked about how she was able to influence the state of mental health of their little patients, and how that newfound mental well-being in turn promoted physical health. He was always expressing how he did not exactly know how she did that, as if she possessed some kind of magic. But she knew that it was merely the power of truth or the divulging of truthful feelings that benefitted the children, or anyone, for that matter. It seemed, though, that not many understood this obvious truism. "What Powell does not know, however," Rupert turned to his wife, making sure that she was not left out in any way when he was passing out compliments, "is that for all of your formative years, Lucas, you were living beside your sister, Isabel, who taught you all there was and is to know about the equality of women, if not their superiority." Rupert smiled broadly at the sister in question, who smiled back at him.

Lucas laughed. "I am not sure if I could put into words what you and I, Rupert, have learned from women and about women. But somehow, I think that Miss Nightingale has had something to do with our acknowledgement of their unique capacities. Certainly, the good lady's actions and her writings influenced the thinking of Isabel. And then...well...she was Gwynne's most exemplary teacher in everything to do with healing and nursing...and nurturing. Wouldn't you agree, Gwynne?" But it was Isabel who formulated a response to this question.

"You know, when pondering what it is that Gwynne does to heal the sickness of her ailing patients, I am reminded of what little Malcolm once said in class with all the other children. We were talking about the differences between a doctor and a nurse."

"My my, dear sister, you do have interesting discussions in your classes. Aren't you supposed to be teaching them grammar and proper pronunciation?"

"That is exactly what I am teaching them when we are having those 'interesting discussions', as you have so aptly called them." Gwynne laughed at Isabel's perspicacious response to Lucas's query. Isabel was certainly right.

"Then what did Malcolm say, Isabel?" Lucas was obviously eager to find out how the boy saw the different roles of the different genders.

"He said, my dear Lucas, something absolutely stunning and most insightful. He said that the doctor heals the outside of the patient, and that Nurse Gwynne heals the inside."

"That's it, then," Rupert intervened. "That is precisely what Gwynne does. But I do not think that it has anything really to do with gender or doctoring or nursing. It literally has to do with Gwynne herself. And perhaps that was what the Lady with the Lamp did as well. But not all nurses do it, to be sure. And, I daresay, both Lucas and I are learning from Gwynne how to bring out of the patient what is lurking inside of them, and that we are eventually going to become healers of the inside, too. At any rate, I hope so."

Both sister and brother murmured their agreement with Rupert, and Gwynne suddenly became aware of the fact that she was no longer perspiring with fear and anxiety over the coming interview with Miss Nightingale. She realized that she did have something to be proud of and that her accomplishments, despite having to do with the intangible and invisible, were tangible and visible to others.

*

The four of them were seated in Florence Nightingale's drawing room, Lucas and Gwynne together on the settee to the left of the doorway, and Rupert and Isabel on a settee facing the door. When Miss Nightingale herself would enter the room, she would probably go to the armchair closest to the fireplace and therefore have a view of the entire room and her company. They had been talking ever so diligently, thought Gwynne, in the carriage, but once they had entered the hallowed halls of this particular healer of the soul, they all remained silent. Lucas held her hand in his, and she noticed that Rupert and Isabel were also seeking this form of comfort from the other. She could almost say that for the first time today she felt happy, comfortable at any rate, although perhaps her heart rate was slightly elevated. She discovered that she really wished to see her teacher of old, to talk with her not as a student, but as an equal now, ready to engage her on subjects about which she had acquired a great deal of firsthand knowledge. And she just wanted to really know how the Lady was faring since their return from the war. Gwynne wanted her to be happy and healthy, full of life and eager to share her precious views. Gwynne also knew with certainty that Lucas, Rupert, and Isabel would make a favourable impression. She was sorry that she had doubted them earlier in any way. Her fears had had much to do with the separation from her baby and her discomfort at having to stay away from Eleanora for what seemed far too many hours. But she deserved this audience with her distinguished mentor. It was definitely time. Eleanora would survive.

The door opened now, and the swishing of skirts could be heard behind the servant who preceded his mistress into the room. And then she was there in front of them, the woman about whom they had been talking so fervently just minutes before. They all rose and she and the Lady in question instantly moved towards each other—long-lost comrades in battle.

Miss Nightingale took her hands in hers. "My dear Nurse Gwynne, it is so exciting to see you again. It has been far too long."